I0678915

BIG HOSE

NEW YORK TIMES AND *USA TODAY* BESTSELLING AUTHOR

JASINDA WILDER

BIG HOSE

JAKE

I SQUEEZE THE BARBELL AS HARD AS I CAN, BRACE MY core with a deep breath in, and push the bar up off the brackets. Maksim and José stand behind the bench, spotting my lift; I've got 315 on the bar going for 5 reps, and at that weight, two spotters are needed to effectively ensure my safety. I focus on keeping my lower back pressed into the bench—none of the powerlifter back-arching leverage nonsense for me, just straight, raw power. At six-five, I weigh in at a lean 240, so benching 315 for reps is, if I'm patting myself on the back, pretty fucking impressive.

I lower the bar slowly and under control, touch my pecs with it, and grind it back up, growling through gritted teeth. A second rep. A third. Fourth. At the top of the fifth repetition, I know I'm gonna struggle to finish. I get the bar down, working like a madman to keep it from bouncing off my chest. Halfway up, the bar just...halts. My arms shake.

"Come on!" Maksim shouts in his guttural Ukrainian accent. "You got this, bro! Push, you little bitch!"

I snarl like a cornered lion and let my back come off the bench, exerting every last ounce of power I have—and the bar raises centimeter by centimeter. My vision tunnels, and like during an intense fire, I feel my whole world focusing in on one thing—moving the bar. It's as much mental now as it is physical.

I get my arms *almost* straight.

"You need a spot, amigo?" José says. "I think you got it. It counts. Come on."

"*No*," I snap through a growl.

It doesn't count unless I finish the rep. I suck in a sharp, quick breath and refocus, feeling the strain of 315 pounds on every muscle. My feet are pressed into the floor, my thighs tensed, my abs braced so hard you could smash a rock against them.

Finally, my arms lock out straight overhead, and I let Maksim and José help me rack the bar.

I'm dizzy.

But I fuckin' did it—315 for five reps.

"Howson!" Captain O'Shaugnessy calls my name from the doorway to the office area. "My office."

Shaking my head to clear the dizziness, still breathing hard and sweating, I grab a towel and my shirt and head for the office. I take a seat in the captain's office, dabbing at my face. "What's up, Cap?"

Captain Larry O'Shaugnessy is a fit sixty-five years old, trim and hard and wiry, still fully able to dress out and work a hose, with salt-and-pepper hair and a neat all-white goatee. He flips a pen in his fingers. "Mackenzie over at Station Five needs an extra man. They're down a few guys with some sort of nasty bug, and they can't field a full second crew. I know you're at the end of your twenty-four on, so I'm not gonna insist. But I know you, and I figure you'll go."

I nod. "Sure thing, Cap. Let me grab my gear."

He clicks the pen, spins it, clicks it again. "I should warn you, Mack said they've been busy today, so don't expect to sit around pumping iron all shift."

"They need me a full twenty-four?"

"No, they've got a couple guys scheduled to come in later tonight. They could call 'em in early, but those guys have been covering for the sickies, so Mack wants to spell them. You'll put in another ten or twelve, I'd say."

"Fine by me. You know me, Cap—I'm always good to go."

"Yeah, you're an oversized version of the Energizer Bunny, Howson."

I laugh as I lever myself to my feet. "Except I'm not pink, fluffy, or cute."

He cackles. "I dunno—all that chest hair you've got, you are kinda fluffy."

"Oh fuck you, Cap. You're just jealous you can barely grow that peach fuzz you call a goatee."

He strokes his goatee—in reality, it's a nice goatee. We just give each other shit like it's part of the job. "Hey, now. Don't go mocking my goatee, Howson. I'll have you doing probie work for a month of Sundays, son."

"Probie" is department slang for probationary firefighter, or the newest of the new—just out of training and not a full-fledged firefighter yet, who are often hazed with doing the shitty jobs the rest of us more senior guys don't and won't.

I hold up my hands. "You made fun of my chest hair. I was just giving what I got."

"Truce, then."

I smirk. "I dunno about a truce, but I'll agree to a cease-fire." Cap massages his left bicep, something he's been doing off and on, lately. I point at him. "You seen Doc Llewellyn about that, Cap?"

He waves me off. "Bah. I'm fine. Just a little ache. Sore from out-lifting you, is all."

I splutter a laugh. "Yeah, okay. I just benched three-fifteen for five, Cap. The day you can lift *half* that, I'll voluntarily do probie work for a month."

Cap winces, pops the cap off a bottle of NSAIDs, and chews one, rinsing it down with what must be eight-hour-old coffee. "Get over to Five, Howson. The crew you're filling in on is a lot of rookies, so show 'em the ropes, huh?"

"Aye-aye, Cap." I give him a two-finger salute and go gather my gear.

Once my shit is loaded onto the back bench of my big black Power Wagon, I head over to Station Five. There's a probie scrubbing out the back of a bus—what we call an ambulance. The soapy water is coming out pink, which means the last call must have been a messy one. A fire crew is sorting out their equipment, checking over hoses, inspecting, sampling, and refilling oxygen tanks, the usual. I set my gear next to what is clearly the rookie crew's engine—it's the shiny, sparkly one that gets washed several times a day because the experienced crew is given most of the calls.

Not how I'd staff the crew—the veteran crew would bitch about being broken up, but you have to balance out rookies and veteran firefighters, or you get a crew going on a call and not having any fuckin' clue what to do.

I head inside and locate the captain's office.

I knock on the frame of the open door. "Captain Mackenzie."

Captain Jeff Mackenzie is on the heavier side, his body more used to jockeying the desk rather than the hoses. Balding blond, clean-shaven, peering down his nose through half-moon readers at his computer screen.

He looks up at my knock, and removes his readers—almost hastily, as if embarrassed to be seen wearing them. "Lieutenant Howson, thanks for coming." He mispronounces my name, saying it *HOSE-son*, instead of *HOW-son*.

"It's Howson, sir," I correct. "Reporting in."

He nods, tossing the readers onto the desk and leaning back precariously far in the chair, which squeals in protest. "Right, right. Larry says you're his best."

I shrug. "If he says so, sir. I just do what I can."

"Well, I got a crew of rookies that needs a kick in the ass. I know you're only here for one shift, but we're having a busy day, we're short men with a stomach bug, so I'm hoping you can whip 'em into something like shape."

"I'll do my best, sir. Not sure how far I'll get in one shift, but I'll do my best."

"All I can ask, right?" At that moment, an alert comes in, the klaxon buzzing, red light coming on, a voice over the PA announcing a medical emergency. "That's you, Howson. Get your crew."

"Sir." I leave the office at a jog and find the veteran crew already in motion. "Rookies, this call is us."

The veterans pause, eying me. One of them, a grizzled, hard-eyed man who must be a twenty-year veteran, glares at me. "Who're you?"

"Filling in from Station Four," I answer. "Come on, boys, *move!*"

The rookies scramble, getting into the rig in admirable time. I let the engineer on the crew take the wheel, and we move out, lights and sirens going. The engineer, a younger guy in his mid-twenties, drives pretty well, making no major mistakes and getting us to the scene in good time. It's a heart attack, a Hispanic male, mid-sixties.

They do fine—stabilize the patient until EMS arrives to transport him to the hospital.

The bus shows up only a couple of minutes after we do. The driver is a woman, her partner a tall Black man, good-looking, with a precisely trimmed goatee. The woman is…gobsmackingly gorgeous. It's not like me to be distracted on the job, but Roger, the driver of our rig and the most senior and experienced of the rookies, did a damn good job stabilizing the patient.

She's also just fucking gorgeous. Damn near a foot shorter than me, but curvy as fuck—even the utilitarian EMS uniform can't disguise the heavy swell of her tits and the generous bubble of her ass. Her hair is black as night, glinting bluish like a raven's wing, braided and hanging halfway down her back. Italian heritage, for sure, her skin like caramel and coffee-with-cream. Eyes like molten chocolate. Every movement she makes is quick, efficient, and no-nonsense. While her trainee evaluates the patient, she checks his knowledge with probing questions, guiding him to the correct answers. They get the patient on their bus and she takes the wheel.

There's a moment, then—she's halfway behind the wheel when her eyes fix on mine. It's a split second, but our eyes meet and something shocks me. It's physical. Like static electricity zapping you—I used to wear my church socks and shuffle around the house touching doorknobs, waiting for the zap. Sometimes, I could even get a little bluish spark to go off. This medic's eyes meeting mine has a similar effect on my brain—a quick, startling zap.

Then she's slamming her door closed and the engine is groaning as she shoves it into gear and hauls away, flipping on her siren and flashers—and the moment is broken.

Those medic blues never looked so good as wrapped around that woman's fine-as-fuck body. Goddamn.

"L-T?" A hand nudges me.

I shake my head. "Let's get back to the station. Come on."

"L-T. Your radio." The voice is young—barely old enough to shave, maybe a month out of training—not Roger, the driver.

I frown. My radio has been squawking in my ear, I realize—and here I am, ogling and drooling like some lovesick probie. The fuck is wrong with me?

"*Engine Sixteen, respond.*"

I realize that's us. I was listening for Engine Four, my usual crew. "Go for Sixteen," I respond.

"Single vehicle accident near your location, corner

of Pine and Sixty-third. M-V-A, medical event—caller believes a heart attack." A pause. "It's Captain O'Shaugnessy."

I'm behind the wheel before dispatch has finished speaking. Pine and Sixty-third is less than four blocks away, and I haul ass. Blast the horn as I barrel around a left, swerving into oncoming traffic. Beside me, Roger braces as I yank us back across the centerline and far right around another car that hasn't gotten over yet.

Then we're there—Cap's truck is wrapped around a telephone pole, the hood smashed into a V, spewing steam, windshield spiderwebbed. The caller is at the driver's door, cell phone at his ear, trying like hell to yank open the crumpled door.

I shove him unceremoniously out of the way, not waiting for the rookies to show up with tools—I use brute force, snarling like a cornered lion as I wrench the door open—this is where my strength comes in useful, where all those reps pay off: the door comes free with a creaking squeal of metal. Inside, Cap is slumped over the steering wheel, bleeding from a shallow abrasion to his forehead. Barely conscious.

Instincts and training kick in—I'm barely aware of my own actions or words as I rally the rookies into action. After ensuring there are no cranial or spinal injuries, we pull Cap from the car and I begin CPR; he's not breathing.

"Come on, Cap," I growl between chest compressions. "Come on, you ugly old fuck. Come *on*."

Someone has the CPR kit, and I let him take over—I can recognize that I'm not objective. Sirens shriek closer. Cap coughs, then moans—he's alive. Thank fuck.

A bus halts, sirens shutting off, flashers still spinning. I help move Cap onto the stretcher and hop on with him.

The attending medic is a young female I don't recognize. "He's stable," she protests when I climb in back with them. "You're not needed for transport."

"He's my captain," I explain. "I'm riding with him." It's not a question.

She checks his vitals as we pull away from the scene, reports to the hospital.

"Cap?" I say, feeling his pulse at his wrist. Thready; I wouldn't classify him as stable, by any means. Alive, for now, but no guarantee he'll stay that way. "You there, old man?"

His hand pulses against mine, gently. He's there.

"We've got you, Cap. You're gonna be fine."

We reach the hospital, and I hop backward out of the bus, hauling the stretcher out after me, the medic scrambling to keep up. Triage nurses meet us.

"Sixty-five-year-old male, thready pulse," I report, filling in the rest of the vitals.

And then he's being whisked away to an OR.

Shit, shit, shit.

Minutes later, Maksim, José, and Jimbo show up, squealing to a stop in Jimbo's personal truck. Entering the ER at a run, they spot me.

Maksim is in first—tall at six-two, he's built like a tank, no neck, boulder shoulders, and bear paw hands. His hair and beard, both dark brown, are buzzed to the same length all over, and he bears a wicked scar on his face from his time in the Ukrainian army—he saw combat in the East, and after things settled somewhat, he emigrated here and joined the fire department immediately; he'd served on a fire crew in Kyiv before combat called him to the East.

"Heard about Cap on the radio," Maksim says. "Were you the responding?"

I nod, wiping at my face. "He's alive. It was his heart." I shake my head, pinching the bridge of my nose. "He was massaging his left bicep when he sent me to Station Five. I should have made him go in then."

Jimbo, burly and brown-bearded, claps me on the shoulder. "Hell, Jake, you know you can't make Cap do shit." He sighs. "He's a thirty-year veteran. You think he'd know what left arm pain means."

"He does," José says. "But guys like him, they never think it means that for them. My old man was the same way. Shrugged it off and said he was fine. Then he was gone."

José is a fire plug of a man, under six feet but what he lacks in height he makes up for in sheer indomitable will and raw power. Covered in tattoos, he's a hardened veteran of the streets in Quito, Ecuador. He gives zero fucks, takes no shit, and lives for the job, just like both Maks and me. The three of us are inseparable, even when we're not on duty.

"Cap is gonna make it," I insist. "He squeezed my hand. He heard me, he knew me."

I simply cannot sit around the ER waiting for him—I have a job to do, and I have to do it. I hitch a ride to Station Five with my guys, find my temp crew refueling the rig and replenishing the medical kit.

"How's your cap?" Roger asks.

I shake my head, shrug. "Alive. I think he'll make it."

"I'm sure he will. Captain O'Shaugnessy is a legend."

Damn right he is—not just in the house, but through the whole city department. He picked me for his crew when I was probie and he was crew chief, made me lieutenant after he hit captain. He's groomed me to take over the station for him, someday. I just...I didn't expect it to be for another five years at the minimum.

Everyone at Station Four knows I'm in line to be captain, and everyone is ready for it. They know me, they know my qualifications. I'm first into a fire, every time, and last out, every time. I get my guys in and out, and I get the victims out.

I'm suddenly not feeling ready to be in charge of Four. Not yet. Not like this. I wanted Cap to pass the baton through retirement, with all honors and ceremony. Not this heart attack bullshit.

The rest of the shift is busy—good, I guess. Keeps my mind from dwelling on Cap's condition. There's a five-car MCI on the interstate—the rookies' first mass casualty incident. A small, easily managed house fire with no casualties. A DOA single-car MVA—multiple vehicle accident—caused by an impaired driver who fortunately only took himself out, the bastard. Sorry, not sorry.

By the time the next shift arrives, I'm exhausted, hungry, and surly. I've been on duty and active for over thirty hours by now, and there's only been time for half a fuckin' bowl of shitty-ass probie pasta.

It's José's day to rattle the pans back home at Four, and I bet there's some tasty-ass chimichangas leftover. I almost head there just to find out, but my need to check on Cap takes priority.

Still in my blues, I drive to the hospital and locate Cap's room. The ward nurse is a salty old bird with a hard-on for visiting hour rules, and even I can't sweet-talk her into letting me so much as peek in on him.

"He's stable, and you can visit him during visiting hours," she says, her voice raspy and croaking; she's a diminutive little thing, coming barely to my chest, but she's not scared of me a bit. "I don't care if you're the pres-ident or the pope, the captain needs his rest." She has the audacity to glare at me like I'm back in eighth grade at the Catholic school Mom shoe-horned me into, after I got ex-pelled from the public school for fighting. "You can wait in the waiting room, or you can come back. Your choice, but you're not getting in to see him, no way, no how, and don't think you can intimidate me, you big gorilla."

I hold up my hands palms out, surrendering, only just keeping my already fraying temper in check. If there's one thing I know, it's don't piss off the nurses. Especially the crusty old lifers like this one.

I park my ass in the waiting room with a Dixie cup-sized Styrofoam cup of three-day-old coffee, prepared to wait the two hours until visiting hours open up. And wait I do. Fortunately, I brought paperwork I've had backlogged, and spend the time catching up on that.

Salt Bird pops her head into the waiting room, a

cardigan draped over her arm, purse in hand. "The on-duty nurse is still clocking in. If someone was to somehow sneak past the nurse's station to check in on his friend, I don't think anyone would notice." She winks at me and vanishes.

I stuff my paperwork back in the folder and hustle to Captain's room. He's crunching on ice and watching the news; when I enter his room, knocking on the frame as I slip in, he mutes the TV with the remote attached to the bed.

"Jake," he says, scootching up higher. "You snuck past Helen, huh?"

I grin as I spin a chair around to straddle it, arms crossed over the back. "She popped into the waiting room as she was leaving to let me know I could sneak in between shifts."

"Hope you didn't waste your time waiting to see my old ass, Howson."

"I had to catch up on paperwork anyway. Only spent an hour or so." I jut my chin at him. "Told you you should get that looked at. How are you?"

He winces, shrugs. "Lucky to be alive, I guess—in more ways than one, what with my cardiac arrest leading to a wreck. How am I, though? Pissed. This isn't how I wanted to retire."

"No shit, Cap. Me neither."

"How was it with the rookies?"

I shrug. "It was fine. He's got all the rookies on one team, which ain't how I'd do it, but I ain't station chief there, so." Cap doesn't reply to that, which I find suspicious. "What aren't you saying, Cap?"

He shakes his head. "Not my place to say anything."

"Well now you gotta, goddammit. What?"

"I spoke with Bruce." This being Bruce Wells, Battalion Chief. "He snuck in earlier. That or even Helen can't say no to a Battalion chief."

"Out with it, Cap."

A sigh. "Nothing's decided for sure, but I have a feeling Bruce is gonna move Mack over to head up Station Four, and promote either you or Kyle Kennedy up to captain of Five."

"I've been in to be captain of Four for a year, Cap. Why would he do that?"

"He feels Four needs the more experienced hand at the tiller. Move around the crews at Five and it'll be fine being run by a new captain. I know you've had your heart set on running Four, and I hate to see you disappointed. You're a damn good firefighter, and you'll make a hell of a captain. But Bruce has to do what he feels is best for the Battalion, and I can't disagree under these circumstances. I'm gonna be out of commission for a while, and this is going to force me into medical retirement. I won't be able to mentor you the way you'll need."

I grit my teeth to keep from cursing a blue streak. "Obviously, I'll do what's needed. I may not like it, but I'll accept what Chief Wells decides is best. Don't have much choice, do I?"

Cap makes a face of commiseration. "I know you will, Jake. Your time will come, okay? If not now, then soon. You know Captain Yates up at One is nearing retirement, too."

"God, Cap, Station One is a shitshow. Yates should have retired five years ago."

Cap laughs. "And that's why they'll need a strong young captain to whip 'em into shape."

I groan. "God, you've cursed me, Cap. Now Wells is gonna send me to One."

Cap laughs again. "One isn't so bad. They've got some good lads. I think Yates is just tired and too damn stubborn to retire. Plus, I think he's dreading being stuck at home all day with his battle-ax of a wife. That woman scares the shit out of me."

I cackle. "I met her once, at a fundraiser banquet. Battle-ax is putting it nicely."

Cap snickers. "We shouldn't speak ill of the unfortunate."

"Unfortunate? The woman's face could strip paint off a barn at fifty paces."

"And Yates's could do the same at a hundred paces, so they're well matched." Cap winces again. "You oughta get a good night's rest, Howson."

I laugh. "Meaning you're tired but too macho to say so."

"Oh, just get the hell out of here and let me be."

I take his hand in an arm-wrestling grip. "I don't like seeing you hooked up to all these wires, Cap. Get your ass better so we can sit on your porch and drink beer."

He nods. "Remember, you didn't hear nothin' about nothin' from me, yeah?"

"About what?"

"Good man. Now get."

I leave him, and head for the parking lot. The only

parking spot I could find was near the ER entrance, so I head through the ER. As I'm on my way out, an ambulance squeals to a jerky stop, sirens silencing, and the driver's door flings open.

It's the medic from earlier, the curvy one with the long-ass black hair. I'm closer, this time, and up close, she's even more stunning. Her face is perfectly symmetrical, her eyes huge and brown, her lashes thick, lips plump and in a naturally perfect cupid's bow. And shit, the way her medic blues fit her insane curves leaves my jaw damn near on the floor.

She doesn't even register me standing at the entrance, mere feet away: there's a godawful ruckus coming from the back of the bus. She yanks open the rear doors and heaves herself up and in.

"Mr. Wilson, you need to calm down." Her voice is hard, commanding. Short-tempered. "If you keep kicking up a fuss like this, I'm going to be forced to sedate you."

"I DON'T GIVE A FUCK, YOU DUMB BITCH! LET ME GO! LET ME GO, GODDAMMIT!"

The medic goes flying backward out of the bus, landing on her heels and quick-stepping backward. Instinct takes over, and I lunge forward, catching her in my arms. For a split second, I'm just holding her. She's equal parts taut and firm, lithe and soft, delicate and warm. And for that split second, she seems tempted to just...relax into my arm. Let me hold her.

A spark jolts through me, like I grabbed onto a live wire. My skin tingles, my hair stands on end, and my lungs seize, breath whooshing out of me.

I'm hard as a fucking diamond, behind my pants.

The split second is gone, and she's rocketing out of my arms like she felt the shock as clearly as I did. She shakes herself like a dog shaking water off, storming forward with her fists clenched.

"That's *it*, Mr. Wilson," she grits out between clenched molars. "I *told* you."

Mr. Wilson is a wiry old white guy, with a shock of hair that looks like he stuck his fingers in an electrical socket. He's wigged the hell out, thrashing like a madman despite being restrained by the gurney straps. The other medic, the young Black man from earlier, is trying his damndest to hold the old man down, but it's like trying to wrestle a wet horse.

I grab the sexy medic's arm and hold her back. "Let me."

"The fuck I will," she snarls.

I'm already climbing up and into the bus, ignoring her protests. I latch onto the patient's wrists and pin his thrashing feet to the gurney with my hips. I fix him with my *you're gonna listen like it or not* glare, and make it clear no amount of thrashing is going to budge my iron grip.

"Cool the fuck off, old man." I growl the command. I let go of one of his wrists, pinioning them both with one hand, and hold out my empty hand. "Needle."

I feel the syringe slap into my palm.

"You got two options, here, pal." I flick the cap off the needle and press the tip to the outside of his skinny little bicep. "One, you quit the tantrum and get yourself treated like a goddamn adult. Option two, I jab this shit into you, and I can't guarantee how gentle I'll be. You feel me?"

He stills, but his eyes snap with defiance. "Get off me."

"Wrong answer." I press the needle harder. "Last chance."

"Fine, goddamnit, fine. That shit constipates me."

I snicker. "Then quit acting like a child."

"I don't need no ambulance. I'm fuckin' fine."

The Black medic coughs a laugh. "You had a stroke two weeks ago and you just overdosed on Vicodin. You're *not* fine."

I blink. "How is he alive? Much less upright and pitching a tantrum?"

The medic shrugs. "Hell if I know. Bastard isn't human."

"I heard that you goddamn—"

I silence him with a glare. "You better not fucking finish saying what I think you're about to say."

He holds up his hands. "I wasn't gonna say *that*. I ain't no racist."

"Get out of my bus," a female voice says from behind me.

I climb backward and out, turn to face a very pissed-off but still drop-dead sexy medic. "What's his story?"

She just glares at me. "I didn't ask for your help."

"You'd be the one getting stitches if I hadn't caught you."

She just glares. "My bus, my patient."

I hold up my hands. "Fine, sorry for nothing, then. Damn."

She reaches for the syringe still in my hand. "Give

me that." She snatches it from me as I extend it to her. "You can't threaten patients. Who the fuck trained you?"

"If the patient is acting a fool and risking the safety of the medics trying to help him, I sure as fuck can. I didn't threaten him, anyway. Not with anything you weren't about to do."

She goes nose to nose with me—well, nose to collarbone, since she's several inches shorter than me; her glare is impressively intimidating, but it's somewhat undercut by the fact that as she sidles up and stands nose to nose with me, holding her ground and glaring fit to murder, her breasts press against my chest, and that's all I can fucking think about.

"*My* bus," she repeats, slowly, furiously, "*my* patient. Go back to your fire and your hoses and leave me the hell alone."

I hold her gaze and try like hell to keep my eyes from wandering down to her generous, button-straining chest.

I fail.

Her hiss of disgust is…well, if it could be used as a weapon, I'd be dead.

She presses all five fingers of both hands into my chest and pushes me away, eyes stabbing murderous fury into mine. "Go…*away.*"

I back up slowly, holding her eyes. "You're welcome." I wink at her, shooting her the grin which, according to the guys at the station, is guaranteed to melt panties at fifty paces.

She growls like a cornered raccoon; her panties are decidedly *not* melted.

I hold up my hands palms out. "Damn, girl. Don't shoot. I was just trying to help. It's instinct."

"Well take your instincts and *fuck off*." She pivots away from me, heading toward her bus, where the Black medic is currently wrestling the gurney down, the patient still muttering imprecations under his breath.

Fuck, fuck, and double-fuck—the girl is all curves. If her tits were about to pop the buttons off her shirt, her ass is popping the seams of her uniform slacks. Not tall, maybe five-six, five-seven at most, she's one hundred percent hot-as-fuck, mind-altering, cock-hardening, dead-sexy curves.

I don't even try to not stare at her ass as she helps pull the gurney off the bus. I can't not stare—it's a biological imperative.

She stops and shoots a glare at me over her shoulder. "Quit staring at my ass."

"I'm trying, I swear. Not my fault you've got an ass that don't quit."

There's a muffled cough from her partner, and his eyes cut to mine, expressing amusement he dares not otherwise let her see. "We'd better get Mr. Wilson into treatment before the sheer stubbornness that's keeping him alive wears off."

I finally manage to rip myself away from the sexy medic and her hypnotic ass. Head for my truck, climb behind the wheel, start the motor…and go nowhere.

She's pushing from the back end while her partner

pulls from the front—I just can't resist one last long, lingering look as she vanishes inside.

"That is one hell of a woman," I say out loud.

She hates me, but goddamn is she gorgeous. And honestly, the fiery fury of her is intoxicating. I don't know her name, but I know I'll be dreaming about her tonight.

JOVIE

AFTER A FOURTEEN-HOUR SHIFT WHICH SAW MAYBE twenty whole minutes of downtime, I finally drag my exhausted carcass up the stairs to my loft. I lock my door behind me and lean back against it, trying to decide which need is more important: food, a shower, or sleep. I'm not certain I have the energy for all three.

Groaning, I stumble for the kitchen, roughly yanking my hair out of the braid and shaking it out. Yeah, too damn tired to cook. I should have stopped at a drive-thru, but I hate fast food and I wasn't sure I'd stay awake that long. I grab a premixed protein shake from the fridge, and a protein bar to go with it. Shitty nutritional choice, but I can barely keep my eyes open—food is a necessity, seeing as our lunch break was interrupted by a multiple fatality shooting at a warehouse on the east side. More of a necessity even than food is showering off the stink of blood and death. It's part of the job, I'm used to it, inured to it. But I have to shower it off at the end of the shift—*have* to.

I wolf down the bar, washing it down with the shake—they're both gone by the time I'm in my bathroom. I strip down, twist on the hot water, and brush my hair out while I wait for it to warm up—the condo building is old, and the hot water takes a hell of a long time to warm up and reach my unit. Once my hair is shiny, I put it up in a bun—washing it takes for freaking ever and I only do it on days off.

I groan in relief as I step under the hot spray—I don't even bother adding any cold to the stream, since this is as hot as it's going to get and I like it turn-me-into-a-lobster hot. I just soak for a few minutes; it may not get any hotter, but it'll last forever. It's a tradeoff I'll accept.

Once I start lathering up, my brain starts off-loading tension from the day. Flashes of various calls burst behind my eyes as I scrub myself: a gunshot wound to center mass that won't stop bleeding; a kid with two broken legs who thought he'd start parkour by jumping off his roof; several car accidents of varying severity...

And him.

The goddamned enormous firefighter from the hospital at the end of my shift. Tall as a tree, broad as a grizzly. I couldn't fit both hands around his biceps with my fingertips touching. When he caught me? For a split second, for a literal eye-blink, he was just holding me, and it felt like heaven. He was solid as a rock and radiated warmth. He held me like I was nothing—and I may be short, but I'm dense. All this curve I'm packing hides a shit-ton of muscle, so I'm not exactly a featherweight. He held me like I was a teddy bear.

I swear to god, when he held me, I felt an electrical current jolt between us.

I can see him in my mind's eye as clearly as if he was standing in this shower with me right now.

Abort, abort—danger, danger!

Do *not* think about the fireman naked in the shower with you.

No.

It doesn't matter that he was six-five in his socks, or that he was built like a god. His hair was blond, sun-kissed, tousled, messy, sexy, perfect, begging for fingers to run through it. His eyes were the deepest blue you've ever seen, somewhere between sapphires and the deep blue sea. It didn't matter that his stubble was just right, not quite a beard, not quite looking unkempt—lickable. Kissable.

It didn't matter.

I don't date firemen.

I don't date firemen.

I *do not* date firemen.

But who said anything about dating, right? It's a big city. I'll likely never see him again. So who cares if I indulge a little? Let my mind wander, just a little. Right?

He's just a jake. Probably from the other side of the city. If I do happen to bump into him again, I'll just ignore him.

So there's no harm, no foul in letting my tired imagination picture him naked. His hair would be wet, looking darker and pasted back over his skull. Water would drip down his face, off the chiseled, granite jaw, and down his chest. And god, that chest would be...oooooh, come to mama. All hard muscle, dense and springy, perfectly curved, carved from marble. Underneath the pecs, his abs would be…maybe not washboard. He's not gonna have that kind of body—he doesn't have the time to count all those calories and macros it would require to get a massive body like that down to that kind of body fat percentage. His abs would be defined, but more like hard-packed slabs of slate, stacked one atop the other. Abs you could break your fist on. The water would run in trickling rivulets down between those abs, sluicing over his V-cut and down thighs the size of my waist. Thick, hard, tree-trunk thighs. The kind of thighs that can run up ten flights of stairs carrying forty-five pounds of gear.

Between those thighs?

A cock to make a girl faint.

Dangling forward, heavy fat tip pointing at the floor, it'd be just the right size. Not an elephant dick I can't possibly fit inside me, but still plenty big enough. How big is big enough? You know it when you see it. And in my dirty little fantasy, his is perfect. He just looks at me, and the sight of my naked body is all he needs to start going erect.

He doesn't speak—he won't ruin the moment with stupid words. His hands reach for me, bring me to him, and he pretends to kiss me, nipping at my lips, teasing me. I hate that, and I love to hate it—when a guy does that, fake-kisses me like that? I lose my goddamn mind. I dunno why. But this firefighter, who is, frankly, sex on legs, does it. In my imagination.

My response? Shove him down to his knees. And you know what he does? He goes, and he goes *down*. His tongue is nimble and quick and eager, and all he wants to do is give me orgasm after orgasm, until I'm just about dead from them. And then, finally, I'll take mercy on him, and let him touch me. Let him put that big, fat, thick, hard cock inside me….

I whimper as my fingers help me along with the fantasy, standing facing the showerhead, one hand braced on the wall, the other between my thighs, water beating down on the back of my neck and running over my face and down my body. My legs are braced wide, my spine bowed upward, head hanging between my shoulders, as I reach climax, picturing the huge hunk of man-meat pounding into me.

I come with a soft whimper, and then a loud, teeth-clenched scream. God, even in my fantasies, the man makes me come like a champ.

Too bad it's a fantasy, and all it'll ever be.

Because…

I don't date firemen.

I catch my breath, and then straighten, wash off some more, rinse, and get out.

Legs still jellied from my orgasm, I do the bare minimum of toweling off, and fall into bed still tangled up in my towel.

I may or may not dream of the firefighter.

It's not as busy, today. Thank God. There's a full, unbroken lunch break, which we spend in a Jimmy John's parking lot, noisily crunching on chips and waiting for a call to come in; DeShaun prefers AM news radio, which is weird as hell, but I have a talent for tuning out the radio, which I discovered when paired with a long-term partner who would only listen to the local classical music station. And look, I can appreciate classical music. Really, I can. But all day, every day, no breaks? I nearly went nuts before I learned how to just tune it out and focus on hearing only my own inner monologue.

There's a call to an apartment complex with an elderly woman having trouble breathing, and a young man in need of a thumb reattachment due to an accident involving a table saw.

And then it comes in: "Six-two-four-six, respond to a building fire on Madison and Fiftieth."

DeShaun answers while I jerk the shifter into gear, fire the lights and sirens—DeShaun pulls up the location on his phone's navigation app, and I focus on getting there as fast as safely possible.

When we arrive and see the fire, I know this is going to be a bad one. It's a multi-alarm fire, a whole apartment complex blazing. Smoke and flames pour from windows on three levels—there are half a dozen fire engines in place already and sirens howl, announcing more on the way. We're the first EMS bus to arrive, and DeShaun and I are immediately swarmed with smoke inhalation and minor burns—I set DeShaun to triaging, sorting out the patients by severity. As residents of the complex continue to evacuate, more busses arrive, helping us process the huge number of victims involved.

Our bus is parked a few feet away from the incident commander's truck, and I hear him respond to a radio call announcing all residents have been evacuated. The firefighter's focus, then, turns to containment, and I lose track of time as we deal with abrasions and burns and inhalation and the myriad injuries which occur in an incident like this.

There's a scream, then, from one of the patients. "There's someone still in there!"

All eyes focus on a window at the very top of the building, a small hand waving a bright blue blanket.

"Those upper stories are all but gone," I hear the incident commander say. "Do we have a ladder truck…no, shit. By the time we get one here, that kid'll be DOA."

"I can get her, sir." The voice is familiar.

No, no, no.

I risk a glance—yep, it's him, all seventy-seven inches of him, decked out now in full turnout gear. He's already hiking his oxygen tank higher on his shoulders, nestling his breathing apparatus to his face, smashing his helmet lower on his head. He snatches a set of irons, ignoring the incident commander's protests.

He's in through the front door at a run, straight into flames and smoke.

"Goddammit," the commander snarls. "Heroic motherfucker is gonna get himself killed."

I don't think anyone on the scene breathes for the next several minutes. The hand and the blanket vanish. It seems like silence to me, even though the scene is deafening—the roar of the flames and the gush of the hoses, hissing of steam, shouts and radio cross-chatter, sirens of busses leaving with victims in need of further care at the hospital.

There's a chorus of shouts and cheers, which I only just barely refrain from joining—the huge, heroic douche-bag emerges from the building, wreathed in flames and smoke. He has a bundle in his arms, wrapped in a fire blanket—his own oxygen mask is on the victim's face. He jogs over to my bus, hands me the child. A small Hispanic girl, no more than three or four, still clutching her blanket. Her eyes are wide and scared, the mask too big for her tiny face. I gently remove the firefighter's oxygen mask and replace it with one of our own.

"DeShaun," I say, "take over with her. Check her over."

"Got it." His big hands are gentle as he takes the girl from me.

The firefighter is bent over, gasping and hacking. I guide him to sit on the bumper. "Sit." I place his mask on his face. "Breathe."

Those big, deep, blue, stupid, incredible blue eyes fix on me. "It's you." His voice is a deep rasp, smoke-roughened, powerful.

"Yep."

He drops the mask. "I was first engine on scene and in charge of evacuations. Tank is empty."

I bring another portable oxygen tank from the bus and hand him the mask, turning on the flow once he has it in place.

"What's…" he pauses, drops the mask, and coughs for a minute straight, then replaces the mask. "What's your name?"

I can't help a narrow-eyed glare. He's flirting? Now? "Save your breath."

He taps the mask with a gloved finger. "I'm getting all the oxygen I can handle. I'm fine. What I need is your name."

"Jovie Martin."

He gives me that smile again—the one he gave me yesterday at the hospital. The grin that damn near set my underwear on fire. I viciously suppress my instinctive, biological response to that deadly dangerous grin of his.

"I'm Jake."

I arch an eyebrow. "A firefighter named Jake, huh?" *Jake* is an old slang term for firefighters.

He laughs, but the laugh turns into a coughing fit. Someone hands him a freshly-cracked bottle of Ice Mountain, and he sips rather than gulps until the bottle is empty. "Yeah, a firefighter named Jake. The irony, huh?"

I can't help a look at his name tag on his left breast. "Wait, really? Your last name is Howson?" I say it *HOSE-son*.

He rolls his eyes. "No, my last name is *HOW-SON*. Jake Howson."

"I'd go with *HOSE-son*, personally."

"You'd go with Hose-son?" His grin widens, and I realize I just walked into a pile of shit. "Like, on a date? Sounds good. I'm off Friday at five, so…dinner at six? My place? I'll cook for you."

"Not what I meant. Good try, but not in a million years." I step away from him. "You're clearly fine. I have patients to transport."

He just grins. "Why not, Jovie Martin?"

I glare. "You're not my type. Just go with that. Goodbye."

"I feel like you've had it out for me since the moment we met." He winks at me—fucking hell, that wink. It should be douchey and stupid and ridiculous, but somehow it's not. Somehow, it makes my panties melt even worse than the stupid grin. I don't let that show, however. "And what about me isn't your type? I'm everyone's type."

I feel like that's probably not a lie or an exaggeration on his part—those cheekbones and that jawline alone would see to it.

"Well for one, you're cocky—definitely not my type. And two, everything about you isn't my type. But mostly, I just don't like you. Now, if you're not going to take smoke inhalation seriously, get off my bus and go bother someone else."

He removes the mask, replaces his helmet, and backs away from me. "You drive a hard bargain, Jovie Martin."

"There's no bargain. Not interested."

He just grins at me, and then turns away. In a moment, he's lost in the scrum of firefighters working to finish off the blaze.

DeShaun, sitting with the little girl, still, smirks at me. "You *like* him."

I shoot a glare at him. "Stuff it, Howell."

He just snickers. "You're in *de-NIII-allll*," he sing-songs the last word.

"I said *stuff it*, Howell!" I stab a finger at him. "Shut

up, or I'll make sure you get paired with Abramson, *permanently*."

Sheila Abramson, a Karen of all Karens, a total bitch, arrogant, bossy, lazy, and incompetent. How she hasn't been fired is anyone's guess, but she should be. No one wants to work with her, and so we rotate who has to work a shift with her—it's supposed to be my turn next shift, but I'll totally finagle a switch just to teach DeShaun Howell to keep his mouth shut.

DeShaun holds up his hands in surrender. "All right, all right."

He doesn't say anything else, but I can feel him laughing at me.

Methinks the lady doth protest too much.

Shut up, Shakespeare. What do you know?

He's a douchebag. Winking. Grinning at me like a simpleton's smarmy grin is going to make me drop trou right at the fire and worship him. Or whatever it is he thinks that grin is supposed to do to me.

Did I feel something when he grinned at me? Sure. Was it disgust? No. But it may as well have been. It means nothing.

He's attractive, yeah. I can admit that. I can even go so far as to admit that he's the most attractive human male I've ever laid eyes on. Doesn't mean shit.

Jake fucking Howson. Fuck him and his giant muscles and his stupid blue eyes.

Wait, no. *Don't* fuck Jake Howson and his stupid giant muscles and stupid giant blue eyes. Definitely don't. That's not happening.

Not even in my imagination—not again, at least.

He won't ever know that I flicked my bean while picturing him eating me out. That's my little secret.

There's no way he can know, right? That I used him like that? He can't see it on me, even if I keep seeing him in my mind, naked instead of geared up in his turnout.

I'm not doing that again, anyway. I'm not.

It doesn't matter that he didn't even hesitate to go into that burning building. Not at all. I mean, sure, it's his job. But that was risky as hell, even for a firefighter. He had to have literally sprinted up eight flights of stairs, through smoke and flames to find that little girl, and then sprinted back down, this time with his oxygen on the girl.

Fucking heroic.

And I don't even really buy into the hero-shit. I'm a career EMS in a big city: I've seen everything. I've seen policemen sacrifice themselves to save people. I've seen firemen go into burning buildings and not come out. I've seen medics run unarmed into what amounted to a war zone, working on victims while bullets continue to fly.

This guy is nothing special.

So then...

Why, as DeShaun and I finish up at the scene and transport the last victim to the hospital, is he all I can think about?

I should not have indulged in that fantasy last night—because now it's all I can think about.

Argh.

I'm not going to see him again. Once is a chance meeting. Twice is a coincidence.

The universe isn't so diabolical as to throw Jake Howson and me together again.

Right?

Because—say it with me, now:

I…DON'T…DATE…FIREMEN.

Not now, not ever.

No matter how panty-melting his grin may be, no matter how fiery those sexy blue eyes are. No matter what. It's a rule for life, in my world. And it's a rule I will not break. Not now, not ever, not for anyone. Especially giant, heroic, handsome firefighters with ironically well-suited names.

JAKE

I AM, OBVIOUSLY, NO STRANGER TO THE OCCASIONAL bout of smoke inhalation. It always sucks, but it's part of the job. What really sucks about it, though, is that it means I get benched from the exciting stuff—tasked with executive work, paperwork, inventory, and shit like that. I prefer to be in the field, manning the hoses and attacking the fires. Which sometimes makes me question my own drive to make captain. I'm still in my prime—at the tail end of it, maybe, but I can still kick anyone's ass on the training course with one hand tied behind my back.

I'm back at Station Four, my home base, rustling up dinner for the crews—it's my day to cook and I take it very seriously, so I'm fixing my famous Howson's Hearty Beef Stew. And by famous, I do mean it. Among fire crews, at least—guys from other stations have been known to find excuses to swing by to get a bowl of it, so when it's my day to cook, I always make enough for a medium-sized army.

My usual crew, José, Maksim, and Jimbo, are

borrowing a new guy from Station One, and I'm filling in as acting captain. A good sign, I hope. A medical call goes out, and my crew heads out to answer it. The other crew is going over equipment after answering a minor grease fire in a hole-in-the-wall burger joint.

I'm stirring, taste-testing, and fiddling with the herbs when I hear the kitchen door open behind me—I assume it's one of the guys hoping the stew is done. "Not ready yet," I say, not turning around. "Give it an hour. There's leftover chimichangas from José's day if you're that hungry."

"I think I'll wait for the stew," a deep, smoke-hoarse voice says.

I freeze—I know that voice: Bruce Wells, Battalion Chief.

I set the spoon down and turn to face him, keeping my face stoic. I know what this visit is about. "Chief, good to see you." I extend my hand, and we shake.

Bruce Wells is a man's man, past sixty but still brawny and powerful and fit. He has severe burns distorting the right side of his face, and the rest of his body, but that's not visible—he earned those burns rescuing no fewer than six of his crew from a collapsed warehouse. He could have and probably should have transitioned careers, but he refused, and made Battalion Chief within a couple years, and his performance in that role has earned him the respect of everyone under his authority, me included.

Not least because I was one of the guys he rescued—I was trapped under a beam, watching fire march toward me, and none of my hard-earned strength could save me. Then came Chief Wells through the smoke and flames, levering the beam off me and hauling me out-side...only to go right back in for the rest of his guys. We should have lost someone that day, but we didn't—not one firefighter, all because of Chief Wells.

So, if he puts me at One, or Five, or doesn't pro-mote me at all, I won't like it, but I'll cooperate without a word of complaint, because he's earned my trust and my respect.

Not all commanders can say the same.

I pull a bowl from the cabinet and ladle the chief a heaping serving. "It should stew a bit longer to be perfect, but it's close enough."

He sits at the table and blows across the top—I sip coffee and wait.

Neither of us is in a hurry to broach the reason he's here, so silence extends as he wolfs down the piping hot stew at a pace only a firefighter can.

Finished, he slides the bowl away. "Best stew I've ever had, Jake. I don't know where you got that recipe, but goddamn, son, it's amazing."

I laugh and sit at the table with him. "I'll give you the secret, Chief—it's a family recipe passed down through my mom's side. She never had a daughter, just me, so she taught it to me."

"Well, you best make sure you pass it on to some-one, because that's a recipe that deserves to live on." He gestures at the industrial coffee maker. "Grab me a mug, would you?"

I pour him coffee, black, and resume my seat. "So."

He eyes me. "You talked to Larry."

I shrug. "I visited him, yeah."

"Crusty old fuck couldn't keep a secret if his life depended on it." He sighs. "It's not a secret, I just didn't want a bunch of rumors floating around when I was still thinking about it."

"You know what I want, sir. But you know my dedication is to the job and the department." I sip coffee, then, and wait him out.

"I do know what you want, but I can't give it to you, Jake. I'm sorry."

I nod, keeping the disappointment out of my face and my voice. "I understand, sir."

"This station is…well, none of them are more important than the others. But…I started here. I made Captain here. And a lot of the more critical calls requiring the most experienced men go through here. So in one sense, I need you here, because you're one of my best men. But I've got a dearth of leadership. Larry is gonna be on the mend for a while. We might be able to use him administratively, but even that's gonna be a minute. Don't let him fool you—that heart attack was a big one. How he even survived it is a goddamn miracle."

I nod. "I know it, sir." I wince, shaking my head. "I saw him working that arm, Chief. For days. I saw it. I knew what it meant. I should've—"

He lifts a hand. "Let me stop you there, Jake. Larry is a grown-ass man, an experienced medic and firefighter. He knows the signs. Shit, his own old man died of a heart attack. He knew better. He just ignored the signs. It's not on you. You're not responsible for him."

I groan, wiping my face with a hand. "I know, sir. I do. I just…"

"Worrying and feeling responsible for everyone is just your nature." He taps the table with a fore knuckle. "And that's why I'm here. Because you're gonna make a hell of a captain, Jake."

"Just not at Four."

"Right. You know as well as I do that Captain Yates is sort of…well…"

"Overstaying his welcome?" I suggest.

He laughs. "Yates is a good man. A good captain. But I think he's too stubborn to hang up his hat on his own, so I'm gonna have to nudge him." Serious eyes fix on mine. "One is a good place for you, Jake. It's a good mix of veterans and rookies—and the rookies are good. It's gonna be a great place for you to learn the ropes of being Captain." He points at me. "It's gonna be an adjustment, because I know how you feel, from experience, about being in the field, getting into the shit yourself. You're pretty young for the job, but I know you'll do it well."

"So Captain Mackenzie is coming here, and Kennedy is taking over Five?"

"Right."

"Well, tell Kennedy, from me, that the first thing he'll need to do is mix up the crews. Mack has the rookies together and they need an old hand to even things out."

Wells just regards me evenly. "Kennedy knows his shit, and so does Mack. And so do you." He removes something from his coat pocket, sets it on the table, and slides it to me: the double-bugle lapel pin of a captain. "Congratulations, Captain Howson."

I take it, look at it. "Thank you, sir. I mean it. Thank you. I'll do the job to the best of my ability."

"You've never done anything less in all the years I've known you." He stands up, extends his hand to me. "Report to Station One on Monday—after today's shift, you've got three days off."

"Yes, sir." I shake his hand, mixed feelings running through me.

"Congratulations, again. And remember, you're not doing the job in a vacuum, Howson. You can come to me with questions or for advice. Larry, too."

"I will, Chief."

He leaves, then, and I sit at the table, looking at the lapel pin in my hands.

My old crew returns, then, and Maksim barges into the kitchen with José in tow, the two bickering about some boxer or other. They see me at the same time, with the pin in my hands.

"Captain Howson!" Maksim claps me on the back. "Congrats, bro!"

José is more intuitive. "Where'd he send you?"

I remove my lieutenant pin and replace it with the captain pin. "One."

My friends exchange looks. "So...who's coming here, then?" Maksim asks. "Figure it would be you, huh? You and Cap...uh, Captain O'Shaugnessy had that all worked out, I thought." His accent renders the name *oh-shaw-NESSY*.

"Chief Wells has other ideas. Mack is coming here, Kennedy is moving up at Five, and I'm going to One. Yates is retiring or moving to central admin or something. I report to One on Monday."

They're both quiet.

"Gonna miss you, bro," Maksim says, eventually. "We can still post up at The Far Bar for beers, though, right?"

I laugh—The Far Bar is a local watering hole for all of the station crews, being centrally located in the city and run by a retired firefighter and his wife. You can always find at least two or three crews decompressing there after shift, and the boys and I are no exception.

"Yeah, Maks, you know it."

Will we, though? Will I change because of the job? Only one way to find out, I guess.

I spend the weekend at my cabin—a tiny, one-room shack on the edge of a little lake, upstate. No electricity, no plumbing, just a fireplace, an old rowboat, and whatever I bring with me. I bought it a few years ago as an escape from the city, and whenever I have more than twenty-four hours off in a row, I go there. Sit either on the rickety old dock or out in the middle of the lake, pretending to fish, and enjoying the quiet.

This weekend, though, my thoughts are anything but quiet.

The promotion, you assume?

No.

A certain black-haired, fiery-tempered beauty of a medic.

She's in my brain like a parasite, refusing to leave me the fuck alone. That fucking hair, thick and glossy and blacker than the midnight sky. That damn chest of hers. She must have a devil of a time finding shirts to fit, because she wears her shirt tucked in tight like regulations require, but her tits are so out of control that her buttons are at risk of becoming lethal weapons, should one pop off.

I roll in my bunk and try to sleep, but my idiot caveman brain keeps conjuring idiotic, impossible, never-going-to-happen scenarios about her.

Like, she just shows up here at my cabin, standing in the doorway. She'd be wearing…well, the scenario varies. Sometimes it's her uniform, which I eagerly rip off, scattering buttons ricocheting off the walls like stray bullets, and her massive, plump tits would spill out into my hands. Other times, she's in one of those old-timey white silk slips. Hair down, loose, like a storm-black thundercloud around her gorgeous face. She prowls toward me, curves swaying and jiggling as she peels the slip off over her head and straddles me.

That one really gets me.

Leaves me sitting bolt upright in my bed, gasping for breath, cock hard as a rock against my belly, straining inside my boxer briefs. Outside, dawn is still creeping at the horizon.

I can't get Jovie out of my fucking head.

My cock won't relax.

My mind won't stand down.

I lay back, close my eyes, and try—simply out of sheer desperation—to meditate my way to a state of calm, non-arousal.

Nope.

Behind my closed eyelids, all I can see is Jovie, standing in front of me, uniform button-down straining, hair braided—all done up and professional, clean, tight, nothing out of place. Fire in her eyes. I grasp the edges of her shirt at her throat and yank. Buttons ping and clatter off walls, windows, and floor. The shirt splays open, and her tits spring free—this is where the fantasy becomes truly fantastic, because in my mind, she's not wearing a bra. In reality, I know there's no way she'd ever not wear one under her uniform. She couldn't, just due to anatomical logistics. But fantasy is fantasy, okay? And in my fantasy, I rip her shirt open and big, bare tits fly free, bouncing and swaying, long and thick, round, heavy, perky and pert despite their almost impossible size. I seize them, fondling and cupping. In my fantasy, just my touch makes her moan, a breathy, porn-star groan of desire.

I sit upright again, eyes flying open at the moment of the fantasy when her head tips back and her mouth drops open as my expert touch drives her fucking bananas.

If she knew I was fantasizing about her, she very well might stab me in the eyeball with a pair of hemostats.

I can't fucking stop my brain, though. My libido. She just drives me insane, and I can't seem to do shit about it.

Maybe if I just indulge. Just *once*. It'll get her out of my mind.

I resist, though.

Stand up out of bed and stomp outside, angry with

myself for being so damn weak-willed. It's chilly, pre-dawn fog writhing along the ground, over the grass and curling on the surface of the water. I only own a sliver of land around my cabin, but there's no other cabin on this particular lake, nor even within ten miles of here. So I'm totally alone.

I stand on my dock in my underwear, deep breathing, willing my mind to banish the image of a topless Jovie Martin. Instead, however, all I manage to do is further it. Picture her tossing the ripped shirt off. She'd be frustrated, needing more, and she'd yank open her pants, shove them down. Thick, strong thighs, caramel and soft. White panties. Simple, plain, nothing special. But so sexy. Cupping a plump pussy, wet with need for me. For my touch. My mouth.

Her hair is loose, in my mind. That, her hair loose rather than braided, is almost as much of a turn-on for me as the fantasy of her bare breasts. Why, I dunno. I guess I've got a thing for her hair. I groan again, rubbing at my face until stars burst behind my eyes. Yet still, I've got Jovie Martin naked in my imagination, and now she's all but begging me to drop to my knees and make her come.

Fuck.

I can't help it.

She's too fucking gorgeous, and work has been so busy the past few weeks that I haven't had time for any fun, not even a hookup with one of the bottle-blond hose-hoes from The Far Bar.

So I'm overflowing with testosterone and libido. That's all this is. I need to get laid, and this whole stupid fantasizing about a medic who seems to hate the very sight of me will be over. In the meantime, I have to do something about this monster ramrod of a hard-on. I could drive nails with the thing—it fucking hurts.

I shove my underwear off and toe them aside, stand naked on my dock. Grip my cock in my fist, and let my mind have its filthy, sinful way with my imaginary version of Jovie Martin.

At first, I focus on making her come. That's always my first priority. Make her come, first and hard. Get a girl off once, and get her off *well*? She'll want more. And she'll be a lot more likely to be generous in her pursuit of more. In my mind, Jovie orgasms like a champion— writhing and screaming, riding my mouth like I'm a prize racehorse and she's a jockey. She won't be totally shaved—a little triangle of fuzz, maybe, or a nice narrow landing strip. I like it that way. I like my women to be *women*. Call me old-fashioned, I dunno. Just my thing. I like the way a little bit of pubic hair feels against my face, on my tongue. Weird? Maybe. I don't give a shit—I like what I like, okay?

Once I've gotten Jovie off a time or three, she'll be all sweaty and flushed and panting, hair wild, huge tits heaving. She'll shove me away, and that's when the real fun starts.

I plunge my fist around my dick, squeezing hard, roughly jerking myself. The ache builds, and I picture her moving to her knees in front of me. Tossing her hair over one shoulder and looking up at me as she takes me in her hands. Now my touch loosens, not squeezing as

45

hard but sliding as fast as my hand can move. Her lips press against my cock, and her tongue is light and wet...

Fuck.

I come with a shout, before I even get to the part of the fantasy where she actually blows me. Stream after stream of cum shoots out of me, into the lake, and I curl forward over myself, working the climax until I'm limp.

I straighten, gasping, watching my cum floating on the water.

I expected to feel better.

Relieved.

No more errant, and all-consuming thoughts of Jovie.

I'm an idiot.

I'd be hard again in a matter of minutes, if I let myself resume the fantasy. I can see her still, where I left her in my mind's eye—on her knees, lips around my cock.

See?

Dammit.

I dive forward and spear into the water—well away from where I, errr, contaminated the water. It's cold, a shock to the system. I pull myself under the water, stroking and kicking until my lungs run out of air, and then I surface, gasping, and finish the lap across the lake and back more slowly. By the time I reach the dock again, I'm huffing and puffing—it's a pretty big lake. But I'm more in control.

Sort of.

I pack up and head back to the city. As I reach home and gather my things, preparing to report for my first day at the new station, I resolve to put Jovie out of my mind. No matter what it takes.

In all likelihood, I won't see her again, anyway.

My first day at Station One is, thankfully, a slow one. I have a meeting with the crews, inspect the station from top to bottom, inside and out, take inventory, inspect the trucks, have the crews run tests of all hoses, check oxygen tank mixtures, mask seals, everything.

I don't have time or mental space for anything but work, thankfully. The rest of the week is the same, getting acquainted with my guys, responding to incidents and learning how to be the on-scene commander instead of the one to rush in. Like Chief Wells said, it's an adjustment.

At night, when the lieutenants on shift are in charge and I'm at home—a weird, disorienting change in my schedule—avoiding letting my mind go into the dangerous and addictive territory that is Jovie...it's tricky.

Porn helps. Somewhat. But even then, she takes over.

God, what's wrong with me?

I need...

What I need is to get laid. I'm working too hard and not playing enough—a habit of mine since childhood.

I find out when Maks and José and Jimbo are all off and arrange to meet them at The Far Bar. I'm in street clothes—I have a radio, of course, because now I'm even more permanently on call. José and Maksim enter a few minutes after me and join me at our booth.

The Far Bar is a hole-in-the-wall, a shotgun floor plan, narrow frontage but it runs way, way back clear the next alley over, a short length of bar near the front door and booths along both walls, low ceilings, a juke-box, dartboards, and pool table near the back door with the restrooms.

Our booth is right near the bar, and we belly up, order pitchers, and get to the good stuff—ribbing each other, telling tall tales of our exploits and dirty jokes, trading rumors and gossip…checking out the menu of girls scattered about the bar, each one angling and jostling for attention.

Hours pass, and I finally feel halfway normal.

And then the bell over the door dings, and my heart leaps into my throat.

Jovie Martin, accompanied by two women who are every bit as sexy as Jovie, in their own ways. Where Jovie is all curves, short and stacked like a porn star, one of her friends is the opposite, tall and svelte, with a delicate build. The other friend is somewhere in between, more medium height and carrying most of her curve in her backside, which, I admit, is pretty damn magnificent. A quick check-out of her companions is all that is. I have eyes for Jovie, and Jovie alone. She's in street clothes, too. Tight jeans with frayed hems at her ankles, wearing street-wear version of ballet shoes. The jeans must have a hell of a lot of stretch to them, to fit her thighs and ass like a glove like that. Her top is a white button-down, the front tucked behind a thick brown belt, the top few buttons undone.

Fuck me.

I'm done.

Done.

Her cleavage is mind-altering. High, but heavy. Perky, yet ready to explode out of the confines of the buttons at any second. One wrong bounce and the poor overworked button holding her boobs in is going to shatter. A lot of trust is being placed on that one button. I can't help but stare—and a primal, caveman part of my hindbrain is actively willing that button to fail.

Her hair is half up, half down, and that's what sends me into a real tailspin. From the temples up, she has her hair tied back, the rest left down around her shoulders, brushed to a glossy, raven-back shine. A simple gold chain drapes around her neck; whatever charm or pendant there might be has vanished into the shadowy chasm that is the valley between her breasts. Simple gold hoops adorn her ears, three on each lobe. Her purse is a tiny black clutch with a long strap, barely big enough to contain a phone and some cards, I'd bet.

"Jake?" I become slowly aware of a voice calling my name.

A hand shakes my shoulder.

"Jake!"

I start, and turn away from the door. Maks is staring at me, hand on my shoulder, looking at me as if I've grown a second head. "What?"

"You good, bro?" His wide, honest face is worried.

I laugh, rub the back of my neck. "Yeah. Yeah, I'm good. Tired, I guess."

José snorts. "Yeah, right. You was starin' at that girl

who just came in. The short one with the *grandes tetas*." He looks at me, then at her. "She saw you lookin', too. She don't seem happy."

I keep my attention on my beer. "She's coming this way?"

Maksim's eyes widen. "The word that comes to mind is murder."

I huff. "Yeah, we've had…a couple interactions. I'm not her favorite person."

José cackles. "A woman who *ain't* trippin' on her own feet to get in your bed? *Dios mío,* I don't believe it."

I toss a crumpled-up bar napkin at him. "Shut up, douchebag."

"You." Her voice is pissed. Sharp as razors and cold as ice.

I spin on the bench and meet her eyes. Her eyes, I tell you. I'm looking dead into those big brown eyes, and nowhere else. "Hi, Jovie."

"Why is it you're suddenly everywhere I go?"

I shrug. "You must be following me."

She doesn't quite snarl. "You wish."

I grin at her—not *the Grin*, which last time only pissed her off even worse. "I mean, I *might* wish you were following me around if you were nicer about it."

She huffs—a sudden sharp out breath, and I immediately fail the don't-look-at-her-chest test. "God, you're annoying."

I sip beer without looking away from her eyes. "I mean, you came to *my* table."

"We're just here to unwind."

I gesture at Maks, José, the two empty pitchers, and

50

the clean, empty rocks glass containing our keys—our reminder to get a Lyft. "Same here."

"Why do you have to do it *here*, though?" She almost sounds…whiny. Even that is hot.

"We're firefighters?" I gesture at the wall behind us, which is plastered with framed photos of firemen, old patches, battered helmets, and rusting sets of irons. "And this is our bar. Why are *you* here? I dunno about your friends, but I know you're a medic. Not a firefighter."

She manages to crank up the glare wattage to zero-kelvin levels of unfriendly iciness. "My stepsister is the head of the ER, and my best friend is an EMT like me." She gestures in turn—the tall one is her stepsister, and the shorter one her best friend.

I grin even harder, turning up the wattage of my own smile as fiercely as she's turning up the coldness of her expression. "And you're more than welcome here. You may not be firefighters, but you *are* emergency services. And that's good enough for me."

I lift a hand and whistle for Rick's attention—he shuffles over with a fresh pitcher for us; I gesture at Jovie and her companions. "Their first round is on our tab, Rick."

Rick, portly, with a balding ponytail, nods. "You got it, Jake."

Jovie's silence manages to convey intense loathing. "Don't buy us drinks."

I set my beer down and stand up to my full height. Her eyes follow me…up, up, up. I tower over her, and I'm satisfied to note her eyes widen a little—and I may be mistaken, but she may have even swallowed kind of hard. And…is that a faint blush I detect? Certainly not. She's of Italian heritage or I'll eat my helmet—her skin tone is olive-brown enough that a blush can be hard to see.

"I'm not your enemy, Jovie." I edge closer, until our bodies are nearly touching—I can almost feel that bolt of electric energy again, and I'm sorely tempted to touch her just to see if I'll feel it again. "I don't know why you seem to hate me, and if I did something to piss you off, I'm sorry for it." I gesture at our booth. "Why don't you and your friends join us? I'll even let *you* buy *us* a round, if you don't want me buying them for you."

She doesn't answer, her jaw set hard and molars grinding. She inhales, swelling her chest. I only just barely, by sheer willpower, manage to not look down. A wisp of inky hair drifts in front of her face, sticking to her moist lips.

I watch my hand lift and order it to drop back down. The hand disobeys me. Continues to lift.

My fingertip touches her cheek, and she flinches as if struck.

Or…as if she felt the lightning bolt spark of electricity, same as me. The moment my fingertip brushed her cheekbone, I felt it. Like sticking scissors into a socket—something my dumb ass did, once, and thank God I was wearing rubber-soled Converse or I'd have been Kentucky Fried Jake.

The jolt travels through my arm, soaks into my very bones and blood. I shiver, suck in a breath…but the spark keeps going. It buries itself in my gut, sizzles down between my thighs—and hardens my cock into something that resembles a steel I-beam.

Her lips part.

Time has stopped.

I brush the single strand of black hair away from her face, tuck it behind her ear with the rest of her hair.

For the space of a single eye blink, she topples forward against me. Breasts squashing against my chest, our hips touching.

Her eyes fly open wide and she gasps—she feels my erection.

The eye blink passes, and she pushes away from me.

Storms out of the bar, not even waiting for her sister or friend. They look from me to the door as it closes behind her, and then hurry out after her.

Holy shit, holy shit, holy shit.

"God*damn*, bro," Maks says. "What the *hell* was that?"

José answers. "*That* was sexual tension you could cut with a knife."

"She hates me," I answer—even to myself, I sound shell-shocked. "I dunno why, but she does."

"I think she *wants* to hate you," José says, amused. "She tryin' to, at least."

"So far, she seems to be succeeding." I slump to my seat. "Fuck me, she's gorgeous." I cover my face with my hands and try to breathe normally.

"She ain't ugly," José says. "Her friend ain't bad, either. Honey had *culo* for days."

"The tall one looked like my first girlfriend," Maksim says. "Back in Ukraine. Not so much to hold on to, but I could throw her around. She liked that, when I put her this way and that, you know?"

I barely hear them. Barely remember what her companions looked like. I can feel the spark, still. I hadn't imagined it. Every time we touch, it feels like I'm grabbing onto lightning itself.

And I've barely touched her.

What would it be like to have a handful of her flesh?

Fuck. I'm in serious trouble.

JOVIE

"JOVIE, SLOW DOWN!" THIS IS LIA.

"Why are we leaving? That bar was *it*! I've never seen so many sexy firemen in my life." This is Erin.

Erin, my stepsister, catches up first, her long legs moving her faster at a walk than I can run, unless I'm *running*. She's a brunette, with a little red in her hair in the right light, and big green eyes. A self-proclaimed member of the Itty Bitty Titty Committee, Erin is stunningly beautiful—she should have been a supermodel. She has the looks and the build, but her brains and ambition took her in a different direction—med school. She graduated high school at sixteen and was doing her rotations by twenty, had a permanent spot in the ER by twenty-one, and head of the entire department by thirty-one.

Lia, my best friend, catches up a moment later. Lia is my partner in crime, and more of a sister than Erin, even—I've known Lia since pre-school, whereas Erin only came into the picture when Mom remarried around my nineteenth birthday, three years after Daddy's death.

I'm close to both, but Lia is like half of me. We can have whole conversations without saying a word. We both lost our fathers the same day, in the same fire, and we swore a blood oath together that we'd never date a fireman.

I know she gets it.

Erin? Not so much.

An EMT like me, Lia is nearly my twin—we're both third-generation Sicilian, with identical long black hair, brown eyes, and Italian complexions. We're twins temperamentally, too, with hair-trigger tempers, high-octane libidos, intense and possibly overdeveloped senses of independence, and a proclivity for a work-hard-play-hard lifestyle.

Erin likes to think she can keep up with us, but she can't. We'll be carrying her lightweight Welsh ass home and putting her in bed, and then keep partying. When you do the job we do, unwinding properly is critical. A nonnegotiable. You gotta wash away the images, you know?

Lia is in front of me, grabbing me by the arm. "We're going back."

"We are not."

"Are too." She shakes me like a rag doll. "DID YOU SEE THE MAN-MEAT IN THAT BAR?"

I try to remain calm. "Yes. I saw."

"Did she see? She was tits-to-chest with the meatiest man in the whole damn place!" Erin says. "They had a *moment.*"

"There was no moment." My voice is *too* calm. My eyes fix on Lia's. "We *don't* date firemen."

"Date? No. Fuck six ways to Sunday? Yes." She gives me one more little shake. "Your dude's friend with the tats was looking at me like he wanted to do very bad things to me, and girl, I am *here* for it. Hump and dump all the way, baby." She pokes my nose. "I know for a *fact* you've hooked up with a fireman. Last May, after the fundraiser banquet. The Black one."

I shake my head. "I was drunk by the time we left, and he was too much of a gentleman to take advantage." I shrug. "I was embarrassed, so I never told you we didn't hook up."

"Good lord, Jovie. Details. You would have fucked him if you'd been sober."

"Sure. But that's a hookup, nothing more. He wasn't even from here—he was from Wisconsin and ended up attending the banquet with a buddy."

Erin seizes on my gaffe. "Meaning, there's something more there with the blond god you were flirting with."

I glare at her. "He's not a god, we weren't flirting, and there's *nothing* there."

Erin and Lia exchange glances, then turn their gazes on me.

"Jove—honey. Baby. Darling." This is Lia, and she only starts like that when she's trying to lay out something for me that she feels is glaringly obvious which I am missing. "You *like* him. You need to admit it so you can handle it. Why? Because he's a fireman, and—say it with me now—*WE...DON'T...DATE...FIREMEN*. But you *do* like him. I can see it, Erin can see it, and I'm pretty damn certain both he and his two hot friends can see it. You're the only one who can't, and only because you're in denial. Which is not going to solve the problem."

"I don't like him," I grumble.

Lia sighs—an expression of long-suffering amusement. "The sooner you admit it, the sooner you can get to the real work of moving on."

Erin rubs my shoulder as if I'm bereaved and in mourning. "Which you can only do once you've admitted the truth."

"There is no truth except he's obnoxious and stuck-up and ridiculous and entirely too macho."

"You're Italian," Lia deadpans, "there's no such thing as a too-macho man."

"Ha ha ha," I snark back. "Real fuckin' funny, Lia."

"Who's joking?" She gestures at me with a flick of a finger. "He had you so worked up back there, I swear, you could scoop the sexual tension between you two with a freaking spoon. You were, as my ex-boyfriend's Jewish grandmother used to say, *verklempt.*" Her finger swipes the air vertically, indicating my body. "You were all pushed up against him, staring up at him like you wanted to climb him like a tree and do deliciously terrible things to his gargantuan stud-muffin body. I mean, yes, if looks could kill, he'd be dead. But if looks could kill, you'd be naked and getting fucked up against the wall of the bathroom in that bar, right now."

"That makes no sense." I glare at her. "It's untrue, and it makes literally less than zero sense."

"It doesn't have to make sense to be true." She smirks

at me. "That's not the first time you've had an interaction with him, is it?"

I roll my eyes. "No. He keeps popping up in my life all of a sudden. And every time, he's more obnoxious, self-assured, ridiculous, and aggravating than the last time. I want nothing more than to never lay eyes on the man again."

Lia, damn her, knows me all too well. "And can you honestly and truthfully tell me you've never thought about him? Not once? Not even for ten seconds? You've never *once* thought about ripping that shirt off him and licking his absolutely enormous muscles from his shoulders all the way down to what I'm sure is a mammoth, colossal, throat-ruining cock?"

I choke on my shock—you'd think I would be used to the things Lia says after knowing her for almost thirty years, yet still, she manages to shock me. "Lia Maria Elisabetta Rossi!"

She shivers, giggling. "Oooh! I got *both* middle names! That one was right on the money!"

"That was disgusting!"

"Only if you're a prude, and you, my dearest love, my sister from another mister, my most darling of friends, are most assuredly not a prude." She leans close, whispers conspiratorially—in a stage whisper. "I know for a fact you *love* gobbling cock. You can't get enough. In fact, when you go too long without a cock in your mouth, you get cranky. And you're cranky. Which means you need cock. In your mouth, in your hands, in your tight little hoo-ha. You want it, you need it, and you're madder than a kicked bee's nest that you want *his* cock. Because he's off-limits."

"Stop talking about cocks, *Lia*," I hiss.

"Why? Are you starting to picture his?" She holds her hands one atop the other, fingers spread wide as if gripping the shaft of a softball bat, using her sultriest dirty-talk voice. "I bet it's fucking *huge*. Lots of purple veins popping out. Big, fat, plump head just *dripping* with precum."

"Whooooo boy," Erin breathes, gasping, shrill. "Girl, you're making *me* verklempt, and he's not even my type."

Lia waves a hand. "Bullshit. A man like *that* is everyone's type. Yours, mine, our mothers', our aunts', grandmas', my gay cousin Sal."

Erin laughs. "I mean, don't get me wrong, I'd take him for a spin. But my job is so damn demanding, I need a man with a low-stress, boring job. Like an accountant. Or a banker. Or an insurance salesman."

Lia gives Erin a look which communicates wordlessly and yet clearly how idiotic Lia thinks this statement to be. "Nobody fantasies about a *banker*, Erin. You fantasize about a man like that guy back there—six-five and two-fifty of solid muscle or I'm a Smurf, fuck-me blond hair, fuck-me blue eyes, perfect stubble." She shivers. "I mean, shit, he doesn't even know I exist, and I know *I'm* gonna go home and diddle the ol' bean to thoughts of his baseball bat cock."

I cover my face. "You are so embarrassing, Lia. I swear."

Erin, flushing, waves Lia off. "Sure, he's the type you fantasize about. But he's not the type I personally am interested in long-term. I want boring and stable. A man I know will be at home when I get there after an eighteen-hour shift. I want him a little squishy, and gentle, and easy to please. Exciting and rough is fun and all, but when you get down to the nitty-gritty, I want stable and predictable. That's just me."

Lia shakes her head. "Well, we couldn't be more different. Good news for you is, finding a man who fits that bill will be the easiest thing in the world. A woman who looks like you, who's as successful as you? Snap your fingers, girl—ten men will drop to their knees and beg for a chance to make you happy."

Erin grins. "I didn't say an unsuccessful or ugly banker."

Lia cackles. "Good to know even you have some kind of standards." She looks at me, then. "You're awfully silent."

"I'm thinking about how I need at least six shots of tequila to get over this idiotic, juvenile conversation."

"I bet they have great tequila back at that fireman's bar."

I glare at her. "Lia? Drop it. Please."

Finally, she sighs and holds up her hands in surrender. "Fine. Fine! But just so we're clear, I want it on record that you're in denial. And remaining in denial about your feelings regarding the hot-as-fuckballs firefighter is only going to make things more difficult. Your only viable options are to either fuck him out of your system, or admit your feelings to yourself so you can work through them like an adult. Denying the truth is only going to drag things out and will likely end in you doing something utterly stupid that you're going to regret, and I'm going to gleefully laugh at you and tell you I told you so, even if I have to do so while holding your hair as you puke your guts out after chugging four bottles of cheap wine."

I stare at her. "That was a hell of a run-on sentence, number one, and number two, that was bizarrely specific, and number three, wrong."

She holds her hands up again. "If I'm wrong, I'll admit it. But I'm not. I'll drop it, though. For now." She plumps her breasts higher, adjusts the strap of her cross-body clutch between them, and gestures at the sidewalk. "I have tomorrow off, which means I'm here for a long time *and* a good time. Let's go get shitty, girls!"

I put all six-feet-five inches and two hundred and fifty pounds of blond-haired and blue-eyed perfection that is Jake Howson firmly out of my mind.

Firmly.

Firm, like his firm muscles.

Gah.

A week later, I'm on a forty-eight-hour-off stretch. Which means a bazillion trips down to the laundry facilities in the basement of my condo building. Laundry day, in turn, means I'm in my day-off doing laundry and cleaning house outfit: Barbie/Pepto Bismol-pink booty shorts that do not, not even almost, cover my ass, and an ancient, no-longer-white sports bra that is not at all up to the job of containing or supporting my stupidly enormous tits. But my condo is populated mostly by nine-to-fivers and retirees who aren't here in the summer, which means I don't see anyone on my trips down to the laundry room.

I clean, I fold, and I catch up on *Love is Blind* and *RHOBH* and *Dateline* murder mysteries. It's late, past midnight, and I have my earbuds in, cranking away at my rowing machine.

I'm in the zone—reaching the end of my thirty-minute session, dripping sweat and gasping.

And that's when I smell smoke.

I'm not cooking anything.

All my risky appliances are unplugged—as the daughter of a firefighter, I know better.

I hop up off of my rower, grab my phone, and poke my head out of the doorway—smoke curls along the ceiling in thin gray tendrils.

I snag my keys off the hook, toss them in my purse with my phone, stuff my feet into the worn Birkenstocks I've had since ninth grade which I wear down to the laundry—all this takes less than fifteen seconds, and I'm out my door.

I pound on doors on my way to the stairs, dialing 9-1-1. "This is Jovie Martin," I say, cutting off the operator's greeting and rattle off my address. "There's a fire in my condo building, third floor I think, but I'm not sure where it's located." I pass the fire alarm pull handle by the elevator and yank it. "I just hit the alarm. Exiting the building."

The alarm shrieks—the fire is not present in my immediate vicinity, so the sprinklers here remain dormant.

The operator confirms that the fire department

already received the alert and is on the way. By the time I reach the stairs, I'm soaked to the bone.

Others from the floor above me are already on the way down, and we make a sleepy, shuffling parade in varying states of undress as we troop outside. It's a chilly night. Smoke trickles from a third-floor window, but so far does not show signs of spreading into a major event.

The first engine shows up a minute or two later, the crew swarming out of the truck and inside, talking into radios and carrying irons. Another truck shows up, and a third, followed by a pair of fire department ambulances. My instincts as a career paramedic are on high alert, especially when a fireman comes out of the building, supporting an elderly woman I recognize from my floor. She's coughing, having trouble walking. Barely realizing what I'm doing, I'm at her side in a moment, taking her from the firefighter—I ignore the odd look he gives me…it doesn't even register.

"Ma'am?" I help her to the nearby bus. "Can you sit up straight for me, Mrs. Bennet? There you go. Let's get this on you—" I take the portable oxygen from the fireman, who also gives me a strange, confused look, and help her get it on over her mouth and nose. Her eyes are terrified, her frail chest rising and falling swiftly—fear hyperventilation more than smoke inhalation, I think. "Breathe in deeply, Mrs. Bennet. Slow, steady, deep breaths. You're safe, now. It's okay."

"Ma'am?" The fire department paramedic touches my arm. "You should me let check you over."

I frown at him—I'm in work mode, and anything non-work doesn't register. "Check me over?"

Mrs. Bennet tugs at my arm. "Mr. Jell-O." She tries to pull the mask off. "Mr. Jell-O is still in there."

"Mr. Jell-O?" I prevent her from taking the mask off. "Is that a cat, Mrs. Bennet?"

She nods. "He's old. Blind. He sleeps by his litter box in my bathroom." She's panicking all over again, trying to get up, to take the mask off. "Mr. Jell-O!"

I look around for the marked truck and labeled jacket of the incident commander—he's facing away from me, and I jog over to him. It's not until he turns around at my tap on his shoulder that it registers who this is.

"Jovie?" His voice is immediately concerned, his eyes scanning over my body, from hair to toes...and then back up, slowly, pausing at my chest before flicking with a guilty start to my eyes. "Is this your building?"

His perusal is what makes sense of the looks I've been getting—I'm not on duty. I'm a resident. I look down at myself—day-off booty shorts that leave the bottom curve of my ass cheeks hanging out, ragged, sagging sports bra that mostly covers but cannot contain my boobs, hair in a messy bun. The sports bra is white, and old and thin stretchy cotton, and thus nearly see-through. Plus, I'm chilled—hello, major headlights. I could cut glass with how hard and prominent my nips are, and with the white bra, I might as well be topless.

No wonder those poor young firefighters were looking at me like that—I was acting like the lead responding medic...while essentially naked.

All this goes through my head in a split second.

"Mrs. Bennet." I force the words out, but they emerge

as a croak. "Three-ten. She has a cat. He's blind, in the bathroom. Mr. Jell-O."

He immediately transfers the information via radio, listens to the response, then juts his chin at me. "One of my guys heard him yowling—they're bringing him down now, but he's not a happy cat."

Translation: Mr. Jell-O is kicking up a hell of a fuss.

I nod. "I'll get him and bring him to Mrs. Bennet."

His huge, calloused hand circles my arm and halts me. "You're not a responder in this incident, Jovie. You need to let one of my medics check you out." He hesitates. "Medically, I mean."

I arch an eyebrow. "I know what you meant, Jake." I tap the double bugle pin on his lapel. "Captain, now, huh?"

He nods. "Yup. First major incident I'm responding to." He grins at me. "How'm I doing?"

I shrug. "I dunno. What's the situation inside?"

"Small fire in three-fourteen. Looks to be from a candle left lit that was knocked over by a cat. Caught the carpet and it spread rather slowly from there, fortunately."

"Did it spread to any other units?"

He shakes his head. "Negative. Contained to three-fourteen. Lots of smoke, but a pretty small fire, all things considered." He smirks. "Someone called 9-1-1 pretty fast."

"The building alarm was first. Your guys already had the call by the time I got the operator."

His gaze is uncomfortably direct and admiring. "Several residents on the third floor report being woken up by someone pounding on their door even before the alarm went off."

I shrug. "I smelled smoke. I've worked night shifts for so long I can't sleep before one a.m. even on a day off."

He nods. "Understand that. I wake up every few hours no matter what—I'm so used to the alarm going off, you know?" A voice comes through on his radio, and he listens. "Copy, Dawson. Good job. Wrap it up." He glances at me. "Fire is out."

I know better than to ask if I can go home—just because the initial fire is out doesn't mean the incident is resolved.

He sees me shiver and reaches into the open passenger window of his captain's pickup and withdraws a thick navy-blue FD zip-up hoodie. He drapes it over my shoulders and plops the hood over my head—the hem drops to my thighs, nearly to my knees, the sleeves hang six inches past my fingers, and the hood covers my face entirely—it's enormous, and weighs a literal ton, the inside lined with fluffy fleece and the exterior a thick Carhartt blend.

I look up at him from under the hood. "Wow. Thanks."

He chuckles and pulls the hood back so it frames my face, reaches down and zips it up, and then lifts one of my arms up and rolls the sleeve until my hand shows, and then does the same on the other side. "There you go."

It's so fucking warm it makes me angry. It smells so fucking good, it makes me angry—faintly of smoke, strongly of man-smell: soap, deodorant, sweat, that indefinable something that is just purely masculine and utterly intoxicating.

What makes me angriest is that wearing this hoodie like this reminds me in a palpable, physical, emotional way of my father.

As a preteen and young teenager, I was an insomniac. I still am, and it's why I so often volunteer for third shift. I'd sneak out of the house and visit Daddy at the station, and sometimes, if it wasn't a casualty incident, he'd let me ride with him either in the engine or in the incident commander's truck. And I'd always get to wear the big thick crew neck sweatshirt he kept in the truck, or his turnout jacket. It'd be huge on me, and so warm, and it would smell like him. That was, in a way, the greatest comfort I ever knew in life—wearing that sweatshirt, watching him work the incident.

Fuck, fuck, fuck.

My throat closes—the smell is fucking *the same*. Like, does Jake wear the same cologne, or use the same deodorant?

I shuck the jacket like it was burning my skin, toss it at him. "Thanks. I'm fine."

He catches it, looks at me, then the sweatshirt, jacket, thing. "Fine, suit yourself. You looked cold, is all. Just trying to be nice."

I roll my eyes at him, summoning the ice to keep from melting. "I looked cold, huh? You noticed?" I cross my arms over my chest. "Keep your eyes to yourself, Howson." I say his name wrong on purpose.

"Jesus, you're prickly," he mumbles, tossing the jacket back into the truck. "Thought I was being nice. Godddamn."

I almost feel bad. He *was* being nice. And for the sixty

seconds I was able to handle wearing that damn jacket, it felt nice. Comforting and homey.

Like a drug, for a closed-off, diamond-hard bitch like me.

Drugs are bad. Just to be clear. I avoid them at all costs. Both the illegal kind, and the others. Like a warm, comforting, familiar jacket that makes me feel like a little girl all over again.

I fight the shivers, keeping my arms crossed over my chest, both for warmth and to hide my pokey nipples as much as I can. I head over to Mrs. Bennet, who has Mr. Jell-o in her arms, petting his wet fur. He's a soft, pale gray, with blind, milky eyes, and he looks pissed at the world.

I sit beside Mrs. Bennet. "They got Mr. Jell-O for you, I see."

She nods, stroking her cat's back. "Yes. Thank you."

I shrug. "I just told them. I didn't do anything."

"I don't know what I'd do without Mr. Jell-O. He's my best friend."

"Well, you've got him, now." I'm not good at small talk. "How'd he get his name?"

"My husband, Harold, God rest him. Harold surprised me on our fiftieth anniversary with a kitten. Harold passed a few years later. Harold named him. I'd made Jell-O, because it was Harold's favorite dessert. Well, the kitty was batting at the Jell-O, making it wiggle, you know? And so Harold decided the kitty should be named Mr. Jell-O."

I reach into the bus and retrieve one of the thick scratchy wool blankets and drape it around both of us— Mrs. Bennet is far safer to be around than Jake Howson.

An hour later, during which Mrs. Bennet has dozed off on my shoulder and Mr. Jell-O on her lap, Jake comes over to me. His deep blue eyes regard me. Do they soften, some-how, as he regards me?

"It's clear for you to go home."

I nod. "Thank you, Captain."

"Just call me Jake." He looks at me. "Did you get cleared by a medic?"

"I *am* a medic, Captain Howson. I cleared myself—I was out before the smoke had spread. I'm cold and tired and ready to go to bed."

He sighs. "Would you see someone for help if you needed it?"

"Of course I would. Have to take care of yourself so you can take care of others. Emergency care one-oh-one."

He nods. His eyes are hard to read, at the moment. "I'm glad you're safe, Jovie."

"I was never in any danger but thank you."

A fraught moment, his eyes boring into mine. He wants to say something. But he doesn't. "We're clearing out. I'll see you around."

"I can't seem to get away from you. So yeah, I guess you will."

Later, in bed, I can't stop reliving that moment when I had Jake's jacket on.

And I hear Lia's words about being in denial.

Sleep is slow in coming, and I at least have to admit some portion of my insomnia is due to the memory of a certain pair of virulently blue eyes, and a big rough strong hand on my arm, and the way his jacket felt:

Like a hug.

JAKE

I N MY OFFICE, WORKING ON THE INCIDENT REPORT.
Fortunately, it was reported quickly and was contained
without major injuries or loss of life, or even any major
structural damage.

Of course, as I finish the incident report paperwork,
my thoughts aren't on the incident, even though it's my
first major incident as captain, it's not really remarkable
as an incident, which is good—unremarkable is good,
when you're a firefighter, or any kind of emergency services personnel, really.

I'm thinking about Jovie.

Is that outfit what the woman wears to bed? I mean,
damn. That was a whole lot of not much, and I'm not
complaining.

Her body is…perfect.

She's wicked strong—her legs are powerful, thickly
muscled yet smooth and silky and soft-looking. I know
comparing skin color to food is…I dunno, passé or

something, but I just can't help thinking of caramel. Smooth, freshly pulled, sweet. Her arms are muscular, and her shoulders—the woman lifts, that much is clear.

But that *ass*.

Fuck.

I wipe my face and lean back in my chair, closing my eyes and trying to banish the image of her ass as she walked away from me. The phrase, "hate to see you go but love to watch you leave" comes to mind. Those shorts were…well, they tried and failed at their job of containing her backside. Round, and big. Firm, yet with a nice little shimmy to it at every step—step step, jiggle jiggle; step step, jiggle jiggle.

Dammit. Eyes closed, it's all I see. That ass: jiggle jiggle, as she walks away…angry at me, *again*, for reasons I cannot fathom.

I mean, all I did was give her a coat.

Yeah, I can't and won't try to deny that I absolutely noticed her hard nipples. But she was literally shivering. So I gave her a coat. I don't smoke cigarettes obviously, and I don't think I have a generally offensive personal odor. So why did she rip off that jacket like it stank of shit?

I put it on her, and obviously it was too big—she's five-six on a good day, and I'm six-five in my socks, so yeah, she's gonna swim in it. But for a moment, I swear, she liked the way it felt. The way it smelled. Something. She probably wasn't aware she'd done it, but when I had the sleeves adjusted and all that, she sank into it, turned her head to the side and sniffed. Exhaled, slowly, like the scent was…*good*. Her face softened, eyes closed. Like she was reliving some memory. A good memory. A scent memory—the most vivid and palpable of memories come from scent, and I would bet the title to my truck that something about my hoodie hit a scent memory for her.

I cannot make sense of that woman.

There'll be split seconds before she catches herself where I'd swear she likes me. Sees me. Is attracted to me. Physically, in those moments, she gives off serious I'm-hot-for-you vibes. Her big brown eyes on mine, the way she catches her breath, the way she can't quite look away.

Then something comes over her, and she pulls on this cloak of impenetrable anger, and that moment is gone, and the soft beautiful woman with it. In her place, the icy demeanor of someone who cannot *stand* me, like I offend her with my very existence. Hard, shut down, do-not-approach.

And I don't get it. I haven't even made any crazy, off-color comments or hit on her in some kind of offensive way. She acts like I slapped her ass and told her to make me a sandwich. And trust me, raised by *my* mom? That's the furthest thing from who I am. Mom would get wind I'd done that, somehow, who knows how, and she'd appear like a genie and slap the actual shit out of me until I apologized like a blubbering baby. Worse yet, she'd give me the Mom Look. The *I'm so disappointed in you* look.

But mostly, I'm just not that guy.

I swear I'm not.

So…why does she hate me?

"Cap?"

I'm lost in my thoughts, my reverie.

"Captain Howson?"

I blink, and realize the person is speaking to me. It's

Lieutenant Childers, a twenty-year veteran with no designs on moving past his current rank. Mid-fifties, tall and stout, a lot of heavy muscle and a little padding around it, with a full gray-brown beard and a shaved head.

"Sorry, Chilly, not used to responding when someone calls for the captain." I tilt forward and focus on him. "What's up?"

"Morton nailed a car on the way to a call." He winces. "Bus Three is…it's not in good shape, Cap."

"Shit." Ambulance Three is brand new, meant to replace One, which is aging and in need of retirement. "Be right there."

He nods, slaps the frame, and leaves. I put Jovie and her mercurial attitude out of my mind—putting her insane body out of my mind is far more difficult, but I manage. Mostly.

Sort of.

Bus One isn't totaled, but it's gonna need work which I don't really have the budget for…but this is the job, right? More importantly, I have to talk to Morton. He's a pretty experienced driver engineer with a good record, so I imagine whatever happened isn't his fault.

It's a long morning, dealing with insurance and paperwork. And thankfully, it distracts me from thinking about Jovie.

And her ass.

And those tits…Jesus, those tits. It took every last ounce of my willpower to keep my eyes unglued from them—that bra may as well have not been there, and it wasn't doing much to begin with.

Gah, this is a problem. I haven't had a crush this bad

in a long, long time. And it's been even longer since any-one seriously held out on me, in the attraction depart-ment. By "even longer" I mean "ever."

As in, yeah, the guys at Five aren't wrong—if I'm in the mood for a tussle with one of the girls who frequents The Far Bar, or any other bar, for that matter, it's usually a matter of pointing and grinning.

But I also haven't pursued anyone seriously in a long time.

There was Sara, the English girl from the university who frequented the coffee shop down the street from Five. She played hard to get, but it was very obviously a game she fully intended to lose—and did. She and I had a good time, but she was only here for a year, so when that year was up, the game was up, and we both knew it was coming and were fine with it.

That was six months ago she went back to jolly old England, and I've only made time for a couple hookups since.

God, my brain is going in convoluted loops.

The problem is, I have it bad for Jovie Martin. And she wants no part of it.

Am I pursuing her? No, I'm not.

I don't know how.

I don't pursue.

Mostly, girls throw themselves at me. At me, and into my bed. When I'm the mood, I let 'em. But I take The Job more seriously than anything in life, and I have since I decided I wanted to be a firefighter as a kid. I had a single goal from that moment, and I worked to achieve it. Having achieved it, being the best goddamn firefighter on the planet has been my singular focus. Girls and sex have largely been a matter of easing the need, letting off steam, sating the hunger, a little. Or, at least, taking the edge off.

The thing with Sara was the closest I've ever been to a relationship, and that *was* nice. Different, being with the same person every time for a few months, getting to know her, her body, her particular like and dislikes. I wouldn't say I really connected, and we never talked about deep stuff—it was more of a friends-with-benefits thing than a real relationship.

Why am I thinking about a relationship? Jovie doesn't even *like* me. It's not hard to get, it's leave me alone.

So why can't I shake the feeling that there could be more? That there could be something there? That she's deflecting, or something? Maybe it's wishful thinking, seeing something that isn't there.

I don't know.

I just know I'm freaking infatuated with her. I had that one lapse at my cabin, and I've managed to avoid thinking about Jovie while jerking off, so far.

After seeing her earlier? Not sure that streak is going to continue.

And if I do that—if I jerk off while thinking of Jovie and her goddess curves, and then I see her in person, I'm not sure I'll be able to keep myself from pursuing her.

Which is what she seems to want.

Seems to—*seems*, being the keyword. I'm not sold that she really means it. I mean, no is no, okay? But convincing her I'm not all that bad? Maybe getting her to go out on a real date with me? That's different.

My day officially starts in a few hours, so there's no point going home. I hit the showers—this is an older station, and hasn't yet housed a female firefighter, so the showers are still communal, even if the sleeping quarters have been updated from the open bunkhouse arrangement; I plan to fix both issues, hiring some women after updating the whole inside. For now, though, showering is a communal thing.

Fine by me.

The water is hot, and stays hot, which is nice. I scrub off, rinse off. When I finish toweling, I notice a couple of the rookies sharing a laugh about something.

"What's funny, boys?" I ask, wrapping the towel around my waist.

They shake their heads. "Nothing, Cap. Just an internet thing."

Not the truth, but I let it go. I don't internet. I don't social media. I'm old, old, old school. I use computers for paperwork, and I CAN do things online; I'm not actually old, obviously, I just never cottoned onto the whole cultural obsession with posting about my meals and fake happy bullshit. I got no time for that shit.

Something tells me they were laughing at me. But they're rookies. Whatever. Unless it becomes something, I'm not gonna make an issue out of it.

Besides, I know why they were laughing. I've been dealing with it since I hit puberty. I grew up, both in height and build, and…other ways. So, changing in the locker room for gym class or for football or basketball practice, and later in training and around the firehouse, the first time guys see me in the shower, there are looks. It's not shower etiquette, I know, but…I can't blame them, I guess.

I mean, I'm a *big* dude.

I shrug it off like I have been my whole life.

Dress, and snag some coffee from the kitchen.

Meyers, Childers, and Lewis are all sitting around the table, and the two rookies from the showers—Gutierrez and Milano—are at the counter, fixing leftovers.

I get the ears-burning sense that they were talking about me right before I walked in—all of them.

I sip coffee, and wince. "God, who made this coffee? It tastes like a fuckin' litterbox smells."

Milano lifts his hand sheepishly. "I did."

"Well fuck, Milano, learn to make coffee."

"Sure thing, big…h-h-h-Hoss." That was *not* what he was going to say.

Gutierrez gives him a look, which I read as *what the fuck, dude.*

"Don't call me Hoss. Or Big anything. It's stupid and I hate it." I look between them. "You guys are weird." I dump the coffee into the sink. "I gotta go get real coffee. Chilly, show Milano how to make a decent pot of goddamn coffee, would you?"

I head to the closest coffee shop, a chain place which isn't as good as the local mom-and-pop shop I liked by Station Five. But the coffee is hot and fresh and doesn't taste like cat piss, so there's that.

I'm munching on a bagel by the bay window overlooking the street and browsing through emails on my phone when I hear a familiar voice cussing up a storm.

"Goddammit. What the fuck?" Exasperation, anger,

short-tempered aggravation—Jovie's voice could flay the hide off a bear from fifty paces.

I look up and see Jovie pushing her card into the reader, and then yanking it out when it beeps a negative sound.

"Try swiping it, ma'am?" The clerk behind the counter is maybe fifteen, skinny, and looks terrified of Jovie in an *it-hurts-so-good* kind of way. I get it, my dude.

She swipes it, slowly. *BEEP*. "FAAAAACK!" She shoves the card in the reader again, and hears it beep. "What is the fucking problem with this fucking machine, goddammit? I just want my coffee. I'm late for my shift as it is, and I know there's plenty of money in there."

"I'm sorry, ma'am, I don't—"

She shoves the card in her pocket and just stands there, as if she's willing herself to not rip this poor kid's head off.

I'm across the shop in a couple strides—bagel sandwiched together and clenched in my teeth, paper cup in the other hand.

I toss a five on the counter and pick up the bagel. "Keep the change, kid." I pick up Jovie's coffee, push it into her hand. "Come sit."

"I can't sit. I'm late." She won't look at me.

"Jovie." I wiggle the radio mic on my shoulder. "Just sit. For five seconds."

She's tense, stiff as a board. "Can't."

I balance the remainder of my bagel on top of my cup and wrap my arm around her shoulders, pull her away from the counter and the line of bemused patrons.

She's frustrated, embarrassed…she needs a second.

I pull her to my seat by the window and plop her onto a stool. She complies, but stiffly. Sits bolt upright. Doesn't move. Certainly doesn't look at me.

Her stomach growls.

I pinch off the end where I'd taken a bite, pop it into my mouth. Push the bagel at her lips. "Open."

She shakes her head.

"God, you're stubborn." I can't help myself—I caress her lower lip with my thumb, tracing the plump curve. "Just eat the goddamn bagel, Jovie."

Her mouth parts, and she lets me feed her a bite. While she chews, studiously not looking at me, I remove the top off of her coffee and blow across the top. She takes it black. She finishes the bagel in a few bites, and I put the paper cup to her lips.

"Coffee. Drink." I keep my voice low, calm.

She keeps her eyes lowered, taking the cup from me and sipping, slurping. After a moment, she finally meets my eyes. "Thank you."

"You had a late night."

"So did you. And I'm used to it."

"Then why are you so out of sorts?"

She shakes her head. "Just didn't sleep well." Her gaze flickers away from me, and I may be imagining it, but it seems like she is possibly blushing. "For…a lot of reasons."

My radio crackles with an incoming call, but it's for Three.

She looks at me, then, a long, probing stare. For the span of a few moments, she's just looking at me, seeing me, speculating or thinking or deciding; I can't fathom her thoughts, but they're about me, I know that much.

"Thanks again, Jake." Her voice is just above a whisper.

I shrug. "It's just coffee."

She stands, capping her cup. "It wasn't just coffee. So, thanks."

I shoot my shot. "Maybe we could have coffee together for real, sometime."

She walks away, shaking her head. Doesn't look back at me, answers as she's out the door. "I don't date firemen." It has the ring of finality.

I watch her go, unable to not watch—it's hypnotizing, that sexy sway of her perfect, round ass.

She's gone.

I don't date firemen.

There's a story there.

I feel the pieces—the way she assessed what was going on, the way she alerted everyone but still got herself out with only her purse in hand. The way she knew her way around the scene—I mean, sure, she's a paramedic and has obviously responded to any number of fires. But there was something else. When she was standing there with me—*what's the situation inside?* She knows her way around a fire, or knows someone who did.

Someone who didn't come back from a fire.

I don't date firemen.

That feels like a gauntlet being thrown down.

I finish my coffee, head to the counter for a refill. The kids here never charge me, but I always toss a five into their tip jar.

The kid behind the counter is staring after the door through which Jovie recently left. I laugh, knock on the counter in front of him with a knuckle. "Give it up, kid. A woman like that? She's out of both of our leagues."

He looks up at me, startled. "Oh! I wasn't—I... she..." a wordless stammer. "Is she your girlfriend?"

I cackle. "Fuck no. Starting to wish she was, though. She's something else, ain't she?"

His eyes are wide. "She'd eat me for breakfast. But she sure is gorgeous." He eyes me. "She's for sure out of *my* league. I'm not sure anyone's out of *your* league. You look like you could probably get, like, Kate Upton or... Emily Ratajkowski."

I laugh. "Appreciate the vote of confidence, kid." I reach over the counter and shake him by the shoulder. "Pro tip for you? Don't let 'em know you think you're out of their league. You may be, and you may think you are, but *they* don't have to know that. Just flash 'em a killer smile and give 'em your best line. They don't go for it? So what? There are other girls in the world, and you've got time."

He sighs with a laugh. "You make that sound *way* easier than it is." He shakes his head. "And not all of us look like *that*." He waves at me.

I pull my phone from my pocket and flip through photos until I find one of me at fifteen—Mom sent it to me just the other day, which is the only reason I have it on my phone.

I show it to him. "That's me at fifteen. Six feet tall and a tub of lard with acne, bad teeth and no friends."

"Sweet Metallica shirt, though."

JASINDA WILDER

I fist-bump him. "You like Metallica, huh?"

He nods. "Hell yeah." He peers at the photo. "So when'd you go from that to that?" He points from photo to me.

"It wasn't overnight. I played football from pee-wee, but when I started sprouting upward instead of just horizontally, the basketball coach got me to join for something to do in the offseason. Turned out I liked it, and there was a lot of running around. Plus, all the guys were in the gym after practice, so I started lifting. I only played football because I was already huge for my age and could push kids over without even trying. Basketball required athleticism. Which I learned I actually had...once I shed the layer of padding. Not that big kids can't be athletic, that was just my experience. By the time I graduated, I was my full height and had packed on some muscle. I still had acne, but I *did* have friends."

He sighs. "Cool story, bro, but I don't play sports."

"Why not?"

A shrug. "I just don't. I never have. I'm fifteen—they're not going to want some gump who's never played before on the team. Plus, I always suck in gym class. At basketball, at least."

"Okay, well number one, fooling around in gym class doesn't count. You need instruction. Number two, you're tall. They'll want you, if only just to stand under the basket and grab boards—rebounds, meaning when someone misses a basket. Number three, you don't know what you'll like until you try it. It might be scary at first, but you'll be glad you tried."

"You think?"

I nod. "I know so. I sucked at basketball when I first tried. I was on JV, and I was on the bench. But I worked, and practiced, and got better, made varsity junior year and was a starter senior year. I wasn't setting any records, but I was on the team, dammit. And those were my friends."

"If it doesn't work, I'm not giving you free coffee anymore." He smirks.

I laugh. "That's fair. But you gotta give it a fair shake. Don't half-ass it—go at it with your whole ass."

He snickers. "All right, fine. Tryouts for summer league are next week anyway."

I lift the coffee as my radio crackles, someone at the station calling my name. "Gotta go, kid. And remember—you *are* in their league. Don't let anyone tell you otherwise."

"What if I never get any better looking?" he calls after me.

I laugh as I back out the door, shrugging. "Then get rich!"

His snort of laughter is the last thing I hear as I hit the sidewalk, answering the call on the radio.

Her unit number is on file as part of the report from the 911 operator. So, my actions the next morning are not creepy or stalkerish at all. I promise.

I buy a brand new Stanley thermos—you know the

kind: your dad took it hunting every fall, tall and green with a screw-on silver lid—had it filled to the very brim with fresh, piping hot coffee, and set it by her door with a little note. Nothing weird, just a little...note.

Then, I go to work and try not to see if it will play out the way I hope.

JOVIE

I'M ON FIRST SHIFT ALL THIS WEEK, WHICH IS disorienting as fuck after two weeks of third shift. But hey, better me taking the fill-in shifts than one of the single moms on the staff who need consistency. So, I take the shitty, all-over-the-map shifts.

I wake up the next morning running late and dragging ass—I couldn't fall asleep, and when I finally did, it was almost two in the morning and I had to be at work by seven for my twelve-hour shift. Okay, I can deal—except I woke up at six forty-two a.m. and the yard is fifteen minutes if I hurry. I scrape my hair into a bun, jump into yesterday's uniform, and grab a protein shake from the fridge. No time for coffee—I'll have to stop and grab some later, after my shift has started. No time now.

Some days, though, I just wake up and know it's going to be a busy day. I can feel it in my gut, and that feeling is never wrong. And this morning? I feel it. Which means I'm not going to get coffee.

I thought I was cranky yesterday?

Shit, I'm going to be damn near unbearable to be around today—I'll have to preemptively apologize to DeShaun.

I snag my phone, keys, and purse on the way out the door—my boot kicks something hard, which thunks and then rolls away.

I lock my door and then look to see what I kicked: a huge Stanley hunting thermos. My dad had one of these—he'd pour a full pot of coffee into it every time he left for a shift. After he died, Mom gave it to the guys at the department to remember him by, and as far as I know, that thermos is still hanging on the wall of the office at his old station.

My throat closes. It's not—is it?

No, it's not—this one is brand-new. Full of coffee, too.

There's a half sheet of spiral-bound notebook paper taped to the outside. Masculine scrawl in thick, dark Sharpie lines:

Jovie,

I know how I get without coffee. Take this thermos to the coffee shop where we last saw each other and they'll fill it for you for free, on me, anytime.

Now, something to think about: I'm taking my lunch break today at 3pm. I'll be on a bench at the park on Tenth and Forrest. I'll have sandwiches. If we simply sat and

had coffee and sandwiches and talked for a few minutes, it
wouldn't be a date, right? Just saying.

Jake

Fuck.

I peel the note off, fold the tape over the edges, fold the note, and put it into my pocket. Head to work, pouring a capful of burn-my-mouth-hot coffee as I ride the subway to work.

That thermos is a literal lifesaver, it turns out. My intuition that it's going to be busy turns out to be dead on: there's barely time to restock supplies and clean up after a run before we're off to the next one. And so it goes, the whole day. No time for lunch, or anything. Just call after call.

By the time 3 p.m. comes around, that shake is all I've had all day, besides the coffee.

And, coincidentally, our last call put us right at Tenth and Forrest.

Across the street from the park is a sandwich shop— one of my favorites, although I rarely get across to this side of town to visit it.

We park on the street, and DeShaun points at the sandwich place. "I'm gonna grab a bite. You coming?"

At that moment, I see Jake exit the shop with a brown paper sack in hand, and a thermos like mine in the other. He crosses the street at a jog, taking a seat on a bench in easy view of the road. He's in his uniform, the sleeves stretched around his massive biceps. Ball cap on his head, hiding his hair and making him look...I don't know. Sexier than ever, somehow.

DeShaun follows my eyes. "Aww shit. It's the fireman you for sure do not have any kind of a crush on."

"Shut up, DeShaun."

"He looks like he's waiting for someone."

He is, very obviously, waiting—holding the sack on his lap, glancing at his watch, scanning the street. He sees the bus, and a grin spreads across his face. He holds up the paper sack—I can almost smell the grilled corned beef Rueben inside that bag.

DeShaun opens his door and hangs a foot out but doesn't get out yet. "Jovie, just get your ass over there. The man bought you a sandwich, and I been listening to your stomach gurgle all damn day."

I lift the thermos. "He left me this, this morning, too."

"The thermos, *and* the coffee?"

I nod, feeling a little sheepish. "Yeah."

"And you ain't even gonna go over there and say thanks? I *know* you're a better woman than that." We've never talked about it, and he certainly hasn't said so in as many words, but I've suspected since our first shift together that DeShaun is more attracted to Jake than to me. So, his next words are unexpected. "A man that fine, who's giving you thermoses full of coffee—which you have shared with me, I might add? Girl, you best get your ass over there. He don't play for my team, but he's fine enough that I might be willing to try anyway, if you don't *get your ass over there.*" He says the last few words through gritted teeth, flicking his hand.

I stare at DeShaun. "Really, right now?"

He shrugs, slides out. "What? You know I'm gay. I don't have to, like, come out to you."

I laugh. "No, not 'really right now' that you're gay, 'really right now' that you're threatening to, like, try to make Jake Howson turn gay if I don't go talk to him."

DeShaun laughs. "You're being dumb. I gotta motivate you somehow."

I grumble under my breath. "You're the worst parts of a man *and* a woman at the same time—meddling *and* belligerent."

DeShaun laughs and claps as he walks away. "You know it!"

I leave the bus running, take my thermos, and reluctantly make my way to Jake's bench. I sit beside him, feeling tension and something bizarrely and frighteningly like adrenaline blazing through me—just from being this close to him.

"Hi." My voice is low, a murmur. I'm stiff, tense, teeth gritted, heart pounding.

He regards me, an amused grin on his face. "Relax, Martin. Jesus. You're so stiff I could iron my shirt on you."

"Are you calling me flat as an ironing board?" I regret the teasing, flirtatious question as soon as it leaves my lips.

He arches an eyebrow. "Stiff as one, yes. Flat as one?" He shakes his head. "Jovie, you're about as flat as the Rockies, sweetheart."

I'm a grown-ass woman. I should *not* be blushing.

"Shut up."

He just snickers. "Ooooh, a real zinger of a comeback." He puts on a deep, mocking tone. "Shut up." He laughs, digging into the sack and coming up with two sandwiches. "I don't know what you like or don't like, so I got two kinds I like equally." He lifts one. "Turkey and brie on sourdough," and then lifts the other, "or a corned beef Reuben on rye."

I hesitate. "You really like them both the same? Or are you just saying that?"

"I never just say things. That's one thing you should know about me: I always mean what I say and say what I mean—unless I'm joking, and I never joke about food." He extends both sandwiches to me. "So really and truly, pick which one you want. I will happily take the other."

I eagerly take the Reuben. "These are my favorite sandwiches in the whole city. I just rarely get over this way to get them."

"Same."

"Thanks for this." I unwrap the wax paper, inhaling the scent of the grilled sandwich. "I used to have these sandwiches with my dad," I say, shocking myself that I'm saying this. "I had soccer practice in the park every Saturday morning. Mom would drop me off, and he'd meet me here and we'd have a sandwich together."

He nods, taking a huge bite, chewing a few times before speaking. "Which station was he out of?"

"One." I answer without thinking...and then my brain catches up. "Wait, hold on. How the hell did you know he was a firefighter?"

I dig in, waiting for his answer, which only comes after a second enormous bite—the half is nearly gone in those two bites.

"It's written all over you. The way you asked about the situation inside, the other day, the fire in your building. You were either in the department yourself, or someone you were close to was." He shrugs. "The way you said you don't date firemen clinched it for me."

I pour coffee into the cap and take a sip. "How so?"

He mirrors my action, filling his own cap and washing down his sandwich with it. Shrugs again. "Just you. The way you are. Not my business to know, and I'm not asking you to share. If you want to, I'll listen. But I can read between the lines just fine, Jovie. I don't need to tell you your own story."

I'm angry.

He's so damn insightful and….and *caring*, and not at all the arrogant, mouth-breathing prick I want him to be. "How am I, then? What's my story, if you think you know it so damn well?"

He regards me, holding the second half of his sandwich in one hand, silver mug of coffee in the other, feet kicked out and crossed heel over ankle. "I didn't mean it like that."

"Like what?"

He sighs. "Jovie, you're getting defensive. If you want to have a conversation, we can have a conversation. But we can't if you're gonna react like that to everything I say. I may be making mistaken assumptions. I dunno. But even if I am, I swear I'm not making them out of any kind of…I dunno, villainous intent or some shit. I'm not the bad guy, here. I like you. I respect you professionally. I think you're hot as fuck. But *Jesus* are you prickly."

I turn away from him and eat. Sip coffee. Calm the raging inferno of emotions inside me. He's right—I am being kind of bitchy.

I just…I don't *want* to like him, and he's not making that easy.

"I can't correct your assumption if you don't tell me what you're assuming about me."

"Your dad was a firefighter. He didn't come home, one day. And, naturally, that fucked you up." He waves with the half sandwich. "That's the short version. The long version is up to you to tell me, or not."

"Why should I?"

"I didn't say you should."

"Do you want me to?"

"Only if you want to."

"Why are you so damn agreeable?" I snap. "God, you're *so* fucking annoying."

"What, you want me to be a dick?"

"Yes!" I shout. "I do!"

He arches that eyebrow. "Wow. Okay. I mean, I can be a dick. Comes all too naturally to me. But I don't feel like that's gonna get me what I want."

"Which is what?"

He leans close, dropping his voice to a murmur I have to lean in to him to hear. "You. Naked. Screaming my name and begging me to fuck you harder."

I flinch away to glare daggers at him. "Yeah, there's the dick attitude I was expecting."

He just grins—the Panty-Melter 5000, I hereby dub that grin. "You asked for it."

"You think I'll ever beg?" I lift my chin. "You couldn't make me beg on your best day."

My heart pounds, my skin tightens. This is dangerous territory. Yet, somehow, it feels safer than talking about

Dad. My nipples go rock hard behind my sports bra—it's my thickest, most compressive and supportive one I own, so there's no way he can see them pebbling. I hope.

He leans even closer, his lips touching my ear. His whisper is hot, huffing. "Give me five minutes with my face between those big beautiful thighs of yours, Jovie, and I'll make you forget your own name." He nips the lobe of my ear, making me start, gasping the breath I wasn't aware I'd been holding. "And then I'll make you beg for more." He kisses the side of my neck, behind my ear. I can't breathe. "And *then*…I'll make you beg me to stop."

"I'm not going to dignify your ridiculous claims with a response." I resist the need to cross my thighs in order to contain the pulsating heat between them. "I don't beg. Not for you, not for anyone, not for anything."

"You haven't been with me yet."

"Nope." I resolutely look away from him, work on the last of my sandwich. "Nor will I."

"Those nipples tell a different story."

I look down—the traitorous bitches, they're visibly erect, dotting my shirt *through* the bra, *and* through the shirt. So ridiculous. It's a curse, I tell you.

I growl and refuse to cover myself. "Doesn't mean shit."

He laughs. "Okay, sure. Keep telling yourself that—maybe you'll eventually believe it. I don't."

"I don't care what you believe." I finish my sandwich, throw back the last of the coffee in the cap, screw it in place. "And on that note, I'm out of here. We're supposed to be posting up near the library."

He lets me get a couple steps away. "Hey, Jovie."

I stop, turn around. "What?"

He crumples the bag with our wrappers inside into a ball and tosses it effortlessly into the trash can ten feet away, then joins me. Bumps his hip against mine. Leans down for one last parting-shot whisper: "Think of me when you get home tonight. Think of me with my face between your thighs, making you come until you don't know which way is up."

I gasp, an involuntary reaction.

His fingers slide down my chest, against the slope of my breast, and then retreat—he put something in my shirt pocket. But god, so close. My nipples ache, they're so hard.

I have to say something back. Something clever. Something witty.

"I already did that. You were okay." I walk away, focusing hard on not swaying my ass too much.

I can feel his eyes on me, though.

"Stop staring at my ass, Howson," I call over my shoulder.

"I can't. Sorry, not sorry. I happen to believe that works of art are meant to be appreciated."

Goddammit. That's a good line.

I have no choice but to let him have the last word, mainly because I think my comeback wasn't as good as it had sounded in my head. Because now he knows I thought about him.

I get into the bus, behind the wheel, securing my thermos where it won't roll around. DeShaun is finishing his lunch, polishing off the last of a bag of Doritos, a bottle of iced tea sweating in the cupholder.

I point at him. "*Not*—a…*word.*"

He pops a chip into his mouth, dusts off his hands, turns up the radio—a classic Britney song, to which he begins silently grooving. Gestures wordlessly for me to go.

I just shake my head. "I hate you."

It's after eight by the time I get home. I have another twelve-hour shift tomorrow followed by two days off, then another trio of twelve-hour shifts. But for now, I'm home.

Dreading the chore of fixing food for myself—but I know I have to; today was brutal, and the sandwich with Jake was the only real meal I've had all day. I just…I don't have the energy.

I'm contemplating simply falling into bed fully clothed when my buzzer goes off. I groan, trudging to answer it. "Who is it?"

"I have a Door Dash for Jovie Martin?"

Ugh. Seriously? It has to be from Jake. Who else could it be? Both Erin and Lia would just bring me food, and Mom would just come over and cook until my fridge was full.

It can only be Jake. The thoughtful bastard.

I buzz the delivery guy up, pulling out a five for a tip. He's young, Hispanic, good-looking. He has a whole pizza from a local carryout-only place with a reputation for having some of the best deep dish in the city.

He pulls a receipt from his hip pocket and glances

at it, then at me. "There were instructions to give you a message."

I sigh. "Okay?"

"'Just say fuck it,'" he reads. "'Eat the pizza, Martin.'"

I hand him the five. "Thank you."

He pockets the money and turns away with a smile. "Thank you, ma'am. Have a good evening."

I take the pizza to the couch, grab a beer from the fridge, and sit down. Pop the beer and open the pizza: white pizza, with tomatoes, pesto, and grilled chicken.

DAMN THE MAN.

I stare at the pizza. My mouth waters. I am tempted, for approximately five seconds, to *not* eat it simply out of spite and contrariness. It's got nothing to do with keeping my ass the size it is, although that is why I tend to avoid pizza and pasta on the whole. It's entirely about him.

But hunger wins, easily.

"Fuck it." I pick up a slice and dig in, groaning in ecstasy. "He seems to like my big ass anyway."

Wait.

Hold up.

No, no, no. I do *not* care whether Jake Howson likes the size of my ass.

I don't.

Shut up, nipples, you don't get a say—and lay down, dammit, it's just pizza.

But it's not just pizza.

It's the most perfectly timed pizza there has ever been. The most thoughtful pizza. How could he possibly know I needed food I didn't cook, tonight of all nights?

How did he know I'd need coffee like I needed my next breath this morning?

How did he know about that sandwich shop?

How did he know I like white pizza best?

I wipe at my lips with my wrist, bumping my chest in the process—something crinkles. I'd forgotten he put something in my pocket, so distracted was I by the proximity of his fingers to my traitorous nipples.

I get a paper towel from the kitchen and wipe my hands, then pull the slip of paper from my pocket.

It's a narrow strip of paper torn from a notebook. There's a local phone number written on it, in that same Sharpie as the note from this morning. Next to the phone number, a scrawled message: *call me. Better yet, FaceTime me.*

Force of habit has me flipping the scrap over, and behold, there's a note on that side too: an address for a condo not too far from my own, and another note: *or just show up. I make a hell of an omelet.*

The inference is clear.

I'm dialing the number before my better sense catches up to my impulsive thumb. It's ringing. What the hell am I doing?

"You called." His voice is rough and deep. And surprised. "I didn't think you would."

"Are you spying on me? Or stalking me?"

He laughs, a shocked burst of sound. "Fuck no. What makes you ask that?"

"You were at the coffee shop when I was having a nervous fucking breakdown. And then this morning, I was running late and didn't have time to make or stop for coffee, and you just happened to leave me the thermos. And then the sandwiches. How could you know my connection to that sandwich shop? I haven't been there in months, because I always get all fucked up in the head when I go, because of Dad. And then you send me this fucking pizza. My day was horrible, just…brutal. There was a six-car pileup on the interstate, and I couldn't save this kid and that sandwich was the only thing I've eaten today, and I'm so fucking hungry I could eat an old shoe, but I'm too tired to make food. And here you go, having the best pizza in the city delivered to me—and not just that, but my favorite kind of pizza." I swallow hard, shoving the emotions down. "So I ask you again—are you stalking me?"

He sighs. "I promise you, I'm not. I swear on my own father's grave, I'm not. I just have a good intuition, maybe. But, I can take a stab at explaining the coincidences. I was just at the coffee shop that day, getting coffee. That was a pure-luck scenario. As for the thermos, my old man was a prison guard, and he brought a Stanley to work every day—the one I use is his. And I figured, as much as you work, you could probably use one. So I just went with it. I didn't know your schedule in particular, but I know EMS scheduling and I figure if you worked Monday and yesterday's early shift, you'd be working it again today. Just an educated guess. Your name and address were on the incident file from the nine-one-one call you made which is how I knew your address. And as for the pizza, I know how I feel after a long day. The white pizza was just a guess, again—you just don't seem like a red sauce and pepperoni kinda girl, I dunno."

I sigh, sipping beer. "Good guesses, you're saying."

"That's all it is."

"What about the sandwiches?"

"Oh." I can almost hear the shrug. "That's my favorite spot for lunch when I need to get away from the chaos, and that place is my favorite lunch place. I had football practice at that park on Saturday mornings. Dad and I would get sandwiches after, since he was usually off Saturday mornings."

I laugh. "Wait, wait, wait. You had football practice at *that* park, Saturday mornings? When was this?"

"Uhh, I'm thirty-two, and that was when I was… eight? Nine? So twenty-three, twenty-four years ago? Which would make it…late nineties?"

I laugh, a desperate, resigned sound. "I remember watching the boys play football on the other field. I'd get yelled at by my coach because I was watching them instead of playing. I just thought football looked like so much more fun than soccer."

He laughs. "You're shitting me."

"Nope."

"You said something about that this afternoon," Jake says, "but it didn't really register, at the time."

"So you're saying we played on the same field at the same time?"

He laughs. "I guess so. I actually remember this girl that used to stand on the sidelines and stare at us. Short, with black pigtails. Number twelve."

My heart leaps into my throat. "That was me."

"No shit."

"What happened to your dad?" I ask, between bites. "Just curious. Don't have to answer."

"He um…he died in a prison riot in 2002."

"Holy shit. My dad worked that incident. Putting out the fire they started in the cafeteria, and getting wounded officers and prisoners out after it was suppressed."

"Yeah, um. He was ground zero, where it started. One of the first guards to go."

"I'm sorry."

"Yeah, thanks. It was rough. He was a great dad."

I eat, and wait, but the question I'm expecting is not forthcoming. "You're not going to ask?"

"Nope." I hear him chewing. "Told you I wouldn't. Up to you to volunteer information."

"You're not curious?"

"Of course I am. But that shit is personal. And hard to talk about. I know from experience, obviously."

"And yet I just asked you."

"If I minded you asking, you'd know."

I sigh. I've eaten half the pizza, and I'm full. I sit back with my half-finished bottle of light beer and put my feet up. "The Causewell warehouse fire in '06."

"Ohhh, shit. Some of the old-timers still talk about that one."

"Yeah." My eyes burn. Still, after sixteen years. "He, um. He was a lieutenant. He was offered a promotion to captain that year, but he turned it down. Wanted to stay with his crew."

"I've got a guy like that. The stations live and die by the lieutenants, and the career LT's even more so."

"Yeah, that was Dad. He just…he lived for the job.

Me and mom, too, obviously, but we both knew that in some ways, the job came first." I sniffle. "If he'd taken the bugles, he might be alive."

"Knowing the kind of guy he must have been, I doubt it. From what I hear, that blaze was…it was…" he sighs. "He'd have gone in anyway, if he saw it starting to come down. He'd have gone in, no matter what his rank, to save his guys."

I cough, to stifle a sob. "Yeah."

"What was his name?"

"Joey Martin."

"No shit? Your old man is Joey Martin?"

"Yeah."

"I'm Captain of Station One, Jovie."

"Wait…you are? Of One? I thought you were in Four? Or Five?"

He laughs. "I started at Four. Worked one shift at Five to cover. Got promoted and put in charge of One."

"So…you know my dad?"

"Well, not personally, no. But the old-timers here talk about him. Chilly especially."

I choke. "Chilly is still there? Childers?"

"Yeah, he's one of my lifer-LTs."

I think about that thermos. "Is, um…is Dad's thermos still around the station somewhere?"

He groans, a long low sound of dawning comprehension. "That's your dad's."

"It is, then?"

"Yeah. It's in a shadow box on the wall of my office. Along with Bruno Rossi's favorite White Sox hat."

"That's Lia's dad. My best friend, from the bar that night."

"Short one or tall one?"

I can't help a laugh. "I'm the short one. Lia's the mid-sized one, and my stepsister Erin is the tall one."

"Well, they're both in reference to you, so to me, Lia's the short one, Erin's the tall one."

"Papa Rossi's hat is there, too?"

"Yeah. You and Lia are welcome to come see."

"Yeah, I..um. Maybe."

"You haven't stepped foot inside since, huh?"

"No."

"And thus your life motto, don't date firemen."

"It's not just a life motto. Lia and I took a blood oath on it."

"Damn." A sigh. "So I don't stand a snowball's chance in hell, do I?"

I don't know what to say. "Not really, no." My lungs, lips, and larynx betray me: "Or, at least…you shouldn't."

"When I gave you my phone number, I was expecting sass and sexting, not…all this."

"Sorry to disappoint you. I can insult you, if you want."

"Not disappointed, not at all." I can hear the grin in his voice. "But go for it. Hit me with your best shot."

"You're far too pretty for your own good, Howson."

"That's more of a backhanded compliment."

"Your stupid Panty-Melter Five Thousand grin doesn't work on me."

"My what?"

"The ridiculous grin you do, when you think you're being charming and sexy."

He cackles. "And you've named it the what, now?"

"Panty-Melter Five Thousand."

"Because it melts your panties every time I do it?"

"Not mine in particular, no. That's the intent. But what I'm saying is, it doesn't work on me. You're not going to melt my panties off with it."

He muses. "I see, I see." I hear a devious tone enter his voice. "And how do I know it's not working on you?"

I can't help a laugh. "I'm not showing you my underwear, Jake."

"Hmmm." A pause. "Wait, hold on, I have an idea."

"Oh jeez. Now what?"

My phone dings, and I pull it away, put it on speaker. I have a message from Jake. A photo. I open it up, and it's a selfie of him from the shoulders up. He has a devilish smirk on his face, and I can't deny, at least in the safe confines of my own head, that it's a hell of a smile. His wild blue eyes spark with intensity and mischievous humor.

"I call that one the Bra-Burner Eight Hundred. Guaranteed to scorch off your bra in seconds or your money back."

I must be sick in the head—it's the only explanation for what I do next. I take a selfie, making a wry smirk, pulling the strap of my bra up away from my shoulder. Send it. "Didn't work, I'm afraid."

He sighs. "Dammit." A laugh. "Worth a shot."

"You think you can show me one sexy little smirk and I'm just gonna...what? Send you topless pics?"

"A guy can hope, right?"

"Yeah, well, keep hoping, Howson. Not happening."
I just hope he didn't catch my little slip.

"Can we revisit how you think my Bra-Burner Eight Hundred smirk is sexy?"

He caught it.

"No."

"You're no fun. Won't show me your underwear, won't take your bra off, won't talk about my sexy smirk."

I laugh. "Gotta keep you on your toes somehow, Howson."

"Yeah, you're plenty good at that."

I yawn, a sudden jaw-cracker I can't even start to contain. "I gotta get some sleep."

"Sounds like it. Well, good night, Jovie."

"Good night, Jake. And thank you."

"My pleasure."

We say goodbye and end the call. I put the pizza leftovers in the fridge, toss my empty bottle, and head for bed. I'm too tired to even rinse off, and you know I'm tired when that's the case.

I barely manage to get my clothes off, and I'm asleep almost before my head hits the pillow.

It's my day off, and I manage to stay asleep until nearly eight a.m., which is an actual miracle of St. Mary. And even when I do wake up, I engage in my favorite part of days off: being awake, in bed and warm and comfy, and not getting out of bed.

I just lay, eyes closed, sunlight streaming through the window, drowsing and daydreaming.

That's my first error—daydreaming. Because where does my mind inevitably go?

Jake fucking Howson.

Things really went from zero to sixty with him in record time, from heavy conversation about our dads to him claiming to be able to make me beg.

But, I recognize that it was likely on purpose, on his part. He seemed to recognize that I was uncomfortable with the conversation, with the weight of it, and he lightened it. With sexual innuendo.

Innuendo? Shit, it was outright seduction. I mean, the man went right past flirtation and right into seduction. Later in the evening, there was playful banter and flirtation, and…god, the man flirts so well.

"Think of me when you get home tonight. Think of me with my face between your thighs, making you come until you don't know which way is up."

I hear his voice, and I can't help but think of him. I can all too easily picture his broad shoulders wedged between my thighs, back rippling with muscle as he delves closer to my sex. His jaw is stubbled and rough against the soft, tender silk of my inner thighs, and then his tongue slithers against my seam…

My fingers are a poor substitute for his mouth, but it suffices to stimulate my arousal. I picture his shoulders moving and try to summon the way his mouth would feel, tongue wet and warm, lips firm. Maybe he'd slip a finger or two inside me, work them in and out just so… his other hand would be drawn to my tits—I pinch my nipple like I imagine he would, roll it between finger and thumb. Faster, my fingers move.

I'm gasping, shaking, quaking—teetering on the edge of climax.

And my phone rings.

As a paramedic, I can't not answer. I grab the phone without looking at it and try to compose myself. "Hello?"

"Figured you'd be a morning person," comes Jake's rough, deep voice.

Shit, shit, shiiiiiit. I have him on the phone, and I was literally just masturbating to him?

"Hi." Fuck, it comes out all breathy and sultry.

"Hello, indeed." His voice indicates that he does indeed note the breathy quality of my voice. "So...whatcha doin'?"

"Nothing." I clear my throat, because I still sound... sexy. Shit, *shit*. "Nothing. "

My phone bleeps and I look at it—he wants to FaceTime me. My thumb, once again, betrays any shred of sense or decency left inside me, or maybe my thumb just hates the rest of me, because it very stupidly and recklessly hits the accept button. Why? Why, why, why? I'm wearing nothing but a pair of blue cotton briefs and a flat sheet.

Fuck you, thumb. Idiot.

His face pops onto my screen—he's shirtless, in bed. Sweaty, hair sticking up in a million directions. "Good and holy god*damn*, Jovie." His voice is low, awed.

"What?" I can only see myself in the little thumbnail—I know I'm fully covered, the flat sheet up to my neck.

"You, is what. You're fucking stunning."

I cackle. "I just woke up, I have no makeup on, my hair is probably a rat's nest…I'm probably all swollen and puffy. And you think I'm stunning?" I laugh again. "You're nuts."

He shakes his head, rubs his jaw. "Sure, maybe. But also, yeah, you're fucking stunning, just like that." He blows out a breath, then smirks at me—the Bra-Burner Eight Hundred. "You were doing something when I called."

"Yeah, sleeping." I'm blushing like crazy. I'm still shivery and flustered—almost coming and then not really fucks with me.

He brings the phone closer and then the view tilts as he rolls to his side. "Lies."

"What were *you* doing?"

"Lifting. I used to lift with the guys, but now that I'm captain, I gotta get it in elsewhere and else-when." He brings the phone closer yet, so his eyes fill the frame. "You were thinking about me, weren't you?"

"No!" I protest, far too intensely. "I wasn't thinking about you."

"You weren't? Not at all?" I can see the grin in his eyes.

That fucking smirk. If I was wearing a bra, it'd be scorching away. But I'm not—I'm all but naked, and it feels far too tempting, far too intimate. The sheet slips lower. His eyes don't miss it. Not hardly.

"No," I whisper. "I wasn't."

"You weren't thinking about…ohhh…say…me, in that bed with you, right now…" his voice drops so low and so quiet it's a faint rumble I have to strain to hear, and strain to hear, I do. "Licking, sucking, teasing? That wasn't on your mind, not even a little bit? You weren't fingering yourself as you think of me eating you out?"

"No." It's a breathy whisper, an obvious denial. "I was doing no such thing." I scoff. "Like I'd touch myself while thinking of you. As if."

"Crazy, I guess. I just had this feeling."

"Your feeling was wrong." I feel the sheet slipping, and whichever part of me is in charge of righting it is clearly on vacation, because I let it slip, and slip...until my traitorous nipples are nearly exposed, poking the thin baby blue material. "I was most assuredly not picturing your face between my thighs, or your tongue devouring me like you couldn't get enough. And I was very surely, most definitely, absolutely *not* mere seconds from coming when you called. Nope. Never happened."

I must be on drugs.

It's the only explanation.

Trick is, it's just him. He's the drug.

"Seconds away, huh?"

"The hypothetical scenario that definitely did not happen?" I clutch my phone for dear life as the sheet somehow manages to escape fully, dropping down to reveal my breasts in their full, absurd glory, nipples taut and hard, areolae puckered. Everything sensitive. "Yeah, literally a couple of seconds. Very rude of you, actually. Hypothetically."

I hear him breathing, but his face doesn't change expressions. Perhaps his jaw tightens a little. His eyes are... well, glued. Staring with unabashed desire.

Finally, he growls, wipes his face with one hand. "*Fuck*, Jovie. Just…fuck."

"Now what?"

"You, woman. You're even more…I dunno. I don't have words. I'm speechless. You. Your body." He swallows hard. "Your tits are incredible, Jovie."

I grin. "Oh, these old things?" I hug them one-armed. "Had 'em for ages."

"What I wouldn't do or give to be in that room with you, right now." His eyes go hot, wild. Scorching. "You'd be over that edge before you could blink twice."

"If I *had* been close, which I wasn't…I'd be really frustrated right now."

The view of him shifts, wiggles, as if he's doing something off-screen. The view then pans out, tilts. Shows his chest—which is goddamned magnificent, and drool-worthy by itself—to his abs—washboard, ridges of iron-hard muscle rippling beneath his chest…farther. V-cut.

I gulp. I see the pink tip, squeezed in his fist. "Jesus, Jake."

"Quit the bullshit game of pretend, Jovie. I got no qualms admitting just thinking of you makes me hard as a fucking rock." He strokes himself, baring a few inches of him, and my breath leaves my lungs in a whoosh—whatever I'd thought he was packing behind his uniform pants, I was drastically underestimating the reality. "I'll tell you the raw truth, Jovie—after I got off the phone with you last night, I jerked off, thinking about you. I thought about you taking me in your mouth and sucking me dry. I thought about you riding my cock. I thought about it, pictured it—tried to imagine what you'd look like naked, and I came so hard I was fuckin' dizzy."

"Jake, god. You can't say shit like that," I breathe, a weak protest.

"Why not? It's the truth. It's also the truth that whatever I may have imagined, it's not anywhere fuckin' close to the truth of how insanely fucking perfect your body is."

I ache. Everything inside me aches, strains. Pulses, for him. For Jake. I need to finish what I started. Need to.

But this is fucking crazy. He's a firefighter, and I took a blood oath.

We're not doing anything. Not actually.

But I *need…*

I groan. "Dammit, Jake. Goddammit." I kick the blankets away and awkwardly wriggle out of my underwear. "I hate you."

"That's okay," he murmurs. "You can hate me. I can handle it." He shifts to lying on his back, and I can see all of him, now, his whole godlike body, his massive cock in his fist, clutched tight. So big. Fuck, so big. "Just let me watch you finish, Jovie."

"Quid pro quo," I whisper.

"Does it look like I'm hiding anything?" he growls. "Pinch your nipples, Jovie. Grab your tits. Play with them—like I would."

I do as he says, because I'm utterly lost to this moment. Fuck the consequences, I need this moment. I don't care. Not about anything except this, right now. My fingers on my clit, circling. My hips begin moving immediately, and I'm reaching the cusp all over again within seconds. I'm heaving, shaking, gasping—I break away from my clit to play with my nipple again, pinching…

"Pinch harder," he orders.

I pinch so hard I squeal, and the intensity of the heat and pressure between my thighs ratchets to unbearable levels. Yet, I cannot come. Not yet.

"Show me your pussy," he murmurs. "Let me see it." I put the camera over myself, and show him—my fingers moving, the slick slip and slide of them through my nether lips. "Fuck, so beautiful. God, I wish I was there. Come for me, Jovie. Make yourself come."

My fingers fly, responding to his command, circling around my clit until I'm crying out and my hips are lifting helplessly off the bed, knees pressing together and splaying apart spasmodically.

I moan—and it's his name on my lips. "Jake—ohfuc-koh*fuck*…Jake, I'm coming, god I'm coming!"

I tense, bridging up off the bed, fingers a blur, shaking all over, gasping and then I can't even gasp, can't make a sound because this is so fucking intense, so surreal, so wrenching…and I know it's him. Because he's watching.

"My turn," he snarls. "Now you watch me, Jovie."

I pry my eyes open and dizzily watch the screen, gasping still—his big fist is wrapped around his cock, the head sprouting up out of the top, then inches of his thick shaft appearing as he drives his fist down. I play with my tits, watching him, pinching and squeezing and kneading—for him, I'm self-aware enough to admit. His hips begin to flex, and his fist moves faster, and then he spits into his hand and smears it on himself, and now his fist is wrenching up and down in a blur, and my core aches all over again. I find myself, with him. Touch myself as he jerks himself to the edge. I watch, greedily—watch the purple veins and the fat round head which now weeps pre-cum, and I watch his hard abs tense as he curls forward even as his hips drive up into his strokes.

"Slower," I breathe. "Slow down."

He slows. Growls. "Fuck, Jovie. So close."

"Where would you be coming, if I was there with you? Where would you put it?" No angel, I—never pretended to be, but this, with Jake? This is a whole new level of debauchery and depravity.

"All over those huge fucking tits of yours, Jovie."

I cup them in my arm, prop them up for him. "Right here?"

"Yeah…god, Jovie—they're so perfect." He's wild, now, grinding his fist on himself slow and hard. "I wish to *fuck* I was there with you."

"Let me see you come, Jake." I'm there with him, again. Writhing, whimpering.

"Oh fuck, right now. I'm coming, Jovie."

"That's right. Say my name when you come all over my tits." He grabs a Kleenex and cups it over the head of his cock, preparing to catch the stream. "Don't. I want to see. I want to see you come."

He tosses the tissue aside and strokes himself once more, twice…and then he snarls. "Jovie—*Jovie…*"

He comes, then. A thick stream of it jets out of him, laying in a stripe up his stomach, all the way up to his chest. He's not done—more cum spurts out of him, not streaking as far, pooling at his navel. Again, and again, until it's just dribbling out of the plump pink tip, string-ing into the pool of it on his stomach.

And I…I can almost feel it on me. Almost see him, above me, painting me with his seed. God, it would be so hot.

I want it.

I want him. I come again, a second wrenching or-gasm ripping through me as he finishes.

He's panting. "Jesus."

"The name's Jovie, actually."

He bursts a laugh, breathless. "Right, sorry—Jovie." He reorients the phone to show his face. "That was…"

"Unexpected," I finish for him.

"Yeah."

I'm at a loss for words, then.

"Believe it or not, I've never done that before."

"What, jerk off?" I quip.

He snickers. "Ha ha. No, like, on the phone."

"Me either."

"It was hot." His eyes search mine—looking for re-gret, or signs of an impending case of the pricklies, maybe.

"It…was," I admit.

"Would be hotter if we didn't have these stupid phones in the way." He grins, just an open, honest, gen-uine smile. "You, me, and the sheets, and not a damn thing else."

I swallow. "Hot. Yes."

"Are you warming up to me, Jovie Martin?"

I shake my head. "Nope. Still can't stand you." My eyes give my words the lie, though.

I hear a radio crackle in the background. "Shit, that's

me. Gotta go." He moans a laugh. "God, I'm a mess." He tilts the phone to show me the mess—he came a *lot*.

I laugh. "Have fun cleaning *that* up."

"You wanna come over and do it for me?"

"You have to go, Jake. Your guys need you."

"Right, right. Next time."

I can't agree to that. I shouldn't have done this. I swore an oath—a blood oath, with the woman who's closer to me than blood. I can't and won't break it.

But Jake is...

Intoxicating.

Addicting.

"All right, I really gotta go. See ya 'round, Martin."

"Bye...Howson."

The screen reverts to my lock screen—Lia, Erin, Mom, Mom Rossi, and me, on vacation together to Martha's Vineyard last year.

I am in *so* much trouble.

Because I know for a fact I'm not going to be able to resist Jake. But I also know I'm not going to break my oath with Lia.

Which means this is only going to result in someone—both of us—getting hurt.

Why?

Because I'm not blind or stupid—this is way more than just attraction and hormones and libido.

I groan, and slap myself in the face. "I'm such an idiot." Then I get a whiff of my fingers, and wrinkle my nose. "Shower time."

I do think about him in the shower, although I manage to stop from giving myself a third orgasm. Just barely.

Okay...fine. Maybe I do get another one in. But it's just a little one. Not as good as the one he helped me give myself.

Nothing has ever been that good, and he wasn't even the one touching me.

Yeah. This spells trouble.

JAKE

S TAYING FOCUSED ON THE JOB REQUIRES ALL MY willpower and then some—fortunately for me, things get busy for the next few days; the bad part of that is a busy day for a fire department is generally a bad thing. I lean into the work, throwing myself with what I hope is characteristic drive and focus into learning how to be a captain and incident commander. I call the chief a few times for advice on particular matters and visit with Captain O'Shaugnessy.

He's out of the hospital now, but at home and on pretty strict rest orders; he's always been an active guy and takes pride in his landscaping, which he now is unable to do, so I get a rotation of my more green-thumbed guys from my station and my old home of Station Four to swing by and help Cap keep his yard looking spiffy. I'm not a landscaper, but I am fairly handy, so I cruise by after work one afternoon about a week after my…ahem, *phone call*…with Jovie, and help him catch up on his honey-do list. I also bring the fixings for my stew.

As I'm fixing leaky faucets and squeaky hinges and sagging porch steps, Cap—and I'll never think of him as anything other than my captain—watches me from the kitchen table, sipping iced tea with a speculative look in his eyes.

"There's something you aren't telling me, Jake." He doesn't phrase it as a question.

I set on the counter the wrench I was using to tighten the wobbly base of the kitchen faucet. "Nope."

He just laughs. "Never bullshit a bullshitter, son." He points at me with his sweating glass. "So I say again, there's something you aren't telling me."

I huff, checking the tightness of my work. Satisfied, I fix myself a glass of Mrs. O'Shaugnessy's iced sun tea, and take a seat at the table. "Personal stuff, is all."

He traces lines with his fingers in the beads of sweat on his glass. "Jake, I'm retired, and you're a captain in your own right. I'm not your superior anymore. We're just friends, now." He eyes me. "I like to think I was something of a mentor to you as well as your captain and friend."

"You are, Cap. All that and more."

"Well, then. Out with it. Hit me with the personal stuff."

I can't help a wry grin. "So…there's this girl."

He bursts out in a cackle. "A girl! Of course it's a girl, son. If a man is broody about something, and won't talk about it, it's a girl." He settles, tapping the table with a knuckle. "So who's the lucky woman to the catch the eye of the mighty Jake Howson?"

I frown at him. "Awww, come on, Cap."

He snorts. "At this point, call me Larry."

I shake my head. "I'll try. But I've been calling you Cap for over ten years. Not sure that's easily changed."

"Fine, fine. But who is she? I've known you since you were an eighteen-year-old probie, Jake, and you're discreet about it, but you've always kept your relation-ships...ummm, casual. I don't know that there's ever been a girl that's had a face for me."

I sigh. "She's a paramedic. First saw her at your ac-cident, and then suddenly she's just everywhere I go. I dunno, Cap...Larry—god, that's weird—I just...I can't get her out of my head. I barely know her, in one sense. But I also just...*know* her. I mean, we did sports at the same field at the same time, we just didn't know each other." I hesitate. "Her dad was Joe Martin."

"No shit? He was a good buddy of mine. We used to play poker together—me, him, Rossi, Bruce, and Mack." He sighs, rubs his jaw, which is showing the heavy stub-ble of a growing beard. "Good man—one of the best. The Causewell fire took him and Rossi both, and god, what a tragedy that was. Two of the best men in the whole de-partment, gone at once."

"Yeah, and understandably, it messed her up pretty good. She and Rossi's daughter are best friends, and I guess they swore a blood oath they'd never date a fireman."

This gets a rueful laugh. "Oof. Tough luck for you. She won't give you the time of day, huh?"

I shrug. "Well, that's just it. I think she's mixed up about it. She'll show signs of liking me one second, and then turn into a goddamn ice cube the next. Gives me whiplash."

Cap muses. "That's tricky. She likes you, but doesn't want to like you, because she swore an oath." He taps my bugles. "More to the point, she swore the oath because she lost her dad to the job. The oath is to protect her from going through that again. And Jake, you're married to the job. So her hesitancy to get mixed up with you is probably pretty easy to understand."

I nod. "Yeah, I get that. But...tell that to the rest of me. My head gets it."

"But Little Jake doesn't get it." He grins. "She's pretty?"

I snort. "Sunsets and flowers and paintings are pretty. She's...the sun itself."

This gets me raised eyebrows. "Well I take back what I said. It's not just Little Jake that doesn't get it— it's this." He taps my chest over my heart. "You don't just *like* her." He laughs. "My granddaughter is sixteen, and we were talking the other day. She told me she was catching feelings for this boy at school, and I couldn't help but think that's a pretty damn accurate way to put it, catching feelings." He points at me. "You're catching feelings for Martin's girl."

I groan. "And it's an uphill battle, just getting her to... shit, man, even admit that I'm not the biggest asshole to ever walk the planet. And for every step I take forward, she takes two backward. And I just can't help but wonder if I oughta take the hint and let her be, you know? Like, she lost her dad to the job. She's scared of losing someone else to it, and I get that. It's a damn dangerous job, and just because I've got this," I tap the captain's insignia on my lapel, "it doesn't mean I'm safe. I like her. And maybe I *am* catching feelings. But is it safe for *me* to let myself really like her? I've never had a real girlfriend, Larry. I'm married to the job, and I don't think that'll change any time soon. But…if she's determined to stick to her oath, is there even a point in trying? Is it fair of me to try?"

Captain O'Shaugnessy is silent for a while. "I can't answer that for you, son. It takes a certain kind of woman to love a man who's married to the job, like we are. We're not volunteers. We're not doing it until we get bored and find a new job. This is it. This is everything. The job is everything, and it will be till the day we die. I may be retired, but I'll be a firefighter until I'm in the grave. Sometimes, even now, I have dreams about putting on the gear and going in, and I haven't put on a full turnout in a while." He eyes me. "But as a man who's been married for thirty-two years, I can tell you one thing—it's worth it. Viv didn't take to me at first. She fought me tooth and nail for months, resisting me and telling me no and refusing to so much as look at me. I knew she was the one, and I knew deep down she did like me. So I stuck with it. And eventually, she agreed to go out with me. Just to shut me the hell up, at first, I think. But once I got her to sit down with me and quit wrestling herself, that was it—I had her. And neither of us have looked back since."

I sigh. "Yeah, that doesn't clear things up for me very much."

He chuckles. "Guess not." He swirls his glass, making the melting ice clink and tinkle. "You have to figure out if she's just scared, and if you're willing to work through that.

Sometimes, fear wins. Especially once you've lost someone young, like she did. It may not be up to you, Jake. You may have to put yourself out there and risk your heart for her, and just know that she may not be able to give hers to you. No two ways about that, son. Viv lived every day with the knowledge that I worked a damn dangerous job, that I went into burning buildings and wasn't guaranteed I'd come out. It's a risk. And you may not come out on top. But you also very well may." He shrugs. "I guess what I'm saying is you just have to decide what the risk-reward ratio is, and if it's worth it to you."

I give a huffing bark of laughter. "Sheesh. Casual seems a hell of a lot easier."

He laughs with me. "Sure it is. But think of your accomplishments, Jake—how many of them were easy?"

I throw a dismissive wave at him. "Yeah, yeah. Nothing worth doing or having comes easily."

He shoots me a devilish grin. "Well, now…seeing as you're talking about a woman, that depends on what you mean by *comes*…"

I widen my eyes at him. "Larry! Jesus."

He cackles. "When I was your captain, it wasn't appropriate for me to joke with you like that. Now that we're equals and friends, anything is fair game." He gives me a shooing motion with both hands. "Now get the hell out of here. You're exhausting me."

I lever myself to my feet, say my goodbyes, and head for home—more specifically, the gym in my building.

I consider his words, eyeing the message thread between Jovie and me—we've exchanged a few texts since that glorious, incredible morning, but I know EMS has been busy this week, too, so it's been difficult to connect.

I push through a back-and-biceps workout, still chewing on Cap's advice. I mean, he gussied it up in fancy words, but it really just amounted to *hell if I know, you gotta figure that one out for yourself, son.*

What do I want? Is it worth rejection?

I know I want her, on a physical level. And truth be told, *want* isn't even close to the right word. Not even in the same galaxy. *Need* is closer, but still doesn't touch the burning ferocity of my attraction to her.

And that was *before* that morning.

Now that I know what those incredible tits look like bare? How she sounds when she orgasms? Fuck. I need to get her alone and naked like I need oxygen. It's a non-negotiable. What happens after that is up for grabs. Will she stick around? Will she turn into a prickly ice queen viper? What if real feelings develop between us and she still won't allow anything to actually happen, in terms of…well, more.

What is more, anyway? What does that mean? More *what*? More than just sex? More than just casual? Being in "a relationship?" I don't know what that looks like.

My phone rings as I'm cleaning off the equipment I used—it's Maksim. "Hey, Maks. What's up, buddy?"

"Now you are captain, you don't drink with us no more, hey?" He's had a couple, I can tell—his accent thickens when he's tipsy, and if he's outright drunk, he's liable to lapse into Ukrainian entirely. "José and me, we are missing you, Captain Jake."

"You guys at The Far Bar?"

"*Da*, we are. The girls today here, they are very pretty. One I think you like, huh? The black hair one with these huge *hrudey*." I have no clue what the last word means, but I can guess based on context. "She is here with those friends. This tall one, and the one with the most amazing ass I ever seen."

"I thought you liked the tall one."

"Oh, *da*. I do. I like them tall. This girl, your girl's friend. I like her. I could put her whole little bottom in my one hand. Pick her up on my shoulders and eat her like a peach."

I laugh. "Sounds like I'm gonna have some catching up to do, when I get there."

"You don't say she not your girl. I notice this, my friend."

"She's not my girl, but she's also not *not* my girl."

Maksim laughs. "I am drunk, but I think I understood that."

"I'll be there in a few. Just gotta rinse off and change."

"Okay, we see you, Captain Jake."

"Shut up with the Captain Jake shit, Maks."

"I am only joking you, Captain Jake."

"Yeah, yeah. Save me a seat and get me a pitcher."

"Is already poured. You get here soon, or it will be warm and flat. Or drunk. Like me."

I laugh. "Maybe drink some water, buddy."

"*Nyet*. Is not that kind of day, Jake." There's a dark, serious tone in his voice, layered under his natural, indomitable good humor.

"Ten-four," I say, understanding without having to be told what he means. "See you soon."

JASINDA WILDER

I rinse off in record time, scrape some hair shit through my hair and leave it messy, dress in what I think of as my good jeans, and my favorite polo shirt, a blue one that girls say brings out the color in my eyes. Cologne, too. Hopefully just enough, and not too much.

Tuck the front of the shirt behind my belt, stuff my feet into my boots and leave them loosely laced. The Far Bar is, ironically, only a few blocks from here—Station One and The Far Bar are both closer to my condo now than Station Four was when it was my home base—so I opt to just walk. When I get there, the doors are open and music spills out along with the chatter of voices and bursts of laughter, and flashes of light.

Jovie is here—I recognize her voice through the din, somehow.

The bouncer, Eddie, knows me and nods at me. "Maks is in one of his moods," he says.

"Shit." I know what that means, and so does Eddie. "Thanks, I'll take care of him."

It means Maksim had a bad day—and a bad day for emergency service personnel means someone died. Thus the serious tone in his voice. Mostly, Maks handles it like the consummate professional he is. But sometimes, the burden of it all gets to even the best of us. And when that happens, you're there for them. You let them get it out, and you handle them. Maksim, however, has the added burden of combat experience to deal with, on top of the everyday shit we firefighters bear.

So every once in a while, Maks gets in a mood. It starts out jovial and wild and fun, but inevitably, as the alcohol takes over, his mood shifts. Usually it's sad and dark and broody, but sometimes…he needs me there to corral him.

When I find the guys, I'm surprised to see that Jovie, Erin, and Lia are with them, all five clustered around our usual table, pitchers of beer and empty pint glasses scattered on the table, and a round of shots lined up, waiting for me.

Jovie sees me first, and my heart stops—she actually smiles when she sees me. Despite the smile, the rest of her greeting is somewhat reserved, a friendly nod, like we're merely acquaintances. Better than outright hostility, though, so I'll take it as a win.

There are proper introductions all around, for my sake, since they've clearly had a leg up on getting friendly—the introductions are accompanied by the shots of whiskey.

"How'd this party start?" I ask, pouring myself a beer to wash down the shot.

José gestures at the girls. "They showed up about five minutes before Maks called you. They recognized us, and we got to talking."

Lia flicks fingertips at the detritus on the table. "Most of that is them."

Maks gulps down the last quarter of a pint in one go, belches softly, slams the glass on the table. "Most of that is *me*. And consider yourselfs lucky there is no good vodka here." He sloshes more beer into his glass. "Is good thing you are here, Jake."

"Why's that?" I ask, wary.

He slurps loudly, shakes his head as if to clear it,

frowning. "Don't let me be that guy, okay?" He glances at me. "You know what I mean."

I nod, gently punch his arm behind José's back. "I got you, pal. No worries."

Jovie eyes me curiously. "Should I be worried?"

Maks shakes his head. "Nah, nah. Not you." He juts his chin at a group of probies from Station Six across the bar—they're loud, obnoxious, and treating the waitresses like shit. "Them, maybe."

"Ah, leave 'em be," José says. "You know the ladies here can handle themselves."

"They're punks. They need a little discipline." He glowers at them. "That one waitress, the blond one. She's new. I am watching for them to make a wrong move. The tall shithead, he is the trouble."

"I've got it covered, Maks."

I say it, but I watch the group for a moment and I realize that Maks is all too right—these are all young punks barely old enough to get in here, and they're probably only signing up for the job because they think being a firefighter will get them laid more. The tall one, as Maks pointed out, is indeed the real troublemaker of the group. He's the loudest, the one pushing the others to drink more, to do another round of shots, and it's his eyes that are on the new waitress—a tiny, innocent-looking young thing who's in way over her head in a place like this.

I whip out my phone and make a call—it rings a few times, and then Captain Henderson from Station Six answers. "This is Henderson."

"Jake Howson, from Station One."

"Howson—heard you replaced old Mack. How's it

going uptown?" Brian Henderson has a reputation for being a hard-ass, no-nonsense, my-way-or-the-highway type of leader. Not liked, but respected.

"It's going okay, Brian. Reason I'm calling is I'm at The Far Bar, and I'm watching your probies about to get themselves in a heap of trouble."

"Awww shit. It's Kline, isn't it? The tall one, real loudmouth."

"That's him."

"What's he doing?"

"Well, so far, just being a jackass with too much to drink and a chip on his shoulder. But it's got the look of something that could go south real quick. You know how the guys in here are about the waitresses, Brian—don't fuck with 'em. And your boy Kline looks to be working his way to fucking with a new girl."

"Goddammit." Henderson growls a few more choice words. "I'm upstate, fishing. Can you handle them for me?"

"I can. I just don't wanna step on any toes."

"Smart move, Howson, and I appreciate it. Just treat 'em like you would probies from your station, and I'll handle them when I get back tomorrow afternoon."

"Got it. Catch a big one for me."

He laughs. "I'll do my best. So far, I've caught nothing but a suntan."

"Well, here's to better luck tomorrow."

Right as I'm ending the call, I hear a commotion from the group of guys across the bar. I toss my phone to Jovie, who catches it deftly.

I point at Maks, who's rising from his chair. "Sit down, Maksim. I've got it."

"They are six, you are one."

"True, but even if it did come to that, which it won't, they still don't stand a chance." I grin. "You oughta know me better than that, Maks."

Maksim sits heavily, laughing. "Words first, fists last. I know."

I saunter over to the group—they've got the waitress cornered, hemmed in by their bodies. So far, they're just messing with her, teasing, taking her tray. Being little assholes. But the poor girl looks terrified. She sees me coming, pleads with me with her eyes.

Kline is in the middle, taking up most of the space, his voice the loudest.

I put my hand on the back of his neck like a wayward child and squeeze—*hard*. "What's going on here, Kline?"

He tries to shrug me off. "Fuck off. I don't know you."

I squeeze harder, and he starts to duck down in an attempt to get away. "I know you. And I've got carte blanche from Captain Henderson to deal with you as I see fit. And what I see right now is a punk-ass little boy who's just begging to get his ass kicked." I squeeze even harder, and he grunts in pain. "What I see is a little probie bitch about to get himself kicked out of the department before he finishes his probation. So you got two choices, kid. I'm gonna let go and you're going to apologize to this waitress you're terrorizing, and you personally are going to pay for the entire tab, and you're going to tip her a minimum of one hundred percent of the total bill. That's option one.

Option two, I let go, you turn around and take a swing, and end up in fucking traction. Your choice."

I let go and step back—he spins, fist raised, eyes landing at shoulder height, and then going up, and up. His eyes widen. "Shit."

I have my hands in my pockets. "You gonna take that swing, probie?" I lean forward when he hesitates to answer. "I believe the correct answer here is 'no sir, Captain Howson, sir.'"

He swallows hard and drops his fist. "No sir, Captain Howson, sir."

I twirl a finger at the waitress, who has her round black tray held in front of her like a shield. "Apologize. By which I mean, beg her forgiveness."

"I'm sorry," he mumbles.

"That didn't sound like begging, Kline." I arch an eyebrow at him. "Don't make me take my hands out of my pockets. You won't like that very much."

Kline turns back to the waitress. "I'm sorry. Please forgive me. Please."

She looks at me, then at him. "Yeah, yeah, it's fine," she whispers.

I frown at her. "No, it's not. Next time, bop him with your tray. Eddie'll have your back." I gesture around at the bar. "You can't take that shit in a place like this, honey. You wanna swim with the sharks, you gotta be a shark." I gesture at the probies around us. "Not that these guys are sharks. Baby sharks, maybe. But still, you get my point."

She nods and makes her escape.

I turn to Kline, my gaze taking in his five friends. "This place is special. You treat it with respect. You don't disrupt our fun. You don't cause trouble. We all come here to decompress—*if* you guys make it through probation, you'll find out what I mean. What you need to know is that being here is a privilege. You *get* to be here. And the number one rule is, you *don't fuck* with the waitresses. You're fucking lucky Eddy didn't see that shit, or you'd all be getting your meals through a straw." I scan them. "This is your one warning. And it's already going to cost you— you bet your ass Captain Henderson has heard about this, and from what I know of him, I don't think that's going to go well for you guys."

Their faces reflect that no, in fact, Captain Henderson is not going to like this development at all.

I pin Kline with one last look. "You pay. One hundred percent tip. You smart enough to know what that means, Probie?"

"Yes, sir."

I speak as if he didn't answer. "It means if your tab is one hundred dollars, you pay one hundred dollars and tip her an additional one hundred dollars. Do you understand me?"

"Yes, sir."

I walk away. "No more bullshit."

José and Maks are about to shit themselves laughing. When I sit down, José promptly loses it, leaning against me and laughing hysterically. "You see his face when he turned around and saw your big gorilla ass? God, so fuckin' funny. I think he gotta check his pants, man. Ohhhh shit, that was good." He shivers. "I did a couple shifts at Six with Henderson back when I was new. Dude is scary as fuck. I don't envy those probies one fuckin' bit."

Jovie grins at me. "I thought for sure you were gonna hit him."

I shrug, wave. "Nah. There are better ways of handling things." I can't help a rueful laugh. "Mainly because I gotta be careful who I hit, and how hard. When I hit people, they have a tendency to stay hit, you know? Got me in a lot of trouble when I was a pissed-off teenager with more size than sense."

Jovie's arm brushes mine, looking at me sidelong, across her shoulder. "Oh?" It's a nudge to keep going.

"Yeah, I got expelled from two different schools, freshman year and sophomore year." I laugh. "I didn't figure out how to control my temper until Mom threatened me with military school. So then I started my third school junior year. Basketball helped. But it wasn't just that I got into fights, it was that I tended to win the fights...and keep going. Not good."

"And now you're a master of your temper, huh?" she asks.

José responds for me. "Mostly, yeah. Me and Maks are both older than him, right? So we were veterans when he came into Four as a rookie. He had a temper back then, too. The guys in the station back then were fond of hazing the probies, and Jake didn't take it too well."

I arch an eyebrow at him. "You're not going there, José."

He grins. "Sure I am."

"No, you're not."

He laughs, slugging beer. "They played a prank on him. Stole all his clothes and gear while he was in the shower, tossed it all out into the street, and then hid all the towels."

I groan, covering my face. "Dammit, José."

Jovie is already laughing. "What'd he do?"

"He walked his ass naked as a jaybird right out into the street. In broad daylight. Didn't even cover his junk!" He moves his forearm and hand side to side like a swaying elephant's trunk. "Big ol' dong was just flopping around, 'bout to take out buildings, knock over busses. Shit was like King Kong gone wrong, man."

"José!" I snap.

He laughs even harder—he's not afraid of me. "I swear to Jesus and Santa Maria, he caused three accidents."

"I fucking hate you," I mutter. "It wasn't three accidents, it was *one*."

Jovie is shaking with silent laughter. "No, no. Seriously?"

José crosses himself. "I fuckin' swear. This nun was crossing the street. She stopped to stare at him, and a van swerved to miss her, and crashed into a parked car. Coming the other way, there was one of those limo busses, right? Guess what it was full of? Horny fuckin' women! A bridal party, like fuckin' twenty of them. All tryin' to get out of the bus and get to him. He got swarmed, and that shit was funnier than anything else. He was legit tryin'ta swim out of this sea of fuckin' horny-ass drunk women. Which caused yet another accident, and that one started a chain reaction of rear-endings, which I count as two distinct accidents."

"It wasn't fuckin' funny," I growl, still sore about it.

"It was sexual harassment, but because I'm a dude, people think it's funny. I had bruises on my junk for days."

Maksim nods sagely. "Is true. I lose a bet, once. Had to strip at a cousin's friend's party, the bachelor party for women. They think I am free meat."

Jovie is still cackling. "And no one thought to help him?"

"We were too busy laughing," Maksim says. "Besides, the police showed up and saved him from the women."

"And cited me for public indecency," I snap.

"Bahhh," José said, with a dismissive wave. "Captain got you out of that. And he also put a stop to hazing."

"Were you guys in on it?" Lia asks.

"Of course we were!" Maksim says, laughing. "I throw his clothes into the street, and José hides the towels on the roof."

Erin just shakes her head. "I don't understand men and the hazing. That's so mean, and humiliating."

"Thank you," I say, gesturing at her. "Someone gets it."

José just laughs. "You replaced Hornby's seasoning salt with ghost pepper flakes, so don't act like you're Mr. Innocent."

"You also somehow managed to switch Coulson's shaving cream with whipped cream," Maksim points out. "I am still not so sure how you managed that one."

"Harmless pranks," I say. "It wasn't hazing, it was a goofy way to welcome the probies. No one got hurt or humiliated."

"Oh, stop," José says, waving at me. "You weren't hurt."

JASINDA WILDER

"Tell that to my dick!" I shiver and cup myself over my jeans. "I have nightmares about that. Twenty horny drunk women all trying to claw me to pieces at the same time. They were like a pack of fucking velociraptors."

Jovie cackles. "I mean, look at it from their point of view: you're drunk and having a grand ol' time with your girls on a bachelorette day out, and suddenly, out of nowhere, there's a giant hunk of naked man-meat, just…right there for the grabbing. What did you expect them to do? Act like rational adults?"

I shake my head and roll my eyes. "Right. But you know those nightmares where you're naked in front of the whole school? It's worse in real life."

"José says you didn't even try to cover up, though," she replies.

I shrug. "I'm not gonna prance around like a scared little boy with a hand over my privates. So yeah, I flaunted my shit. I was dying on the inside, but when you're the rookie getting hazed, you can't show fear. Those fuckers can smell it. If I'd acted like anything less than the big tough confident badass, I'd never have heard of last of it. And shit, there's still the framed newspaper article about it in the breakroom at Four, I think."

"Yeah, it's there," Maksim confirms. "They put a little smiling sunshine guy over your big old monster honker."

I glare at him. "My *what*?"

"Your monster honker." Maksim extends his hands a good foot apart, and then touches his fingers in a circle at least six inches across. It's like this, I swear. I see you in the shower every day, I try not to look but holy fuck

136

Moses, you just can't look away. I am no small shakes, but you make me feel like a little boy."

Jovie is blushing, Erin has her hands over her mouth, shoulders shaking with silent laughter, and Lia is desperately trying to not spew beer all over the table.

José has his head thrown back and is laughing raucously. "Oh shit, Maks. You just mixed up so many fuckin' metaphors, buddy. Monster honker. Jesus. Where do you come up with this shit? No one ever has called a dick a monster honker. Tits are honkers. Dicks are *not* honkers." He looks at me. "Does your dick honk?"

I am biting my lip to keep from laughing, gamely trying to keep a pissed expression on my face. "No, José, my dick does not honk."

Lia, having successfully avoided beer spewage, glances at Jovie. "You tell us, Jove—does Jake's dick make any kind of a honking noise?"

Jovie whips her head around to stare death daggers at Lia. "How should I know?"

Lia does an impressively believable innocent expression. "I dunno. I just thought that you guys have—"

"We haven't." Jovie's eyes flit to me, and then away.

"Yet," I mutter, into my pint glass.

Jovie heard, and her eyes widen to saucers. "Jake!" She hisses.

I take a swig, shrugging. "What?" I say, after swallowing, wiping a foam mustache away with the back of my wrist. "It's no secret to these guys that I'm crazy fuckin' attracted to you." I glance at the other two girls. "I dunno what you told them or didn't."

"I didn't tell them anything," Jovie says, shooting me a warning look. "Because there's nothing to tell."

"Ah," I say. "It's like that."

"There's nothing to *be* like that."

Lia just snickers. "Jove, honey. Baby. Sweet'ums."

José cackles. "Aww shit, you know she mean business when she say it like that."

"You don't even know," Erin says. "This oughta be good."

Jovie glares at the table at large, in an impressive range of aggressive staring. "Is this amusing to you?"

"Yes," Maksim says, now drinking directly from the pitcher. "I am greatly amused. Sweet'ums."

"No." Jovie spikes a finger at him, voice ice cold. "You don't get to call me that."

Maksim shrugs behind the pitcher, still slurping away. "Only joking. Put the finger away."

"Maks, buddy, slow down." I touch his arm to lower the pitcher.

He just glares at me. "Move it or lose it, bub. Not today."

José taps me, shakes his head and makes a slicing motion across his throat. "It was a bad one."

I nod. "Well, just don't make me wrestle you into your apartment like last time."

Erin eyes Maks. Then, she takes a pitcher—which seems to have magically refilled itself—and drinks directly from it, as well. "It was one of those days," she says, pausing to belch softly. "Fuck it."

Lia watches Erin with a worried expression on her

face. "Erin, you're a lush. You're gonna be puking in the gutter in ten minutes at that rate."

Erin set the pitcher down, belching again, her eyes still on Maks. "You know, we're all the same, here."

Maks shakes his head. "Not same."

Erin lifts her chin. "You know what I do?"

"Model for the angels of Victoria, what is it called?" He mutters something in Ukrainian. "The secret. Victoria's Secret, that is the thing."

"Cute, but no," Erin says, blushing. "I'm head of the ER at the hospital, as a matter of fact."

Maks puts the pitcher down slowly, eying her. "This is true?"

Erin nods and jerks her thumb at Lia. "She's EMS like Jovie. So, I'm just saying, Maksim, you're at a table of people who *get it.*" She reaches across the table for him but stops short of touching his hand. "You don't have to be fine. We all understand."

Lia drops her eyes, staring at her glass. "I lost a kid, today. Hit by a car. Wasn't anything I could do, even if I'd gotten there sooner."

Jovie nods. "Semi-versus-Honda on the interstate. The semi won."

Maksim shakes his head. "Was something I could do, but I didn't do it in time."

José's head whips around to look at him. "*Bull*shit, Maks. I was fuckin' *there.*" He stabs a finger at him. "That kid was as good as gone and you know it. We all knew it. If you'd gone in there, *you'd* be gone. You *tried* to get in there—it took fuckin' four of us to stop you, bro. It was gone. The house was *gone.* You get to be upset, man, but you don't get to blame yourself. You did your job to the best of your ability, and sometimes it's just not fuckin' enough."

"His mom…" Maks shakes his head, covering his face. "Her eyes. When she saw me come out without him."

Silence, then. We all know that look.

Lia grabs the pitcher from Erin and knocks it back for a few big chugs. Passes it to Jovie. "To the ones we couldn't save."

Jovie chugs, repeats the toast, passes it to me, and I drink, repeating the toast at the end as well. José does the same; Maks watches all the while.

Then, slowly, he lifts the pitcher high. "To the ones we could not save."

Lia slaps the table with her palm. "And that's enough heavy shit. Can we go back to talking about Jake's monster honker?"

"No." I point at her. "Nope. My dick is not a topic for public discussion."

She shrugs, studiously NOT looking at Jovie. "I mean, it can't be *that* big. Can it?"

I put my face in my hands—a double facepalm. "Lia, come on."

"What? I'm just curious." She remains remarkably expressionless, even as Jovie is getting visibly more embarrassed, flushed, and uncomfortable. "I mean, if it's this gargantuan anomaly of a cock, you probably don't get actually laid all that often, I would think, since it'd be too big to fit inside most women—mouth *or* vagina. So I'm just curious."

"You will have to languish in ignorance, I'm afraid," I say.

"He gets plenty laid," Maksim says, the traitor. "Very plenty. Is really that big. I mean, is why he has the nickname—" he cuts off with a sharp grunt.

I frown at him. "I have a nickname?"

José shakes his head. "Maks is wasted. Don't listen to him."

"Is true. Can barely see straight. I forget what I was saying about."

"What nickname, Maksim?"

Maks shrugs. "No nickname. I am drunk. Ignore me." He makes a shooing motion with his hands. "I must piss. Move."

José and I let him out, and he walks—more steadily than he has any right to, considering how much he's had to drink—to the restrooms.

I fix José with a glare. "What was he talking about? I don't have a nickname."

"I have no idea, Jake." José shrugs. "You know how he gets when he's like this." He slides out of the booth and heads for the bar. "Time to finish the morose bastard off. Garçon! A round of your finest vodka! No, *two* rounds!"

"Bad plan, José!" I call. "Giving Maksim vodka right now is a terrible, horrible, awful, idiotic idea."

José just grins as the bartender slops twelve shot glasses full of top-shelf vodka. "That's why it's such a great idea."

The girls trade looks.

"Why is it a bad idea?" Jovie asks. "What will he do?"

I shrug, hands lifting. "Hell if I know. Anything is possible when you give already drunk Maksim vodka. That's why it's such a bad idea. He could start a fight, he could strip down to his skivvies and dance on the table, he could tell war stories in Ukrainian, he could cry, he could pass out standing up." I shake my head and shrug again. "It's a real crapshoot."

Lia giggles, clapping. "This sounds like fun!"

José arrives with a tray full of shot glasses. "She gets it! It's the most fun you'll have all week—unless he starts a fight, starts crying, or falls asleep." He tips his head to the side. "Although sometimes when he starts a fight, it *is* kind of entertaining. You think he stands no chance, but he always manages to surprise you."

Erin frowns. "Letting your drunk friend get into a fight hardly seems responsible."

José waves her off. "Bah, we never let him get into any real trouble. He usually picks the biggest asshole in the room and knocks their head off." He grins at Erin. "Figuratively speaking."

I rise from the table. "I'm gonna go see what's taking Maks so long."

I find him leaning on an elbow against the urinal, improbably still peeing. "Damn, Austin Powers, you're *still* pissing?"

He gives a wobbly nod. "I do not understand this reference. But yes. I broke the seal and now I am cursed to piss for an age."

I lean back against the counter opposite the urinals. "You okay, buddy? For real?"

He shrugs, seems to finally finish and shakes off. "It just got to me. I will be okay." He turns to wash his hands, glancing at me. "Do you think there is a chance Erin likes me?"

I shrug. "I don't know her well enough to know, Maks. I think she's got a secret wild side, despite that she seems way more buttoned-up and reserved than Lia or Jovie."

"It is the ones that seem buttoned up who are often the wild ones," he points out, speaking carefully—which is how I know he's really wasted: tipsy Maks has a strong Ukrainian accent, and drunk Maks will often lapse into Ukrainian, but wasted Maks speaks English very precisely, without slurring or stumbling over his words.

"That's what I hear. Never tried to find out, personally."

He grins at me. "No? It is great fun. I recommend it most highly."

"I'll keep that in mind."

He laughs. "I forgot—you are all tied up in Jovie."

"I'm not all tied up in anyone."

"You have barely spoken directly to her all night, nor she to you, but you are stealing glances at each other whenever you think the other is not looking. I have seen this." He holds up an index finger. "This means something has happened."

"Nice theory, but no."

He peers at me. "You cannot lie to Maksim. Tell me the truth."

I growl. I hate it when he does that—speaks in third person…and corners my lamentably honest ass. "Nothing actually…*happened*."

"But something did almost happen? Or sort of happened?"

"Sort of."

"And that is what?"

"None of your business."

He laughs and claps his hands. "Oh ho! You will not tell me. You have never not told me about your conquests. This means you *like* her." He nods, sage and wise and all-knowing. "Very well. I accept your silence… *if* you admit to me that you like her more than simply wanting to bury your face in those magnificent breasts of hers."

"If I admit it, will you drop it?"

He just grins.

I groan. "Fine. Yes. I may possibly like her as a person, and not just for her magnificent breasts, which I do very much want to bury my face in."

"Which you have not done. Yet."

"Yet."

He claps me on the shoulder. "Very good. This is good. You work too hard, and you are too serious. You need a woman to lighten you up. Maybe if you got your cock sucked more frequently, you would be more fun."

I shake my head. "I'm not *that* serious."

"Your idea of a vacation is a weekend at that cabin of yours. You have never taken more than forty-eight hours away from work in the years I have known you. You have never had a serious girlfriend except that English girl Sara, and you knew from the very start she was going back to England so she does not count."

"I like my job."

"You are afraid of women."

I laugh. "What? You're nuts. I love women."

"You love their bodies. They are soft, and warm, and fun to be naked in bed with. But you are afraid of how they make you feel, so you keep them from knowing the real you."

I groan. "Oh god, it's philosophical and introspective drunk Maksim. Great."

He laughs, claps me on the back, and pushes me to the exit. "It is all about your father, you see," he says, as if he's my therapist. "It is a kind of reversal. Your mother cared for you in place of your father, and you fear no other woman can ever love you the way your mother did, and you are afraid to try."

"And what, oh great and wise Maksim, does that have to do with my dad?"

"You are smart enough to know he did not abandon you or leave on purpose, so you cannot be angry at him. And your mother did the best she could. But your heart is wounded and grieving, and you have nowhere to place the blame except fate or the world or what have you. So, you shield your heart from further hurts by preventing any woman who might be able to get inside your heart and actually love you from getting close." He waves a hand in a flourish. "If this Jovie stands a chance of getting your heart into the...shit, I forget the word.

145

The circle of rope. The cowboys use them to catch cows."

"Lasso," I answer.

"Yes, the lasso. If Jovie can get your heart into her lasso, then I will help her."

"Don't help her."

"I will. It is my duty as your best friend."

"There's no lasso. I'm not afraid."

"There is a lasso, and you are afraid. It's okay. I will help you grow out of your cowardly man-boy heart and into the brave and fearless manly man heart."

I cackle. "Oh man, Maks. You're really on a roll." I glance at him as we finally make our way away from the restrooms toward our table. "If you're so all-knowing and wise in matters of the heart, why are you still single?"

"Because I have been waiting for the right woman, Jake Howson." His eyes are on Erin. "It is too soon to know for sure, but I think I maybe have found her." He grins at me. "She just does not know it yet."

I notice Erin is pretending to look at her phone but is actually very intently studying Maksim from underneath her eyelashes. "I dunno, buddy. I think she may actually have an idea."

He brightens visibly. "You think?"

I clap him on the shoulder. "Only one way to find out, right?"

He laughs. "I am wise to your game. You are trying to distract me from your problems by focusing on mine. Only mine is not a problem."

"I don't have a problem either!"

"Then leave José to drunk-sit me and take your Jovie away to be alone." He spies the shots on the table. "Well, shit. I take that back. He will need you, because I think tabletop stripper Maks is about to make an appearance."

"No, no, no." I haul him back away from the shots. "You nearly got arrested for public indecency last time, Maks. Don't do it!"

He grins at me. "Would you rather I pick a fight with the assholes from Six?" He points—they're behaving themselves, but the occasional dirty glances I'm getting tell me one little spark is all it would take to start a brawl.

"Can't you just cry instead?"

Maks wrinkles his face like he's going to sneeze, but then his expression smooths out again. "No, I do not feel it." He takes a pair of shots and holds them up. "Only two choices today, friends: fighting, or dancing." He stands up on the bench and props one foot on the table in a Captain Morgan pose. "I'm for dancing. Who's with me?"

Lia is the first to follow suit, grabbing her shots with a sly look at José as she stands up on the bench as well. "I'm all for the dancing."

Erin is quick to join. "As long as no one posts any videos or photos of it, me too."

José is on his feet on the bench as well, doing a quick step jig. "You know I will dance at the drop of a hat, and I will drop the hat myself. We need music, though." He shouts across the bar: "Jimmy! Music!"

Jimmy, the bartender, shakes his big, bearded head,

147

but he reaches to turn on the music. "Just don't break nothin'."

He cranks up the music, a lively Irish jig-and-reel that has Maks stomping on the table in time with the beat, José quick-stepping to fill in the pattern; the women clap, even Jovie, who seems more bemused than anything else. Once Maks heaves himself entirely onto the table, shots still in hand, she climbs to her feet and stomps a foot on the bench in time, as well.

Leaving me, the sole lame duck.

Jovie is nearest me, and she shakes her head, reaches down for my hand and hauls me up onto the bench. "Oh, get over yourself and have some fun, Howson."

I let her pull me up—even though I have no rhythm or dance moves whatsoever, I still do my best to stomp along.

Maks is gyrating and stomping—I have to admit that he actually has some pretty good moves. He holds one of the shot glasses high. "Slava Ukraini!"

We all throw back the first shot together, and I lose the beat in the process.

Jovie just laughs and starts bumping my hip with hers in time with the beat. "You're so white, it's adorable!" She bops her head and bumps me with her hip, eyes bright, vodka sloshing over her wrist. "Like this!" She stomps exaggeratedly, showing me the rhythm.

The song transitions abruptly, from a jig to a reel, or the other way, I don't fuckin' know. It just gets faster, the fiddle melody circling and circling faster and faster. I feel the rhythm, and for once I just let it take over, for once not caring how I appear, if I'm on beat or look stupid—Jovie's joy in the music is infectious, and each slam of her full hip against mine sends jolts of that hot electric energy searing through me, and I can't look away from her, from the pure happiness in her eyes, her utter abandoned presence in *this* moment.

Maks throws the other shot high. "To The Job!" he says. "To the life, the brothers, the sisters, and the only job there is."

Erin puts a hand on a hip and fixes him with a glare. "Hey, what about us?"

"For this toast, you are honorary firewomen. Fire ladies?"

Jovie shakes her head, putting her shot glass up against Maks's. "No, no, I got one." She pauses to think. "To the good cops and the great medics, to the tireless doctors and the fearless firefighters—we put one foot in the grave to keep others out of it."

"Hear hear!" José says.

"Spoken with the morbidity of a career medic," I say. "Hear hear."

We clink and we drink, and my eyes never leave Jovie.

Spilled vodka trickles down her wrist and forearm, and when everyone else has devolved into dancing the table, kicking over empty pitchers and scattering pint glasses, I find myself face to face with her, standing on the bench, bodies flush.

I grab her wrist, turn it over tender side up. I run my tongue along her skin, tasting the burn of the vodka on my tongue mingling with the salt of her flesh—all the way up her forearm to her wrist, and then I turn her hand over and kiss the web of her thumb, licking away the vodka.

I'm on fire.

She's not breathing.

A fraught moment flickers between us, a war between my holdups and hers, my desire and hers. Her eyes are huge and brown, deep and wild.

I take a mental snapshot of her, in this moment.

Tight, stretchy, faded jeans hugging thick thighs and bell-curve hips. Black heels, maybe three inches or so. A loose, blousy white top, the front tucked behind a wide brown belt with a fancy gold buckle. The top, despite being loose and flowy around her waist, hugs her chest and hangs off her shoulders, wrapping around her arms and cutting across the valley of her breasts. Hair pulled back and braided, the braid twisted around itself into a neat bun. So...fucking...gorgeous.

"You take my breath away," I murmur.

Somehow, she hears me. "We're doing this?" she murmurs back. "Here? Now?"

I shrug. "Why not? If not here, then where? If not now, then when?"

"It's a mistake," she says. "For you, I mean. Just... being honest."

"It's my mistake to make."

"You know I can't be what you want, so why bother?" She gestures at a table full of beautiful women openly scanning the bar for someone to pay them attention. "Crook a finger, and you'll have all four of them ready to obey your every whim."

"Been there, done that, bought the t-shirt, burned the t-shirt. Not interested."

"Not as fun as it sounds?"

I shake my head. "Not nearly. Way too much work, and someone always gets left out."

She looks up at me. "You're hard to resist, Jake Howson."

I grin. "I haven't even turned on the charm, yet."

"Oh no? What was that phone call about, then?"

"That was me getting sick of my own imagination. I needed fresh fuel for the spank bank."

She splutters a laugh. "Wow. Nice. So I'm just spank bank material, then."

"Yup."

"And you say you haven't turned on the charm." She fans herself and pretends to swoon. "Oh, Jake!"

I catch her in her fake swoon, and as my arms go around her, she lets herself relax into my hold—swooning for real, perhaps. "I'm not thinking about what I want you to be or the future or any of that. Maybe I should be, but I'm not."

She's leaning up against me, arms upright between us, breasts flattening against my chest, wide brown eyes gazing up at me. "Oh no? Then pray tell, what *are* you thinking about?"

"This."

I kiss her.

I don't normally lead with a kiss—it tends to imply something I don't intend. But Jovie is different. This thing with us is different.

I can't use a line on her.

JASINDA WILDER

I can't *not* kiss her.

Her lips are soft, and warm—she's shocked at first.

But then she slowly relaxes into the kiss, lifting up on her tiptoes, music skirling around us, our friends dancing and whooping—at us, probably. Her fingers curl into claws, dig into my chest—the kiss wilds, heats, our tongues slipping and twirling, and her fingers dig in harder, and I feel her chest swell against mine as she breaks the kiss just enough to suck in a breath…holds it…

And then exhales a soft "Fuck it," and slams her mouth against mine.

To say sparks fly is to call the sun a nice little candle.

I am on fire.

I need more.

I need all of her.

JOVIE

HOLY FUCK.

I have never been kissed like this—not in bed, not in public, not anywhere. Not by anyone.

I'm consumed by it. I forget where I am, I forget who I am. There's only Jake, and his strong lips and his insistent tongue. His big hard body against mine, his firm chest under my hands.

I've been crushing on him all night—stealing glances at the way the sleeves of his polo stretch around his huge arms, the way his shoulders and torso taper to a tight wedge. When he got up to go to the bathroom, I openly ogled his tight hard ass in those fucking jeans. No man has ever worn jeans the way Jake Howson wears those.

His eyes, fuck me, his eyes. There are no metaphors or similes or descriptions to accurately describe the blue of his eyes, the way they shift shades with his mood and his clothes, sometimes look pale as a summer sky, other times azure like the Caribbean, or even almost blue-green like the deep waters of the Atlantic.

His hands, as we continue to kiss, standing on the bench, clutch at my hips, hold me. Pull me closer. I writhe against him, and his grip moves to cradle my ass.

I groan at his touch, break the kiss. Look up at him. My mind knows I'm going to regret this, later, but for now...my body rules. "Let's go."

He hops down from the bench without letting go of my hips, lifts me effortlessly to the floor. He digs into his hip pocket and pulls out a thin bifold wallet, removes a hundred dollar bill and tosses it onto the table, then takes my hand and hauls me away toward the exit, shoving his wallet back into his pocket.

"Yeah girl!" I hear Lia shout, whooping and laughing. "Get you some!"

"Let us know if the rumors are true!" Erin shouts, and I feel Jake's groan.

I use my empty hand to flip them off without turning around.

We hit the sidewalk, and the sudden relative silence is disorienting.

Jake tugs me one way. "My condo is three blocks this way."

"Mine is one and a half the other way," I say, resisting his pull and gesturing the other way.

He pauses, looks at me, and then waves in the direction I indicated. "Lead the way."

It's a bizarre, disorienting moment of normalcy as we walk hand in hand, like a couple, to my condo. He seems to refuse to hurry, even though my stolen glances at his zipper tell me he's *definitely* in a hurry—that zipper is at the end of its lifespan, straining to contain him.

So, we don't hurry. We walk a normal, casual pace, fingers twined. Not looking at each other. I feel every step—my breasts ache with the bounce of my steps, nipples peaked and hard behind my bra, my core throbbing.

From a kiss.

He says nothing, his eyes roaming the street, scanning, watching. It's a pretty safe area—Lia and I have walked back to my place together after a night out plenty of times with never an incident.

So, of course, tonight is the night something happens.

We pass an alley between buildings, and a skinny white guy with fucked-up teeth and dilated pupils steps out in front of us. He has a large folding knife in one hand, open, the edge serrated.

He's jittery, shaking. "Money." He gestures at Jake with the knife. "No funny shit or your girlfriend will watch me cut you to pieces."

Jake drops my hand and steps between the would-be mugger and me. "Not the night, my friend. Really not the night."

"I give a shit? Give me fuckin' money *now*, you big bastard."

"Walk away," Jake rumbles, and I feel him tensing.

Dammit, he's gonna try something, and that'll be the end of the sexy feelings.

I never carry cash in my purse or my wallet, but I always keep some in my pocket for this purpose. I dig it out and reach around Jake, slap it into his palm with a disgusted huff. "Just give it to him, Jake."

Jake extends the cash. "You're lucky, you know."

The man snatches it and backs away. "How so?"

"That cash just saved your life."

"How you figure?"

"I spent all mine, and I'm out of patience." Jake steps forward, his posture threatening. "Take the money and fucking run, you little tweaker bitch, before I change my mind and snap your neck like a fucking twig."

Something must be in Jake's eyes that tell the mugger Jake means business—he turns on a heel and runs, so panicked he even drops the knife to the ground with a clatter.

Jake moves as if to start after him, but I haul him back. "Let him go," I say.

"I should've turned him into toothpaste," Jake rumbles.

I move in front of him. "Haven't you ever heard that discretion is the better part of valor?"

"I just let a pussy fuckin' tweaker mug me." He glances down at me, irate, pissed off, and vibrating with adrenaline. "He took your money."

I put my hands on his chest. "I have no doubt you could have wiped the floor with the poor guy, knife or no knife. But you know what, Jake? That doesn't turn me on. I've responded to knife fights, and I know you have too. It's not pretty. You don't get out of a knife fight unscathed."

He grumbles. "Yeah, I know. But I also have training on disarming people."

"So do I." I curl my fingers in his shirt. "You put yourself between me and him, and that turns me on. But you know what really gets me going? You *listened*. If you'd have fought the guy, I'd have to stitch you up and there'd be a police report, and there goes the night. But instead, I'm out sixty bucks, he's gone, you're fine, and now we can go up to my condo and fuck."

His eyes narrow. "I wanted to impress you with my hand-to-hand combat skills."

I laugh. "I'm more interested in being impressed with your tongue-to-pussy skills."

"Those skills *are* far more impressive, I like to think."

I pull him backward, toward my building. "So come show me. Forget that guy. His life is sad. He's an addict and he's going to end up face down in an alley. I don't care about the money. I know you're more than capable of protecting me—and the fact that you gave him the money and let him go is more of a protection than if you'd taken him on." I let go of his hands and hook my fingers behind his belt, walking backward and pulling him by his pants. "I know you're flush with adrenaline right now, Jake. But just focus on me. Let it go."

"Trying."

I wiggle my hips, dancing as I sing, badly off-key. "'I'm bringing sexy back…'"

He laughs, lunges for me and scoops me up. My legs go around his waist and we catch up against the side of the building next to the entrance. I'm pinned by him, eye to eye, and he nuzzles my throat, forcing my head to tip back. "'Them other boys don't know how to act,'" he finishes, the words mumbled against my neck.

I laugh, burying my fingers in his hair. "You know Justin Timberlake?"

"My mom loves him. Whenever I go over to her

house, she's got his music bumping while she does what-ever, gardening, cleaning, folding her laundry."

I can't help but pet his hair, stroke the back of his neck. "Awww, are you a momma's boy?"

"Hell yeah I am."

I laugh. "That's a hell of a turn-on, too." My laugh turns breathless as his nuzzling of my throat turns into soft light kisses to my exposed shoulder, then my clavicle, and then down the slope of my cleavage. "That…that's *definitely* a turn-on."

He just growls, wordless, an erotic, primal snarl. His face nuzzles lower, between my breasts.

"Jake."

He just growls again, kissing, licking, nuzzling.

"Jake!"

He pulls away, finally, and looks at me. "What?"

"Quit motorboating my tits and take me upstairs."

He barks a laugh. "That wasn't motorboating." He buries his face between my tits and makes a growling sound as he twists his face side to side, making a comically accurate motorboat sound. "*That* was motorboating you."

I cackle, push him away and tug my top back up. Gesture at the entrance beside us. "This is my building, Jake. If motorboating is your thing, let's go upstairs and I'll let you do it as long as you want."

He looks at the door, the steps, the buzzer panel with my last name clearly printed next to one of the round black buttons. "Oh." A little laugh. "Right. That makes more sense. I think your tits short-circuited my brain there for a second."

I lead him up the stairs, fish my keys from my purse,

and let us in. He presses the elevator call button, but nothing happens. Not even a clang or a grind or anything.

He looks at me and I just shrug. "It's an old building," I say. "Unless I have a lot of groceries, I usually just take the stairs."

He drags me to the stairwell and jogs up—I'm fit, and I can sprint up stairs with the best of them, but Jake is on a whole other level—he sprints upward two and three steps at a time.

I laugh as I struggle to keep up. "Jake! Slow down, big fella. I'm not gonna change my mind in the next minute or two."

He growls again, an impatient sound, comes back down to me, scoops me back up with my legs around his waist, and proceeds to run back up the stairs two at a time...equally as fast as if unimpeded.

Fuck yeah, it's hot.

"I'm not afraid you're going to change your mind," he murmurs as we reach the third floor and he beelines for my unit.

"Then what's the rush?"

He halts at my door, eyes on mine as I slide to my feet. "If I don't get you naked in the next sixty seconds, I might just spontaneously explode. That's the rush."

"Oh." I fit my key into the doorknob, twist it open, and then the deadbolt. "We wouldn't want you to explode." I push open my door, spin to face him, already toeing off my heels. "At least, not unless it's in my mouth."

He steps through, the movement a predatory prowl. Instead of slamming the door as I'd half expected, he closes it with exaggerated softness, as if afraid of his own strength. Knowing him, he might very well have wrenched it right off its hinges. He looks superhuman, suddenly, muscle tensed and swollen, chest heaving, arms massive, chest more massive still. Hair a mess from my hands, lips parted, eyes furious with arousal. My sex pulses at the sight of him, immediately soaked…as if I wasn't already drenched.

He crosses his arms in front of himself and rips his shirt off, hurling it aside as if sick of the very thought of it.

Fuck.

Holy…fuck.

The man is a literal god. I stare up at him, at the wonder and glory of his bared torso. He's…sculpted. Instagram couldn't handle him. Magazines couldn't contain him. Movies couldn't do him justice. Every muscle is carved from marble and turned to living flesh—I saw him on my phone, but that's a pale imitation of the real thing, live and in person.

My mouth goes dry, every droplet of moisture in my body flooding south—you could just about wring out my panties, at this point.

"Jake," I whisper his name, step forward. His back is still to the door. "My god, Jake."

He grasps his belt buckle, but I arrest his hands. "Oh no, no way," I murmur, leaning in to press a kiss to his chest, right between his pecs, my hands knocking his away. "Mine."

He laughs, and moves his hands, sliding them to my shoulders as I work the buckle open. His lips touch the top of my head, breath hot as he kisses there—my heart does something funny at that, but I ignore it. Easy to do, as I pop the button of his fly, then drag down the zipper of his jeans. His underwear, stretchy black cotton, surges to fill the V of his open jeans, and I palm the round bulge.

Ohhh lord.

I knew he'd be big, but…damn.

I kiss his chest again, pause, look at him, grinning, telegraphing my intentions.

Bend to kiss his diaphragm, pushing at his jeans so they sag around his thighs, the weight of his phone, wallet, and keys pulling them lower.

"Jovie, wait."

About to sink to my knees, I frown at him. "What?"

He pulls my braid out of the bun, fingers deft and gentle. His eyes ask the question, which I find sweet and endearing—which is disorienting against the raging inferno of my sexual arousal. In answer, I turn to face away from him, and he pulls the hair tie off the end of the braid, and then his fingers slowly and gently work my hair free of the braid. Once it's all loose, his fingers comb through it, leaving my hair wavy and hanging to mid-back.

I turn back around. "You've done that before."

He spins me back around and I feel him expertly braiding my hair—he only does a few inches in demonstration, and then undoes it, combing through it once more.

I turn again and look up at him. "Explain."

"My mom." He smiles—his mother brings a smile to his face…god, be still my beating heart. "She was in a car accident several years ago, a pretty bad one—T-boned. Smashed up most of the left side of her body, left her damn near helpless. Well, she's got this long-ass blond hair, like, I don't think she's ever done more than trim the end in her whole life. And guess who had to learn how to help her with her hair? She was in a cast for months and even after the cast was off, she didn't have enough mobility in her arm to do it herself, so I lived with her for a full year to help her with chores and such. I learned to braid her hair, and did it for her every morning, and took it out for sleep every night."

"That's sweet."

He just shrugs. "She's my mom."

I trace my fingers over his chest. "Well, it's sweet. I am kind of sorry I asked, though."

He laughs. "Why's that?"

"Because talking about moms isn't sexy."

He nods knowingly. "Ah. I see the problem."

"You do?"

He nods again. "I think I have a solution, however."

"Oh? Do tell."

He doesn't tell—he shows. He steps into me, and his fist wraps into my hair, twisting the thick black locks around his fist—my breath catches, a sizzle of aroused fear at being helpless to his grip taking over. My heart pounds. He has me utterly at his mercy—his grip is firm, tugging at my scalp but not causing pain. He tugs my head back, tilting my face up…leans down, and kisses me.

If I'd thought the kiss back in the bar was hot, this one is purely scorching. Demanding my breath, taking it without mercy. Tongue driving into my mouth, lips scouring mine. He owns me in this kiss, devouring me, devouring my soul. I whimper, melt—and then come alive with hunger. Lift up, pulling against his hold, daring him to control me.

He accepts my dare, calls my bluff.

One hand gripping my hair, pulling my head back to press his searing kisses onto my lips, he towers over me, forcing me to arch my back and kiss him almost directly upward, off-balance. Forcing me to trust him, to give over to his control.

I reach up and grasp his face, claw at his cheek, dig my fingers into the back of his neck, pulling him toward me, kissing him with every fiber and molecule in my being.

Arousal pumps through me in waves, crashing through my body with tidal force. My breasts ache, nipples so tight and hard they hurt, pussy soaked and begging for a touch, a hungry, demanding climax clamoring inside me for immediate release.

He hooks a hand in the neck of my shirt and jerks it down, roughly, taking my bra with it. My breasts jounce free and his hand eagerly fondles one, and then the other. I moan as his fingers find my nipple and pinch, roll it between his fingers, flick and tweak until I'm so overwrought that I could come just from that.

He's unrelenting, moving to the other breast, toying with that one until I break the kiss to moan.

"Did I mention I have hypersensitive nipples?" I whisper.

"You showed me, on the phone the other day." His lips move against mine, words soft and felt more than heard. "I watched you play with them and saw how crazy it made you."

He releases my hair and takes my breasts in both hands, fondling, cradling. Drops to his knees. I reach behind me and snap my bra open, peel my shirt up and off, bra going with it. He frames my tits with his hands and buries his face in them, but this time there's no humor in it, nor even reverence. Only pure, unadulterated lust. He suckles a nipple into his mouth, forcing a shrill gasp from me—I've very nearly orgasmed just from nipple play, and often have wondered if, under the right circumstances, I could. I have a feeling I'm about to find out.

His worship of my breasts is all-consuming. I close my eyes and simply feel—his hands, his mouth, his rough stubble and his wet tongue. I gasp, whimper—each new touch takes me higher, each tweak and lick, each twist and suckle making my core throb and my chest ache, a hot wire lancing from my sex to my nipples; the wire is pulled tighter and made hotter with every touch, until I'm gasping and shaking, hips pushing forward, seeking… something. Anything.

"Jake…" I gasp.

He licks and suckles, pinches and twists, kisses softly and caresses roughly, and the live wire connecting my breasts to my sex abruptly snaps.

I curl forward over him, fingers tangling in his hair as a climax concusses through me, a shrill breathless scream ripping out of me. Mouth still fused to one of my breasts, he yanks my belt open, my jeans, and then jerks the jeans down my thighs. He abandons the effort when they reach my knees—I take over, kicking them off. I'm still quaking, gasping, clumsy as I step out of the denim.

Impatient and voracious, Jake's mouth slides down

my belly, kissing and stuttering. He yanks at the sides of my underwear—a tight, skimpy little red thong; the jeans are more spandex than denim, and I didn't want panty lines. Also, I had a feeling I'd see Jake.

Fine, I wanted to see Jake.

Hoped…

Planned…

For this.

The thong catches on my hips, and rather than waste time rolling it off properly, he simply grabs with one hand the skinny little string spanning my left hip and with the other the tiny red V of fabric over my pussy…and yanks his hands apart.

I gasp in shock as air hits my bare sex…the gasp turns to a moan as his mouth grazes my seam. The ruined undergarment hits the floor and I kick it away. His hands knock my thighs open, forcing my stance wider, and he sits on his heels, tongue pressing into my clit.

Still riding the ragged edge of my very first nipple play-induced climax, it takes very little on his part to push me back up to the cusp, but now…oh, now, he toys with me. My hips thrust against his mouth, but he backs away, kissing the lips and licking the seam until I settle, only to immediately suckle my tensed, swollen clit into his mouth and make me wild all over again.

And again.

And again.

I'm grinding against his mouth, seeking the release, the *real* release. Because now that I'm hovering on the razor edge of it, I realize the first one barely counted, a pathetic little puff of nothing when compared to the monstrous hurricane building inside me.

But he continues to tease me with it, keeping me just shy of toppling over the edge, tonguing and licking and kissing, his thumbs prying my lips open so his tongue can find me, only to slow to feathery light kisses when I start to grind against him and whimper.

"Oh fuck, Jake…" I grip his hair and shamelessly attempt to hold him place. "Jake, fuck—goddammit—*please.*"

I realize something, in that moment, as he growls a rumbling laugh: I just begged him to let me come.

"Fuck it." I give in. Grind against his mouth as he flings his tongue against me now, side to side and up and down, fast, relentless. "Please, Jake. I'm begging you— let me come."

He drops away, stopping entirely. "No."

I about pop in shocked rage. "*What*?! You can't stop *now*!"

He just grins, wiping his lips. "Can, and am." He scoops me up, one arm around my shoulders and the other behind my knees, carrying me down the hall to my room.

He throws me onto my bed, where I land with a bounce. For a moment, he just stands at the end of the bed, staring at me; he reaches back and flicks on the light. I'm writhing with need, thighs pressed together and rubbing, back arched to thrust my heavy breasts to the ceiling.

I have no shame, now. None. "Jake. Please." I spread my thighs open and touch myself. "Make me come. Please."

He puts one knee on the bed, one hand, preparing to prowl over me. "Told you I'd make you beg."

"You did tell me, I just didn't believe you. I didn't think it was possible." I reach for him—he's still in his undone jeans, shirtless, boots still on.

He's a beautiful god, crawling over me, shoulders impossibly broad, muscles rippling with each movement, tigerish, graceful, powerful. He kisses the inside of my knee, the divot of my hip, my navel. And then, all at once, he buries his face between my thighs and devours me, sudden and rough and insatiable.

I scream at the sudden assault, driven abruptly and immediately to the cusp of orgasm. I hook my knees over his shoulders, lock my heels together behind his head, lift my ass to get closer to his mouth, reach down and snarl my fingers in his hair, which is just long enough to let me get a good and knotted grip. I cry out as his tongue and lips work me until I'm shaking, helplessly curling upward.

"Oh fuck oh fuck oh fuck oh fuck!" I scream, grinding myself against him. "Jake!"

He growls against my sex, shoves me down to the bed and presses his forearm against the backs of my knees in a bar, pushing my legs away. His other fingers swipe down my slit and find my opening—two thick digits penetrate me and curl inside me to scrape against my inner walls. Already coming, already screaming, he sends me into breathless paroxysms, shuddering and spasming, unable to even scream for the raging force of the climax.

And I can't even move. He has me pinned in place, helpless to stop him even if I wanted to—I can't thrust or flex or shift, can't do anything but endure the inferno ripping through me.

He shows no mercy. Just when I think the orgasm is fading, his licking tongue slowing and his driving fingers withdrawing, he renews his attention, tongue circling with fresh vigor and speed around my clit, fingers slicking in and withdrawing, curling just so—he adds a third finger, spreading and filling me, fucking me with his fingers.

I arch my back, ass driving off the bed to writhe myself against his mouth and fingers, breasts swaying as I scream, breath finally breaking as I come a second time.

Now, finally, he lets me settle back down, gasping raggedly, sweating, whimpering and twitching as aftershocks shake me like a rag doll. He shifts to his knees and watches me, a pleased and self-satisfied grin on his face.

I give him a fake droll glare, panting. "Well…I hope you're…happy…with yourself."

He just laughs. "Yes, I am actually. I've reduced you to a speechless puddle of helpless woman. I feel very proud of myself."

I can't help a laugh, the fake glare dissolving. "Well… honestly, you should be. That was fucking incredible, Jake."

He huffs on his fingernails and rubs them on his chest. "Hey, you know. All in a day's work."

I lever myself to a sitting position. "Work, huh? That was work?"

He takes my hands in his. "I mean, my tongue is pretty tired."

I nod, pat his thigh. "Awww, poor Jake's tongue is tired from all that pussy licking?" I push at his chest, and he allows me to guide him to his back. "Let me kiss it all better."

I crawl over him, straddle him, clasping hands with him and pinning his hands to the mattress behind his head, and I kiss him. He tastes like me, musky and tangy and salty, and faintly of alcohol—which is a heady, intoxicating combination, for some reason. His tongue doesn't *seem* tired to me, eagerly tangling with mine.

I lift up, breaking the kiss. Push his hands over his head. "Stay."

He tucks his hands under his head. "Yes, ma'am."

I slide down to sit on his thighs, rubbing my hands over his stomach and chest, just luxuriating in the privilege of having the work of art that is this man's body all to myself. I trace his pecs, run my fingers in the grooves between his abs. Along his sides, up his ribcage to his arms. Just caress his body, his face, his hair, the shell of his ears, tease behind them, rub my thumbs over his lips. Pause there, at his mouth. Thumbs brushing and grazing, I bend forward, draping my breasts on his chest, and kiss where my thumbs were. Alternate, then, teasing, kissing and rubbing with my thumbs, never letting him get a good kiss in, until he's laughing with frustrated arousal. Finally, my own impatience gets the better of me. I kiss his chin. His Adam's apple.

His hands come to my shoulders and carve down my spine, cup my ass—I replace his hands back up by his head. "Nope. My turn for touching."

He growls in annoyance. "Not getting to touch you feels like torture, woman."

I just laugh, pat his heavy chest. "I think you'll be

okay. Just lay back and relax and try to enjoy letting me be in control."

He heaves a sigh. "You don't know what you're asking, Jovie."

I sit up, hold his gaze. "I think I do, actually, because I'm the same way. The only difference is, you can literally pin me down and take control, whereas because you're so much bigger and stronger than me, you have to voluntarily decide to give me what I want."

"I would never—" he starts.

I lean forward and silence him with a kiss. "I know, Jake. You think I'd be naked and alone in my own bed with a man I didn't feel safe with?"

He sighs. "Yeah, I guess that's true."

"Of course it's true. I'm always right."

"You weren't right about me making you beg."

"True." I hold his hands palms facing me, and kiss each palm, and then place them back up by his head. "Now shut up and relax, Howson. I'm trying to sex you up."

He laughs, body shaking silently. "All right, fine, Martin. Do your worst. Or your best. Or whatever." He tucks his hands under his head again. "I won't move a muscle."

I scratch my fingernails lightly down his chest. "Good boy."

He watches as I kiss his chest, across to his flat nipples, which I flick with my tongue—making him hiss. I kiss, and kiss all over his chest, taking my time.

I scratch his chest. "I like this."

"The fur?"

I nod, kiss across his diaphragm. "Mmm-hmmm."

"Not everyone does. I had one person tell me it was unattractive and I should wax it, because no self-respecting woman would ever want to be with a man who, and I quote, 'looked like a Wookie.'"

I pause, looking up at him. "She said that?"

"Yes."

"I hope you gave her the boot."

He shrugs, makes a face.

"You didn't, did you?"

"Um, no?"

"She must have had big boobs."

He laughs. "Not really, no."

"A big ass?"

"Again, no."

"Then what did she have that would convince you to let her stay after a rude-ass comment like that?"

He just shrugs again.

"Tell me! I'm curious."

"Isn't it, like, a huge faux pas to talk about your past partners when you're currently in bed with someone new?"

I shrug and wave a hand. "I'm not the jealous type. Even if we were, like, an item, I'm not the jealous type."

"Well, there are different kinds of not the jealous type. There's the 'you can do what you want' kind, which is really more of an open relationship thing, or there's 'I'm saying I'm not the jealous type, but if I see you talking to another woman I'll castrate you.'"

I cackle. "Wow. Someone dealt with a jealous girl."

He blows a raspberry. "We went on one date, hooked

up *once*. I never told her I'd call her. I told her at the very outset it was for fun, I wasn't looking for anything—I laid it all out."

"With you so far—gotta set expectations at the outset. I do the same thing."

He tucks my hair behind my ear. "You can keep kissing. I'll keep talking, if you really want to hear."

I touch my lips to his stomach. "Okay, you convinced me."

He huffs a laugh. "Well. The thing with the girl—it was okay. Not great, just okay. I certainly wasn't going to be calling her, you know? Even if I *had* gotten her number or given her mine, which I didn't. So, I was having coffee with someone else, very literally two weeks later. She shows up. Pitches a fit, how I'm such a liar, how could I toy with someone's feelings like that, yada yada yada."

I pause with my lips just above the waistline of his underwear. "Damn. She cray."

"No kidding." He huffs again as I tug at the waistband, moving it down an inch or so, letting it hook on the firm head of his cock, kissing along the left side of his V-cut.

"Back to the other girl," I say, between kisses. "Why'd you let her stay?"

He laughs. "You don't really want to know that, do you?"

"Sure I do. That was a super bitchy comment, and I can't fathom what would make you let her stay, if it wasn't her tits and ass, because correct me if I'm wrong, here, but you seem to like 'em big."

"I like you."

"But in general."

"Jovie."

"You're not gonna hurt my feelings. I'm a tough girl."

"Yes, I tend to be more attracted to big boobs and butt." He sucks his belly in as I lower the waistband yet more, kissing across to the other side. "And you…your body is…fuck. So amazing. So perfect."

"So. If this girl wasn't blessed, as I am, with bountiful boobies and backside, why'd you let her stay after a shitty comment like that?"

"Because she said it while she was going down on me."

I laugh. "Ohhh. Well that makes sense. You're not going to give her the boot until after she's done."

"Right."

"So you let her finish sucking you off, and *then* you gave her the boot?"

"Mostly correct."

"Mostly?"

He laughs. "Mostly."

I pull the front of his underwear away from his body and tug them down a few inches, showing the top of his hard, thick, straining cock. "What does that mean?"

"Jovie…"

"I'm curious. This is fascinating to me."

"I didn't kick her out right away, no."

"She must have sucked you like a goddamn Hoover."

He cackles. "Yes, yes she did."

"And let me guess, you're too nice of a guy to let her suck you off and kick her out. So you gave her a pity fuck."

"Nope, not a pity fuck."

"I swear, you better not have rewarded her with what you can do with that mouth." I rub my hands on his belly just to either side of his cock, teasing.

"Nope. Just the fingers."

"At least you have *some* dignity."

"Men possess absolutely no dignity, standards, self-respect, pride, or cognitive functions whatsoever when a woman has her mouth around his cock." His abs are tensed, his words sounding deceptively casual despite how badly I can tell he wants me to just touch him, finally. "It was only after I regained my higher mental faculties that I realized what a vapid, shallow bitch I'd invited home with me. But, no one leaves without a door prize, so I did the bare minimum and then asked her to leave."

I pull his underwear lower. "Wait, you just flat out asked her to leave?"

"As opposed to what?"

"I dunno, coming up with an excuse. Surreptitiously text a friend to fake a radio call."

He frowns, blinking at me. "Well shit. That would have been much easier."

I laugh hard enough that I have to rest my head on his thigh. "You mean to tell me it never even occurred to you to fake an excuse?"

"I'm a guy who tends to tackle things head-on. Excuses aren't in my nature." His eyes are glued to me, his breathing deep and slow, brow furrowed.

I pull a little lower, and now his jeans and underwear are down around his thighs, exposing all of him. And holy fuck balls. The man is so beautifully endowed it boggles the mind.

I say *beautifully*, not *massively*, on purpose.

I was with a man once who was *too* well endowed, and that was not as pleasant an experience as you might imagine it to be. He could barely fit the tip inside me, and my jaw literally couldn't open far enough to take much more than that either. Maybe I'm just more dainty than other women, in the diameter of my orifices, but it was... bad. I felt bad for him, too, because he was clearly frustrated and handled it with admirable aplomb; we ended the night with nothing more than hand play and awkward goodbyes.

Jake is...

Just perfect.

Our little video call hadn't been able to properly convey the beauty of his man parts—his fist was around it the entire time, and the man has enormous hands, thus obscuring what he was working with.

Now, with no screen in the way, I'm treated to the full glory of his arousal.

I don't know inches, and care even less—I just know that his is plenty long enough. The thickness, too, is ideal, enough that just by looking I know he'll stretch me to perfect ache and then some, without causing pain or discomfort.

I mean, clinical perusal aside, it's just *pretty*. It's a pretty penis. Long, thick, mostly straight with just a slight curve back toward his belly, a plump, round, pink head, lots of lickable veins—so much real estate to play with. His balls are fat and heavy and taut, begging for my hands and mouth.

He's trimmed, but not shaved—my personal preference.

I've drawn the examination out as long as I dare—he's squirming under my intense gaze, flexing his abs and tensing his cock. Begging silently, that little tensing movement is. You know what I'm talking about: how men can sort of flex their cocks? Make them move, just a little, when fully erect? I get the sense that he's doing so involuntarily, as my hands are flat against his belly and pubis, in the valley between hipbones and the root of his cock.

I hold his gaze, now, as I finally gather the soft warm weight of his erection in my hand. He literally sighs in relief.

"Thank *fuck*," he growls, "I thought you were gonna stare at it all night."

I shrug, giving him a lazy stroke up to the tip and back down to the root, pausing again to lightly grip him at the base. "I mean, I *could*," I say, grinning. "You have been blessed with a rather magnificent specimen. What was it you once said to me? Art is meant to be appreciated? Something like that. Well, I happen to agree."

He grins, his hands gathering into fists above his head as I stroke him again, root to tip, twisting loosely around the head a few times before plunging my hand downward again. His grin fades as his eyes close, head tipping back, hips shoving upward.

"You know how many times I've jerked off, imagining you doing this?" he murmurs.

"About as many as I jilled off imagining you doing what you just did?" I respond. "What else have you imagined me doing?"

I stroke him again, slowly, the full length of his massive cock, tip to root and back with a twist at the top, then simply twisting around the head.

He opens his eyes, watching as I adjust positions, pulling my long, wayward hair around the back of my neck and over my lower shoulder, leaning on my left elbow and hovering over him. "Your mouth," he murmurs. "I fantasized about that fucking mouth of yours."

I flick my tongue over the tip. "Like that?"

His upper lip curls, teeth grinding—in any other circumstance the expression would look threatening, aggressive. Now, it just looks…hot.. aroused. Like he's a thread of control away from just roughly fucking my mouth. I almost wish he would.

"That's a good start," he mutters. "You want to know what I want you to do?"

"Yes," I say, gripping at the root, pumping there as I lick the hole at his tip again. "Tell me what you want me to do, Jake."

"I want you to lick it. All over."

I run my tongue from base to tip, up the side, down the other. "Like that?"

"Uh…yeah, like that." He watches, eyes narrowed, heavy-lidded. "Play with my balls."

I cup them as requested, massaging, squeezing as firmly as I dare, tickling them with gentle scratches of my fingernails, and then licking them…ending by taking them entirely in my mouth, which leaves him groaning, back arching.

I let them fall out of my mouth with a satisfied grin. "Like that?"

"That was somewhat….more…than I even imagined."

"Which part?" I ask, licking them with little flicks of my tongue—holding his cock in both hands now, squeezing and twisting while my mouth is otherwise busy. "This?" I then take the full weight of them in my mouth again, plying them with my tongue before letting them fall out and caressing them with one hand, stroking his cock with the other. "Or that?"

"The second part. For sure."

I laugh, and do it again, drawing it, tonguing and mouthing them until he's hissing and shifting. "You *really* like that, huh?"

"I guess so."

I grin up at him. "You don't mean to tell me I'm the first to do that to you?"

"I'm telling you exactly that," he murmurs. "And holy fuck, I love it."

"Good to know." I watch his cock weep, then, pre-cum dribbling from him. "Any other special requests from your fantasies?"

He shakes his head. "I mean…everything?"

"What about this?" I ask, and wrap my lips around the plump head, swirling my tongue over him, tasting pre-cum. "Did you fantasize about this?"

I take him, then. Slowly. Deeply. All lips and tongue. It is, if I do say so myself, insanely sensual. Some of my best work, not to pat myself on the back or anything.

And god, does he respond beautifully.

His hands gather my hair, twisting it around his fist, gripping tightly as if he might do something rough at any moment. Yet, he doesn't. He just…allows. Doesn't even guide.

I let my saliva coat him messily, smearing it over the broad, straining head with my palm before plunging my mouth around him again, one hand stroking the thick shaft beneath my mouth, twisting and pumping around the many inches my mouth can't reach, and with my other hand, I play with his balls.

"Oh fuck, Jovie. Fuck." He shifts under me, thrusting gently, and now his hands pull a little. "Your mouth is fucking magical."

I respond by swirling my tongue around his tip and then plunging deep, until he hits the back of my throat—that's my limit. I'm not a deep-throat girl, and he seems perfectly content and then some with what I'm giving him.

And then his radio crackles—I don't remember him bringing it in here with him, but he must have, and set it on the floor near the bed. "All units, please respond. Multiple vehicle accident…"

"Goddammit," he hisses as dispatch continues to relay the pertinent details, "Worst timing in the fucking world." He groans, pulling away from me and sitting up. "And I feel like an asshole for even saying that."

"I could finish you in ten seconds," I say, even as I let go, knowing he won't allow that.

"I fucking wish I was capable of allowing that, Jovie. More than you know." He's already off the bed and jerking his underwear and jeans back up.

Fortunately for the sake of the call, I never even got as far as removing his boots, so he simply has to button, buckle, and zip, and then jerk his shirt on as he reaches the door. He pauses to check his pockets, turning to, I assume, say goodbye to me.

He's visibly shocked to see me stuffing my ass commando into a pair of uniform slacks. "You're not on call, Jovie.

I have a bra and uniform shirt in hand—I wrangle my tits into the bra and shrug into the shirt, speed-buttoning as only someone with years of experience can do. Within seconds, I have my socks on and my personal gear bag in hand, phone and wallet in the other, along with my boots. I push past him to my door.

"I'm a medic first, Jake," I say, locking the door behind me. "On call or not, I'm responding."

We reach my car, a high-mileage but well-maintained Miata I only drive when necessary, preferring to walk or take public transportation whenever possible. Jake goes to the passenger side, but I toss him the keys. "I have to put on my boots. You drive."

He responds without comment—he looks like an overgrown bear in a circus clown car as he adjusts the seat for his much larger frame. As soon as I'm in, he's jerking the shifter into reverse, tires squealing as he pulls a pro-level J-turn. He thrashes my car to its limits as he navigates us to the scene.

On the way, he addresses the radio. "Captain Howson responding in a civilian Miata…" he glances at me and I relay the plate number. He then fumbles his phone from his pocket.

I snatch it from him. "Who am I calling?"

"Chilly," he answers. "Code is one-four-nine-zero."

I snicker. "Your birthday? Really?"

"And what's your passcode?"

I grin. "My dad's birthday. Zero-six-one-six-six-five."

I find Chilly's number, set it to dialing, put it on speaker, and hold the phone toward Jake's mouth—he moves to take it but I snatch it away, put it back.

Chilly answers on the second ring. "What's up, Cap?"

"I'm responding to the MCI on the freeway, but I'm not coming, from, um, my house. I need my truck. There's a spare keyfob in my desk drawer. Go get my truck from my house and bring it to the scene."

"You got it, Boss." I hear a grin in his voice. "Hey, Martin. Your dad was my fuckin' hero. Anyways, see you guys there."

He hangs up, and I stare at the phone. "So. He knows."

"Were we keeping it on the down low?" Jake asks.

I shrug. "I guess not. We did make out in front of the entirety of Far Bar." I glance at him as he shifts in the seat, plucking at his zipper. "How you holding up over there?"

He shrugs. "I'll be fine." I can tell he's focused on the imminent call, but I can also tell he has…thoughts.

I let it all go myself as flashers light up the night ahead—squad cars, fire department busses, engines, EMS busses.

Only a moment or two after we arrive and park my Miata behind a patrol car, Jake's big man-truck arrives behind us, a gargantuan F-three-million-whatever with knobby tires and a lift kit and a hood scoop, fire department stickers on the rear window, and a single rotating flasher on the roof. Jake is already jogging for his truck, reaching in past Chilly to grab his IC jacket and then jogging for the tangled knot of first responders.

I'm not far behind him, finding the crowd of EMS and immediately throwing myself to work.

Everything else fades away, then, as I lose myself in the work of saving lives.

It's a very, very, very long night.

JAKE

WE NEVER ENDED UP ABLE TO RECONNECT THAT night after the scene was wrapped up—I got pulled one way to write up reports and get my third shift crews resettled, and Jovie was pulled the other, transporting victims to the hospital and dealing with her own after-incident duties. I realized partway through the hours-long response that I still had her keys in my pocket and had a probie with an unexpected blood sensitivity nausea issue find and deliver them to her.

We then continued to miss each other, as I stayed at the station and she went into her next shift early, and then we both crashed separately, with only a brief text exchange between us, both of us too exhausted for anything more.

We chat on the phone briefly the next day, but the day after that is a full moon and thus meant a chaotic twenty-four hours for both of us—me especially. I end up at the station for going on seventy-two hours, catching a couple hours' sleep on the couch in my office and eating some cold leftovers in the truck on the way from one call to another, slugging hours-old, lukewarm coffee while doing paperwork.

My eyes burn and droop as I finally catch a break and can go home. I'm a zombie as I drive home, keeping the windows open and the AC blasting, rock music blaring, all to keep myself awake. I barely make it home, eyes drooping dangerously.

I'm ravenous, in need of a shower…and, weirdly, clamoring for attention above even those priorities, is missing Jovie. Not just the need to finish what we started, and I don't mean literally the act she was doing when we were interrupted, although I certainly wouldn't mind if we revisited that. Just…the whole evening. Being with her. The different side of her—teasing and funny, but also softer, sensual, erotic.

Fuck, she's amazing.

I find myself shuffling around my kitchen aimlessly, thinking of Jovie instead of fixing food.

My buzzer rings. "Hello, yeah?"

A somewhat gruff and possibly female voice answers. "Door Dash delivery."

My brain is in a fog. "I didn't order anything."

"It says here, uh, paid for by a J Martin?" The voice is odd, but I can't place what about it is wrong, and I'm too fried to figure it out.

I smile to myself. "Oh. Well, god bless the woman. Come on up."

I wait at my door, opened and leaning against the frame. I see the delivery person leave the elevator. It's a woman, her head bowed, studying the receipt. She's kind of oddly dressed for a delivery person—plain, skin-tight pink workout leggings and a white V-neck tank top, also tight and molded to her body, wearing a plain white ball cap, hair pulled through the back, carrying a tiny little wallet-purse-thing by strap from one wrist, barely big enough to carry some cards, cash, and a phone, and *maybe* keys if there's only car fob and house key.

I'm so slow of thought that even though some caveman portion of my hindbrain instinctively recognizes her body, it's not until she reaches my door and looks up at me that I realize it's *her*.

And yet, I'm still stupid. "You're a Door Dash driver?"

She just laughs, planting a hand on my chest and gently driving me backward. "Oh, you poor exhausted man."

I let her push me backward—although "let" is a strong word, since I feel about as weak as a day-old kitten. "Oh. You're just bringing me food, because you're an actual angel."

She just smiles up at me, walking me backward to my couch, where my legs hit the edge and I half fall to sit. "Yes, Jake. I'm an angel, here to bring you food."

She hands me the bag—sandwiches from our favorite shop; I smell chicken pesto and a Reuben. She stands there in front of me as I pull the sandwiches out.

"You care which?" I ask.

She shakes her head. "Nope. You pick this time. You have any beer in your fridge?"

I nod, tearing open the Reuben. "Yup. Help yourself."

She has an odd, secretive smile on her face as she heads into the kitchen. I hear the fridge open, bottles clink. Tops pop with a hiss—my eyes are closed as I take the first bite, groaning in blissed-out relief.

"First real, hot food I've had in almost three days," I say, hearing her approach.

"I know. You've had a long week, huh?"

"Long week, really long couple days. My trial by fire as a captain, I guess."

She takes her sandwich and sets it aside on the coffee table with the other beer. Hands me mine, and I take a swig.

And then, oddly, confusingly, she takes my beer *and* my sandwich away. "Hey," I protest. "I wasn't done."

She just smiles enigmatically, and pulls at my shirt. "Arms up."

I cooperate, a glimmer of hope dawning in my mind. "Oh. You're *that* kind of angel, too?"

She gives me my beer and sandwich back, tossing my shirt aside. "You could say that."

For a moment, she just watches me eat.

"Aren't you eating?" I ask, between bites.

She gives me that enigmatic grin. "Yeah, I'm going to eat." She pulls her hat off, removes her hair from the ponytail. "In a minute."

I eat more slowly, watching as she holds my eyes with that small, secretive grin. "In a minute, huh?" I'm dumb, both with exhaustion and now with anticipation of what I hope is about to happen.

Namely, a revisiting of our interrupted evening.

She stands between my knees, gazes at me for a moment. "Yeah, in a minute. Something else I want to do first."

"Oh?" I hope I come across as flirty and teasing rather than simply befuddled and stupid. "What's that?"

She peels her shirt off in a lithe movement, revealing a pink sports bra to match her leggings. I swallow hard, because holy fuck is she gorgeous. My mouth goes dry and I forget everything but her. Especially when she continues the show by slowly peeling off her sports bra, keeping her breasts covered until the last possible moment, finally letting them free with a heavy, tantalizing bounce.

I groan. "Fuck, Jovie. Your tits are like fucking kryptonite, honey."

She laughs, sidling toward me to straddle my legs, bracing her hands on the couch behind my head, dangling her breasts over me, slowly lowering them until her peaked, pert nipples brush my face. "Does that make you Superman?"

"Depends on the day," I answer, moving to set my beer and sandwich aside.

She grabs my wrists. "Ah ah. Just relax." She guides my beer back to my mouth. "Just let me have my way with you, Jake."

"I may be tired, Jovie, but I'm never *too* tired, if you know what I mean."

She slides off my legs and sinks to her knees between my thighs. "Oh, I know. I have no doubt whatsoever that you could rock my world right now. But right now, *I'm* going to rock *your* world."

"Oh," I say, again sounding flat and stupid.

"So just sit back, relax, and…enjoy."

She watches me, my face, instead of what her hands are doing. Which is, rather delightfully, unbuckling my belt and slowly pulling it free, loop by loop, and then rolling it into a spiral and setting it aside. I begin to harden behind my underwear, but focus instead on my sandwich and my beer and Jovie's huge, perfect breasts.

Round, teardrop-shaped, with a plump, parabolic swell at the bottom, nipples and areolae tilted to face slightly upward, the inner edges just barely brushing. I want to bury my face in them and simply fall asleep there. God, I love her breasts.

And wonder of wonders, I get to just look at them. Stare at them to my heart's content—or, to my dick's content, rather. She looks at me looking at her and seems perfectly happy for me to just enjoy the sight of her naked breasts.

Does it get any better? Honestly?

It does.

She thumbs open the button of my slacks and slowly draws the zipper down. Stops there, my trousers unbuttoned and unzipped—she unties my boots, loosens the laces, and pulls them off. Strips me of my socks—which somehow she manages to make erotic. Something about the way she peels them off combined with the sheer relief of simply having your socks off after wearing them for three days straight is well-nigh unbearable.

I polish off the last of the sandwich, wash it down with the last long pulls off my beer—I'm normally a heavyweight when it comes to holding my alcohol, but my physical resources are utterly depleted, and I've had very little to eat in the last few days, so that one beer hits me like a freight train.

Shirtless and barefoot, I wipe my fingers on my pants

front and then finally allow myself to touch her, simply tracing the line of the shoulder blade to her neck, behind the shell of her ear. Her hands rest on my hips, and she nuzzles into my touch, briefly.

"Stop being sweet." She guides my hands to her breasts. "You're distracting me."

I laugh. "Stop being sweet—that's a new one."

"Not all the time. Just right now."

"Noted." I gladly and eagerly oblige her, fondling and caressing her tits.

I can't help my body's reaction to having those lush globes in my hands—my cock swells, prodding against the fabric of my underwear into the opening of my zipper.

She traces the ridge of my erection. "There we go."

She moves out of my reach, tugging my pants off by the cuffs at my ankles—I lift up to let them slide off. She takes the time to fold them and set them on top of my boots. Now clad in only a pair of gray boxer briefs, I wait for her next action.

She re-settles between my knees, runs her hands up my thighs to my hipbones. Caresses up my abs, lovingly tracing my stomach muscles with her fingertips. Smooths her palms over my pecs. Down my sides, tickling now. My hands rest on the couch at my sides—it feels unnatural and almost awkward for me—to simply sit here and be touched. I don't often, or really ever, allow myself to be the receiver of touch unless I'm also doing so in some way. If she's touching me, doing something arousing to me, I'm participating.

This is different. New.

And kind of difficult.

I want to touch her. I want to make her feel good—it's a psychological and biological imperative: TOUCH HER; GIVE HER PLEASURE.

She grins at me as she runs a fingertip teasingly underneath the elastic waistband of my underwear, one knuckle brushing the tip of my erection. "You want to take over so badly, don't you?"

I laugh. "So fucking bad."

"But you're not going to." She arches an eyebrow at me. "You're going to just sit there and let me do what I want. Right?"

"I'll damn well try." I tuck a strand of hair behind her ear, then laugh. "Sorry. Forgot—don't be sweet." I trace a circle around her nipple, instead. "That better?"

She laughs. "Yes. That's better. Just look at the boobies, Jake. Touch the boobies."

I give a long, flat groan, and then speak in a zombie monotone. "Mmmmm. Boooooooo-bies."

She laughs, finally hooking her finger inside the elastic on either side of my cock. "That's right, Jake. Boobies."

She pulls them down in front first, and then I lift my ass off the couch to allow them past, and then she whips them off my feet with a flourish, tossing them behind herself with a whip of her wrist, then displaying her empty hands with a flourish. "Tada!"

I clap. "Brava, brava. An amazing magic trick. Where'd they go?"

She runs her palms up my thighs again, just barely missing my cock on her journey up my torso, and then dragging her fingernails lightly down my chest and stomach, yet again not quite touching me where I so badly want her to touch me.

"And now for my next trick," she says, grasping my cock in one fist. "I'm going to make this dick disappear!"

I can't help a laugh, a stomach-tensing twitch and huff. "Now *this* I want to see."

She caresses my length with both hands, now. "Watch carefully, or you might miss it."

I'm holding my breath as if this is the first time—with her, or with anyone. The anticipation is a tumultuous jumble of need and eagerness and awe.

She holds my gaze as she twists her touch around me one fist atop the other, her fingers gliding slowly downward, my tip sprouting upward. Once more her hands lift, one twisting around the head while the other twists around the shaft, and then plunging downward shallowly a couple times so the pink head pops free of her upper hand.

She leans forward, then. Eyes on mine. "Here we go—I'm going to make it disappear, now. Are you ready? You watching?"

I can only manage a nod.

She frames her lips around the circle made by her fingers, holding my gaze as she lowers her hands and mouth in synch.

I groan as I enter the hot wet heaven of her mouth. "Ohhhh fuck, Jovie. Fuck."

There's no teasing or playing. No edging or toying with me. Neither is she rough or aggressive. She just... seems to want nothing so much as to simply show me pleasure.

And fuck, pleasure isn't the right word. Bliss. Ecstasy. Words fail.

I can only watch in greedy, needy, helpless awe as she keeps her fist synched to the rise and fall of her mouth; with each downward stroke her hands twist—sometimes in unison, sometimes in opposition—her lips stuttering and sliding around me, tongue licking and flicking and swirling, until I reach her throat, and then she backs away until only the head is left in her mouth. She pauses to worship, then, licking, kissing, mouthing the head, probing the tiny slit with her tongue tip, until I'm breathless and gasping and aching, and then she moves to take me all over again.

I wrap her thick black hair in my hands, and she lets me. I hold, grip—follow her movements as if hanging on for dear life.

Which I am.

The orgasm builds in me, and I confess I hold it back. I want this to last forever.

And then she shifts tactics.

Her palm cradles my balls, fondling them gently, her other hand flattening up my stomach and then dragging her nails down again, circling my base with forefinger and thumb; while she does this, she suctions her lips around the head, sucking, and then loosens the suction and toys with me with her tongue.

"Ohhh *fuck*," I growl. "Jovie, *fuck*."

She grins then, a pleased, wicked smile, knowing she's found the thing that makes me craziest. Apparently. I never knew how wild that combination makes me until this moment, until Jovie shows me.

She does it all again. Lips wrapped loosely around the head, framed at the groove beneath my glans while her tongue slathers over the head and down the shaft and back up. Cradling my sac in her hand, massaging and caressing as if they're precious and delicate, her other hand circling my cock at the base and pumping gently, slowly.

She doesn't let up.

Lips, tongue, hands, all working together in slow, deliberate concert. I ache, gasp. Groan. Throb.

"Jovie," I gasp, unable to keep from flexing, thrusting gently. "Fuck, I'm close."

It's impossible to hold back, now. To restrain my base urges. My hands tangle in her hair and grip at the roots, and I guide her to take more. She looks up at me as she allows my guidance, takes more of me, tongue working.

I tense all over, gritting my teeth. "Jovie, fuck—*fuck*!"

She feels it, I know she does. Yet, she pulls away, and her tongue runs up the underside of my cock, licking along the pulsating ridge of the thick vein along the bottom. My abs are rock hard and I'm curled forward, ass lifting up. Riding the edge. Holding back. The need to come is an inferno, a wild volcanic pressure mounting inside me, aching, burning. I don't want to come yet.

I want this to last longer. Her mouth is heaven, her lips magical, her tongue a fantasy, her hands a delight.

And now, teasing me to the very ragged edge, she clutches my balls and my base in both hands together, licking and licking up the underside of my cock from balls to glans, again and again. Then, she grips my cock and mouths my sac, licks, teases, while simply clutching my cock without moving her hand. All the while, the urge

JASINDA WILDER

to let go, to my orgasm rip out of me grows hotter and wilder and more imperative. My teeth are gritted and I'm arched up off the couch, every muscle clamped down as I hold it back.

She's at war with me, I realize—trying to tease the orgasm with soft, delicate gentility rather than aggression and mere speed.

I growl, feeling my climax pounding in my balls, surging through me, dammed at the wall of my willpower, pent up, it feels, in the throbbing head of my cock and the pulse in my balls.

She's everywhere, one hand twisting around the head, the other caressing my sac while her mouth runs sideways up my shaft.

I groan, a long ragged growl of desperation—I'm a heartbeat away from losing control. "Jovie…."

"Mmmm?" She meets my eyes, once again licking the ridged vein on the underside from root slowly up to the tip, pretending like she's going to put me in her mouth, only to return to the base, licking back upward again.

"I…I can't…"

She licks the tip, her tongue going fat and flat, licking away the pre-cum as it dribbles out of me. "Can't what, Jake?"

"Can't hold out any longer."

"You need to come, Jake?"

I nod. "Have to."

She puts her closed, pursed lips to my head, presses a kiss that slowly turns into taking me into her mouth, to the back of her throat, and now the pulse and the ache mounts to impossible pressure. "Right now?"

194

"I don't want you to stop," I gasp, fighting the pressure, holding it back. "But I can't...I can't hold it anymore, Jovie."

She lets me drop out of her lips. "Jake?"

I close my eyes grunt. "Mmm?"

She laughs, a breathy huff. "Jake?"

I open my eyes—her deep beautiful brown eyes are amused, glinting and twinkling. "Stop holding back." She mouths me, once, softly, a wet hot pressure around the tip. "Give it to me."

"You want it?" I murmur.

Jovie licks, responds. "I want it, Jake," she whispers, her lips moving against my glans. "I'm taking it from you, ready or not." Another soft lick, a feather-light tickle of her tongue tip. "Right...now."

On the last word, she plunges me between her lips and her fingers wrap around me, both hands circling my shaft. No mercy, then. No more toying or teasing.

She only takes a few inches of me into her mouth, but her tongue provides additional stimulation, circling and smearing as she pumps and twists and strokes my erection, faster and faster.

I have no hope of holding out, then.

I last all of five seconds.

I can't even manage a warning.

Not so much as a tug on her hair.

I explode, so suddenly and so powerfully that it's silent, my mouth dropping open, spine arching, fists tightening in her hair. It's a wrenching, ripping thing, this orgasm, a nova detonating first behind my balls, and then in my gut, and then pulsing through my cock and subsuming my whole being. She's relentless, then, ravenously devouring my climax and demanding more.

Her lips suction around my cock and her tongue rests flat against the underside, providing a cushion along which I thrust into her mouth. Her hands are loose and gentle around my shaft, her strokes remaining slow and purposeful, twisting and plunging, pumping my orgasm out of me.

A blinding light bursts behind my eyes as I come, and I blink it away to watch her, freezing this moment in my mind, her mouth around me, hands on me, eyes on mine.

Even as I come, she continues to work me to paroxysms of ecstasy, not content with simply making me reach release but insisting on wreaking havoc on me, wresting every ounce of pleasure from me. Pumping every drop out of me. Sucking it all away, licking, tasting.

When I think I can't come anymore, she speeds her fist on me, pumping harder and faster until a second impossible wave crushes me. I'm paralyzed, then, a guttural roar ripped from my throat.

And still she continues.

Soft again. Slow and sweet, gently caressing my now-softening length, licking the tip as errant droplets of cum leak out.

When at long last, I've got nothing left, she places my cock against my belly and sits back on her heels, licking her lips and wiping at them with her fingertips.

I'm utterly limp—my whole body, not just my dick. Limp, boneless—already feeling weak from exhaustion, I'm now totally spent.

"Jesus, Jovie," I mumble. "I think you killed me."

"Turnabout is fair play—I'm just getting you back from what you did to me before we were interrupted."

"It's your turn." I attempt to sit up but make it maybe three inches off the couch. "As soon as I can make my body cooperate."

She straddles me, draping her breasts against my chest, hands resting on my shoulders. "No, Jake."

"No?"

She slides a hand through my hair, shaking her head, touching a soft kiss to my lips. "Nope. I'm going to help you to your bed, and I'm going to tuck you in, and you're going to go to sleep."

I shake my head. "No. I don't—" I grunt as I force my body to work, managing to sit upright with Jovie on my lap, her arms now around my neck. "I don't take and not give, Jovie. It's not how I'm wired."

She just smiles, slides off my thighs and backs away, taking my hands. "Up you go," she says, leading me toward my room.

I fixate on her ass—plump and round yet firm, with a generous helping of jiggle as she walks, dimples showing on the outside of each cheek. Despite how colossally intense my orgasm was, just moments ago, I feel my soul responding to the beauty of her naked body, to the hypnotic movement of her beautiful ass, the curve of her spine, the sensual sinuous sexiness of her back, the strength and softness in her thighs.

She leads me to my room, tossing my blankets back, and climbs into the bed, tugging me after her. I climb in, pursuing her—or trying to. Really, I'm only just barely capable of movement. She goes to her back in the middle of the bed, grasping at my wrists and pulling me to her. When she can reach, she tangles her fingers in my hair, and brings my face to her chest.

"I want you, Jovie," I mumble, even as my face comes to rest on the warm silk of her breasts. "I want to...make you feel good."

She just huffs a laugh. "You will, Jake."

I fight it. There's something wrong with this. What is it I'm supposed to know? Supposed to remember?

Something about how much like home this feels. Something—a warning.

She's home, and there's a warning with that lulling, vulnerable softness blooming within me.

I'm too exhausted to remember what it means.

I just know, as her fingers tickle and tease in my hair, trail and traipse over my shoulders, as her breasts pillow my face, that I am completely and utterly *home*, in a way I never knew even existed.

It's just...right.

And that's...wrong, somehow.

JOVIE

STUPID, STUPID, STUPID.

I'm such an idiot.

He's sound asleep, face smushed into my breasts. He's so soft and gentle and boyish, asleep like this. I never knew how thick his eyelashes were.

Which is why this was such a stupid idea.

I couldn't have just sucked him off and bolted.

Oh no.

I had to go all *gooey* on him.

He just…he needed it.

It started with a desire to simply pay him back in some small way for the coffee and the sandwiches and the various things he's done for me—the things he's done just because, without any kind of expectation of being thanked, let alone because he thought he'd get anything out of it. So I picked up some sandwiches from our favorite place. At first the plan was to just show up and hand him the sandwiches. Plain and simple.

But then on the drive over, I started thinking about the last time I was with him, and how he'd made me come so hard I saw stars…not just once but—well, honestly, I'm not even sure how many times.

And I started thinking about his cock, how big it was, how beautiful. How close I had him to coming, and how robbed I felt of that payoff. I mean, I don't normally *love* the taste or feel of cum, but I do enjoy a guy's reaction to being good and thoroughly pleasured. And I had Jake well on the way to a pretty epic climax.

Which was interrupted.

And he didn't hesitate—not for a second. There was no thought to delaying, even though I could have finished him in a matter of moments. No, he was out the door within sixty seconds of the call coming through, with no thought for his own discomfort.

And that's even fucking hotter, to me.

So that's how I found myself sitting in my car outside Jake's condo building, sandwiches in a sack, picturing Jake's cock throbbing and glistening and ready to blow.

And wanting it.

Needing on a visceral level to finish what I'd started. Needing to know what Jake looks and feels like when I make him come.

That was the start of it.

But I have a bit of a playful side, which I only rarely indulge in and only with people I truly trust—usually Lia and sometimes Erin. Never a man. Which is what makes my impulsive decision to surprise him through deception even more shocking, because I've never shown a man this side of me, before, the quirky, playful, prank-ster side of me.

That was step two.

So when I exited the elevator and caught a glimpse of him waiting in his doorway, looked run ragged and beyond exhausted, things got even *more* complicated.

Listen, I'm a career paramedic. It's safe to say I have an intense, if not overdeveloped, need to care for and nurture. Usually, as in ninety-nine percent of the time, it comes across as HEAL, SAVE. But it's not a protector drive, not like Jake. It's a drive to take care of—the psychology of it goes into losing my dad and my mom shutting down, but that's a different story. The point is, deep down, it's a need to nurture.

So when I saw Jake looking two seconds from literally collapsing, that drive kicked in hardcore.

But, because I'm fucking complicated, it got mixed up with the horny.

Which leads us to step three: Operation Make Jake Feel Good, which was in turn a two-step operation—feed, relax, and soothe via beer and sandwich and hopefully my mere presence; and give him a blowjob he'll never forget, a blowjob so erotic, so thrilling, so sensual, so mind-blowing that he'll be forever ruined for all other blowjobs.

Contingent on part two of this operation is that nurturing drive. It wasn't just about my own pride in my BJ skills—which, I admit, I am pretty proud of, despite not actually using them all that frequently; I don't give out many blowjobs, because I have to really like the guy, because when I do give them, I do so with gusto and enthusiasm; I don't hold back. This with Jake wasn't about that—or not totally. I mean, I did have it in mind to really blow him away, pun intended—if only because he'd gone down on me better than I had thought possible and dammit I'm competitive as hell and I'm not gonna let him win *that* competition.

But back to the other factor in why I did what I did the way I did it: I have no idea.

Nurture played a huge part, but it's all so nebulous and confused that I can't seem to make sense of myself. What I just did for Jake was way, *way* above and beyond anything I've ever done for anyone else. That wasn't just a BJ. That was…something else.

Which brings us to now.

Jake sound asleep on my breasts, my arms around him, listening to him breathe, my heart beating under his ear.

Panicking.

Flat out panicking.

I can't breathe.

I hear a klaxon in my head, in my heart: *DANGER, DANGER, DANGER, DANGER!*

It's all panic. There's no reason, no sense, no analysis.

My hands are shaking, my head is pounding, my heart is thudding against my ribcage so hard and so loudly it physically hurts. My lungs are seized, refusing to open or close.

I have to get away.

I worm out from beneath him—he snuffles, murmurs.

"Don't wake up, don't wake up, don't wake up," I hear myself hissing under my breath.

I shove a pillow under him, and he grabs it, lying on his stomach, face turned to the side. Naked, sprawled on the bed.

God, he's just so fucking *gorgeous*. Even in my panic I can't help but admire him—the broad V of his shoulders and back down to the tapered waist, the hard, taut cannonballs of his ass cheeks, which I just want to pet and nuzzle like…

No.

No.

I slide out the other side of the bed and tiptoe out…

But I'm helpless, a sucker. I go back and cover him up with the blankets.

And that's when the most unthinkable betrayal possible occurs: my fingers trail through his hair, gently, yes, and tenderly, over his temple and behind his ear. His hair is soft and feathery.

There goes the klaxon again, louder than ever, ratcheting the panic into high gear all over again.

RUN, RUN, RUN!

Heart slamming against my ribs, trying desperately to suck air into my lungs, I tiptoe out of his room. His phone is forgotten on the couch.

Damn me.

Seriously. I'm damned.

I could have just plugged it in and been done with it. But no.

What do I do?

I take a topless selfie with his phone. And *then* I plug it in beside his bed, refusing to look at him as I exit his room a third time.

Now I shrug into my bra and tank top, retie my hair back through my hat, gather my sandwich and clutch, and leave his condo, locking the door handle on the way.

I go home.

I eat my sandwich.

All while panicking.

Finally, I strip and get in the shower, and I force myself to process what's going on under the surface to cause the extended panic attack.

Jake.

Holding him.

I was fine when it was just attraction and sexual tension, when it was playful banter and witty repartees and attitude.

I was fine when it was giving in to sexual urges, letting the sexual tension that had been building between us explode into a one-time-only fuck-a-thon.

But that had been interrupted.

And that had thrown the whole plan into disarray—the plan being give in and fuck him. That was the whole plan. The hope being, fucking him would get him out of my system, done with him, not thinking about him anymore, not wanting him anymore because the mystique is gone. The mystery is solved.

Does Jake Howson have as big and beautiful a cock as I fantasized? Yes, and better.

Does he go down with the eager skill and willing talent I dreamed he would? Yes, and then some.

Does Jake Howson look and feel as unbearably erotic and wildly, primally powerful when he's coming in my mouth as I had pictured while fingering myself? Yes, and then some.

Mystery solved.

Right?

RIGHT?

No. Thus the panic.

Because he'd caught my nurture in a vise grip, brought it out with his exhausted puppy dog eyes. He'd dragged it out of me with his sweetness. His insistence on turning around and giving me orgasms when he could barely see straight much less form a coherent thought, let alone stand up on his own two feet…that was just too much. The way he tucked my hair behind my ear? Way too fucking much.

In general, I keep the soft, vulnerable, sappy, easily manipulated heart of me locked inside a box, and that box is wrapped in chains, padlocked, covered with an invisibility cloak, and buried way down deep in the lightless depth of my being where no one, least of all me, can get at it.

One look into those big blue eyes?

The box containing my secret heart was smashed open.

Thus the panic.

Thus the forty-five minutes I've spent in this shower, trying desperately to repair the box, chain it back up, and shove it back down into the Marianas Trench of my soul.

I haven't even fucked him.

We've only messed around. Kissed a couple times. Some oral play.

I CUDDLED HIM TO SLEEP.

In testament to how messed up I am, I put on

conditioner first and then shampoo, and put face wash on my scrubby poof. I give up the attempt at cleanliness and simply rinse off and climb into bed with a towel around my head, otherwise dripping wet and naked and near tears of sheer frustration.

There's only one thing left to do.

Pull the covers over my head and call Lia.

She answers on the first ring. "Girl. You should be sleeping."

"Girl, I fucked up."

"You fucked him, didn't you." A question phrased as a statement, an accusation with a tone of foreknowledge—Lia's specialty. "And it was earth-shattering, mind-altering, pussy-ruiningly amazing. And now you're calling me because you're in emotional trouble, because he's a firefighter, and we have one hard and fast rule of life…" she trails off.

We say it in unison, as we have at least once a week since taking the blood oath: "Never date a fireman."

"You're correct, to a degree." I have the phone on speaker, because I'm too…everything…to even hold it.

"Wait, hold on. Jovie, do you have the covers over your head?"

"Yes," I admit.

"And you just got out of the shower, but you didn't bother drying off, and you have a turban on your head."

"No," I grumble, lying.

She sighs. "It's like that?"

"Shut up."

"The real question here is, tequila, whiskey, or herbal tea, and ice cream, chocolate, or cheesecake?"

The combination I pick will be an indicator to Lia how fucked up I really am.

"Tea. Cheesecake." I drop my voice to a whisper, mortified to hear the words which drop from my lips. "And *The Notebook*."

There's a stunned silence.

"NO."

"Yes."

"Jovie, no."

"Lia, yes."

"Tea, cheesecake, AND *The Notebook*?"

"Yeah," I mutter, miserably.

"Jovie, what the hell happened? Did he dick you down *that* good?"

"Lia, gross."

"Well? It was something. Good dick doesn't lead to *that* combo, Jove."

I debate on even saying it. But in the end, it's Lia, and I'm incapable mentally, emotionally, physically, and spiritually of lying to Lia Rossi.

"We haven't even actually had sexual intercourse, yet."

Now the stunned silence is so thick, so fraught that you could scoop it with a ladle. "He must have the most magnificent cock God has ever bestowed on the male species."

"Yes, he does. But it's worse than that, Lia."

"How can it be worse?"

"Because I'm not fucked up about his cock, that's why. I'm fucked up about *him*."

"Shit." A sigh. "I thought you hated him."

"So did I."

"I thought your attraction to Lieutenant Jake Howson, career firefighter extraordinaire, was purely physical in nature," she says. "I thought you'd nail him a few times and that would be that."

"I thought so too." I pause. "And it's now Captain Jake Howson."

"Well shit, that *is* worse."

"That he's captain?"

"Right."

"How is that worse?"

"Because while the rank means he's for sure married to the job and all that, it also means the risk of him getting hurt or killed in the line of duty is much, much less now that he's a captain, because he's not anywhere near as likely to be the one to go into the fire. And if you're trying to tell me that hasn't crossed your mind, you're even more fucked in the head than I thought."

"It hadn't, actually."

"Fuck me, fuck me, fuck me. This is bad."

"That's what I'm saying, Lia. And you don't know Jake. Not as likely? Sure. But Jake is the kind of man to go in and save his guys or die trying, no matter what."

"Like our dads."

"Exactly like our dads."

"Shit." She groans. "Tea, cheesecake, and *The Notebook*."

"How soon?" I ask.

"Give me an hour. I'm finishing up some paperwork, and then Lisa and I have to clean and restock the bus, but it was a slow day so that won't take long."

"Sounds good. I've got the tea and the movie. You just grab the cheesecake."

A brief explainer of the liquid/treats combo disaster rating system: whiskey is lowest on the scale, for general anxiety, as opposed to beer and wine which are just for general good times consumption. Whiskey is for when a guy I like rejects me, or a hookup turns out poorly.

Tequila is for more acute situations. Such as, I really like a guy—a good-looking, wealthy, charming investment banker type with an impossibly perfect name like Winchester Morgan the Fifth...just for example. And let's say this guy is perfect. On paper, certainly, and the more I get to know him, the more perfect he seems. He's charming, he's well dressed, he's sexy. He likes me. He's also busy and has no issue with my unpredictable schedule. Sex is off-the-charts. He makes me come. He knows his way around a clit. He doesn't pass out after unloading. He can hold a conversation. Then I found out—or, um, theoretically *would* find out if this were a real situation, which it's totally NOT—that he's married to a beautiful, educated woman and they have three perfect kids.

That's where tequila comes in: to forget that cheating asshole. Because if there's one thing I've learned in life, it's that if he'll cheat WITH you, he'll cheat ON you. Not that I've ever knowingly been the other woman, mind you. I'm no home-wrecker.

Tea, now. Tea is for major emergencies which even liquor can't handle. Serious heartbreak. The days at work when you lose a kid, or a partner gets hurt or killed, or something like that. Real heartbreak, real emotional wreckage which even alcohol can't solve, numb, or suppress. The big stuff.

The rating system is further complicated by which treat is chosen. Chocolate is usually paired with whiskey. It's for the minor stuff. For when you need to get your mind off it and let go. You CAN pair chocolate with tequila, but that generally means you're pretty mixed up about what happened, as in you're struggling with it, but you're not sure it's a full-on blackout from the tequila and gain five pounds from the ice cream kind of situation.

Ice cream is for when you're really upset. When you just don't give a fuck that you're gonna have to eat salad and go hungry for a week afterward just so you can fit your ass into your favorite skinny jeans, because you ate a whole gallon of ice cream and washed it down with half a bottle of tequila.

That kind of night.

Cheesecake? Major emergencies only. You're not even going to try to excuse it or make up for it, let alone worry about the physical effects of the indulgence. You simply accept that you won't fit into those favorite skinny jeans for a while, but that's okay, because you're so emotionally destroyed it just doesn't matter.

Herbal tea and cheesecake? Code red, all systems offline, five-alarm fire, all personnel respond.

There's another factor, too—the movie. Mostly, it's rom-coms. *The Notebook?* Well, let's just say you only break out Noah and Ally when things get *really* emotionally messy.

This whole thing with Jake has me so messed up I don't know which way is up, and I can't even explain why exactly, but this is a tea and cheesecake and *The Notebook* level crisis.

Lia breezes in about an hour later with a whole cheesecake, still in her uniform—she has keys to my place, and I have keys to hers. "Get the tea going, babe. I'm just gonna rinse off and borrow some PJs."

I've already got the kettle ready, so I just turn the burner on. Lia's in and out of the shower in minutes—when she says rinse off, she literally means just rinse off, a quick scrub of pits, tits, and bits. She's wearing a pair of my gym shorts, which considering the Kardashian-level ass she's sporting means she's hanging out the bottom. Up top, she's wearing a T-shirt from my drawer of stolen man-shirts.

Don't tell anyone, but I have a secret indulgence: if I stay the night at a guy's house more than once, I steal one of his T-shirts. Not anything from the top of his drawer, not anything obviously a favorite. You always know the ones he keeps just to have in case he's running low, and those are the ones I steal, because those are the ones he won't miss. They're still worn in and comfy and have that distinct and comforting man-smell, and fit perfectly as loungewear, but aren't his favorite with memories and meaning and shit.

I've been caught on more than one occasion, and they always end up chalking it up to a quirky but endearing habit.

It's not weird or creepy. I tried just buying shirts from the men's section, but they're stiff and don't smell right and it's just not the same.

Lia cuts the cheesecake while I pour tea and cue up the movie.

We drink tea, eat cheesecake, laugh, and cry. What we don't do is talk during the movie.

It's not until the credits are rolling that Lia turns to me with her third mug of chamomile-spearmint tea. "So. Spill."

I shake my head. "It's complicated as hell."

"No, it's not."

"Yes, it is."

She slurps noisily, pointedly, staring at me—there is no sound I hate more than someone slurping.

"FINE!" I wave my hands at her. "Fine. Stop slurping and I'll spill."

She sets her mug down on the back of the couch and clutches it with both hands, feet curled up under her thighs, huge T-shirt hanging off one shoulder. "It's really not complicated, honey. It's just something you're having a hard time admitting to yourself, much less out loud to me."

I nod, swirling my teabag in the lukewarm half-inch of liquid at the bottom of my mug. "I know."

"So. He's been gifted with a cock sculpted by the gods themselves—I could have guessed that much on my own. Clearly, he rocked your world with it, in one capacity or another. But…you haven't had sex. You have done *something*, though, because you know he's got a nice dick."

"Nice dick?" I toss back the last of the tea and set the mug aside. "Jon Bristow had a nice dick."

Jon Bristow being the school heartthrob in high school, the guy every girl wanted and every guy wanted to be. Lia and I both ended up sleeping with him—unbeknownst to each other, at the time—only finding out a few years after graduation, sharing notes about guys while drinking. And it turns out Jon Bristow's dong ironically ended up being the standard against which we each measured a man as having a good dick or a not good dick. Jon's was nice, a good length, a good width, a nice shape. Not a *golden* standard, more of a baseline.

Lia arches an eyebrow at me. "Meaning Jake Howson is packing a real python?"

"Meaning, the organ between that man's legs goes beyond phrases like packing pythons and having a good dick." I close my eyes and cover my face with my hands. "Words fail, Lia. Descriptions fall woefully short. Because it's more than size, you know? I mean, obviously size matters, and we all know it. Not the way men think it does, but it does. And we both know from experience there's too big, which is in a way worse than not big enough. Not big enough you can still work with and have fun with. Too big? Not the same." I sigh again. "Jake's is…fuck it. I'm gonna use the word. Jake's is perfect. It's just so… so…*pretty.*"

Lia grabs my wrists and pulls my hands away from my face. "You're waxing poetic about his penis, Jovie. That alone tells me all I need to know." She holds my gaze. "But you said this is about way more than his penis."

"It is."

"So? Spill. And you know *I'm* serious when I'm telling you to skip the physical details and get to the juicy stuff. Why did we have tea and cheesecake, Jovie? You haven't cried once—not about Jake, at least."

I turn away, put my feet on the floor, my elbows on my knees, and my face in my hands. "I can't skip the physical details, because in this case, they matter. And *that's* why we had tea and cheesecake and *The Notebook*."

"Ohhhhh shit."

I tell her in graphic, explicit detail what happened tonight. Every detail. The way he looked at me. The way he tucked my hair behind my ear. The way I cuddled him with my bosom for a pillow, and how my heart freaking melted as I held him.

When I'm done, Lia is silent for a while, staring into space, thinking. Finally, she looks at me. "You showed up unexpectedly at his house after he worked three days straight, with his favorite sandwiches. Sandwiches for which, I may add, you share significant emotional memories with your deceased fathers. You showed up unexpectedly at his house with said emotionally significant sandwiches, complete with an elaborate ruse to surprise him. You sat him down with the aforementioned emotionally significant sandwich and a less emotionally significant beer. And you proceeded to give him, according to you, the blowjob to end all blowjobs, and not just any old blowjob, but a blowjob without expecting or even allowing any kind of reciprocation. A just-because blowjob, you might call it—the most dangerous kind, because a just-because, no-reciprocation BJ is the fastest way to a man's real emotional nougaty center."

I can only nod.

"But you didn't stop there. Oh no, you did not. What did you do? You, topless, with your magnificent breasts on display for his viewing pleasure, led him to bed, took him in your arms, and pillowed his beautiful stubbly face on your bosom as he fell asleep." She turns a look on me. "Do I have this correct?"

"You do."

"Jovie Martin, you are an idiot."

"I know."

"I mean, what did you expect?"

I shake my head. "I don't know, Lia. I don't. I wasn't thinking. I wasn't planning it—it just happened."

"At least you left before he woke up. If you'd been there when he woke up, you'd have been in even worse trouble."

"I know."

"You can't fuck him, now—you do know that, yes?"

"But—"

"No." She chops her hand down over my protest. "No. Can not. No way, no how, no. You *like* him. Fucking him isn't going to get him out of your system, Jovie. If you have sexual intercourse with Jake Howson, there is no going back. Oath broken. You'll be *with* him. It will be a *relationship*. I hesitate to bust out the L-word, but I can just look at you and tell." She turns me back around sideways on the couch to face her and takes my cheeks in her palms. "Even if you keep it dirty and fast and casual, Jovie. Hear me."

"I need it," I whisper. "I need to know. Just once."

She shakes me by the shoulders. "No, no, no. Not even once. Even if you let him fuck you standing up against an alley wall, surrounded by trash and rats and homeless heroin junkies, it will be the end of it for you. You will not just have feelings for him, like you do right

JASINDA WILDER

now. If you have the sex with him, you will fall irrevocably in love with him. You're already more than halfway there, and if I know anything about men at all, he is too. He's going to wake up and you'll be gone and he'll be wondering where his lovely bosom pillow went, and he'll be thinking about you showing up when he needed comfort most and giving him a blowjob he couldn't forget in a million years, just because. And he's going to be all in, ready to jump, how can I make Jovie Martin fall in love with me."

"He's as married to the job as I am."

"Makes no difference. You made it personal. You offered him comfort. If you'd just sucked him off and left, that would be different. But you didn't. You went and made it personal and now you're gonna end up breaking our oath, and that means I'll end up in the same damn boat."

"I didn't mean to."

"Clearly. Thus the issue."

"I'm sorry, Lia. I didn't mean for this to happen. He just…he gave me the best orgasms of my entire life, by far, no contest. And then right when I was bringing my A-game, he got a call. And I couldn't very well let him get away with that? I mean, he didn't hesitate, Lia. He put the call first without a second thought, and he was *right fucking there*. You know how hot that is, to us. And just everything he's done, everything he's said. He's just… he's the real deal, Lia. And I called the station to see if he was there, with some excuse about paperwork, they said he'd left after being on duty for seventy-hours straight. And I've pulled those, Lia. I know how that feels. You're just…totally drained. It's more than physical exhaustion, you know?"

She sighs. "I know, I've pulled them too."

"I know you have, so I know you know. But you didn't *see* him, Lia. Those fucking eyes. He was so tired, so drained, but still wired from forcing himself awake and forcing the focus, you know? He couldn't relax. He *needed* my help, Lia. I *had* to do *some*thing. I had to make him feel better. Had to."

She's quiet a long time. "I don't know how you're getting out of this one, Jove. I really don't."

"But…I can't. We swore a blood oath, Lia. I will not end up like our mothers. I *will not*. Not even for Jake Howson."

"You may not have a choice, now, honey."

I peer at her. "There's always a choice."

She laughs, a quiet huff. "I'm mad at you, girl. Why'd you have to go and fall for a fucking fireman?"

"I haven't fallen for him, dammit."

"Are falling for, then."

"Falling doesn't mean fallen. It's not a done deal. I can still resist him."

She just stares at me. "Jove. Please. Be realistic with yourself. You're not going to, and you know it."

"Fuck. What do I do?"

"Does he know about the oath?"

"Yes. We talked about it."

She groans, face in hands. "Ohmygod. That's even worse."

"I know."

"You have to dump him and play the ice queen. That's the only course of action left to you."

"There's nothing to dump. We had some sandwiches, some coffee. He ate me out, I sucked him off, the end. There's nothing to dump. I'm just going to ice him out. I can't fall for him, Lia. I look at him and I...I see Dad. Not, like, literally. He looks nothing like Dad. Doesn't sound like him, doesn't act like him. But it's the...the attitude. The way I feel around him. It's too much. I just...I have to ghost him."

"You owe him an explanation, Jovie."

"I know, but...if I have to face him, I'm afraid I'll chicken out."

She clutches my wrist. "Jove, you *owe* him an explanation. Be honest. Tell him it's turned into something you're not ready for. He'll have to respect that."

I sigh. "Dammit, Lia."

"You know I'm right. You can't and won't ghost him. You'd try, only to end up accidentally running into him, and oops, you'd fall onto his dick. This way, you have closure. No accidental nookie sucking you back into the trap that is Jake Howson's big blue eyes and mighty wiener."

I growl at her. "Please, Lia. This is hard enough. Talking about his mighty wiener is only going to make it worse." I hold out a hand in front of her face. "Also, never refer to it as a mighty wiener again. That's just weird."

"Fine. But talk to him—*in person*." She points at me. "Face to face. Not a call, and certainly not a text. Woman up and do it right."

"Fine."

"In a public place where there's no chance of

accidentally falling onto his mighty wiener—sorry, throbbing member."

"Lia!"

"What? Is that worse?"

"Yes, that's worse! You're just being mean, now."

"Sorry. Well, no, I'm not. You fell for a *fireman*, Jovie. You deserve *some* ridicule—loving and affectionate ridicule from your platonic hetero life partner. But still."

"I didn't mean to."

"It doesn't matter."

"And I haven't fallen for him."

"You're splitting hairs." She points at me. "No bean-flicking to him, either."

"You can go, now." I point at the door. "If you're just going to mean, you can leave."

"You have to purge him from your system. Give him one inch, he'll give you six."

"More like eight, if not ten."

"Fucking hell."

"Yeah."

"Thick?"

"So thick."

"That yummy vein along the bottom?"

"Delicious. I could lick it for hours."

"Did his cum taste good?"

"Like candy." I laugh. "I honestly don't even remember what it tastes like. I was too busy focusing on the way he looked and felt while coming." I close my eyes—I'm immediately immersed back into the memory; I can almost taste him on my tongue, then. "Salty, tangy. A little musky. Not quite sweet, but very nearly."

She shakes her head. "You're in so much trouble." She sighs. "Just don't fuck him, Jovie. That's the biggest thing. You cannot fuck him. You can still get out of this with your heart intact, maybe…if you just…don't…fuck him."

What I don't tell her in that moment is that *not* fucking Jake Howson feels impossible. I *have* to know what he feels like inside me. I have to know the weight of him on me, his hips pinning me to the mattress, nailing me deeper and deeper with every wicked thrust…I have to know what he feels like beneath me as I ride him like a blue-ribbon bronco.

Ahhh, fuck.

I'm in so much trouble.

JAKE

I WAKE UP ALONE.

I sit up in bed, groggy, disoriented. It takes a minute to even process that I'm awake—that I'm a person, that I'm in the world.

Then finally, after blinking and stretching, my brain starts to grind into motion. Pertinent details begin to spring into mind.

First, I'm naked.

Why am I naked?

I'm not hungover, but I almost feel like it, sans the raging headache, sour stomach, and the spins. A mental hangover. Emotional?

Close my eyes and breathe, force my brain to actually turn on all the way.

Jovie.

Jovie happened.

It all hits me, all at once, like a Mack truck. Shit, like

a NASA rocket gone rogue, smashing full speed into my chest.

She showed up, pretended to be a Door Dash driver...

Ohhh my lord.

The Blowjob.

It deserves the capital letter.

Wait, no, let's go one better: The BLOWJOB. All caps.

That's why I'm hungover—that was like mainlining a Schedule 1 narcotic. Or what I imagine it would be like, at least.

Those tits, fuck. Burying my face in them, getting to play with them, kiss them.

Her mouth. Jesus, that mouth. The way she toyed with me, drew it into something more than merely oral sex. More than just...sucking me off. Way more. What it was, I don't know. But it meant something. Hell if I know what, but something.

I remember her leading me to my bed, climbing in, pulling me after her.

I remember falling asleep on the softest, warmest pillow on earth—her chest.

I remember being...*held*.

But now she's gone.

No note, just gone.

I grab my phone, intending to call her...

She'd accessed the camera from the lock screen and took a selfie. Still topless, those huge, beautiful breasts front and center, her free arm hugged under and around them as she leans slightly forward toward the camera. Her soft, faint smile is…dare I say, almost haunted? I don't know. Like she can't believe she's doing this, but is doing it anyway.

I save the photo in a hidden folder so no one can accidentally see it if they happen to get ahold of my phone. And around a firehouse, you never know what could happen.

I call her.

It rings three times and then goes to voicemail—either she's working, or she just blocked my call.

Shit.

It's early, because I wake up crazy early out of a long habit, so I still have over an hour before I have to get to work. I shower, feeling comically reluctant to wash my cock, as if to wash it would be to wash away the knowledge of what she did to it. Fortunately, I can report that even after a thorough washing, I still have the memory. Vividly so.

Work, and I try to put her from my mind.

Meet José and Maks for burgers and beer—nothing wild, just hanging out. Jovie doesn't come up, nor do Erin or Lia.

They can tell I'm chewing on something, though. I know them, and they know me. They also know me well enough to know when to leave things alone, and this is one of those cases.

Late evening, at home alone again, finally. And I call her.

Right to voicemail.

Shit.

She's freaking out—I can feel it.

Next morning there's a captain's meeting with Chief Wells, which lasts until midafternoon. I grab some food to go on the way back to the station—there's an ambulance parked in front of the station, idling, a familiar Black man in the passenger seat—Jovie's partner. I wave at him, and he waves back.

I wonder why she's here.

The main doors are open; Lt. Edwardson is walking some new guys through checking the mix on the tanks and the seals on the masks.

No sign of Jovie.

Check my office—nothing.

I hear riotous laughter coming from the break room—there she is.

I edge into the partially open doorway.

Chilly is holding court. "So then, so then, Joey fuckin', he jumps! The lunatic fuckin' jumped. Three stories up, floors burning out from beneath him, he jumps from the landing of the stairs down to the next level, like he's fuckin' John McClane. I couldn't fuckin' believe it."

Jovie is facing away from me, as is everyone. She's at a table, sipping coffee and picking at a blueberry muffin as Chilly tells stories about, I assume, Joe Martin, her dad.

I hang back and listen.

"Rossi was just as ballsy, though." Chilly sighs, the humor fading. "Saved my fuckin' life when I was a rookie. There was this backdraft like outta the fuckin' movie, right? I was too raw to know any better, and he saw it coming, yanked me out of the way and outside before I bit it. First big call, and I hadda get saved by Rossi. Chapped my ass good, but shit, that's how you learn, right?"

Jovie nods. "I have a question."

"Shoot." Chilly tops her coffee off. "I'm an open book."

"It's not about Dad, though, it's about Jake... ummm—Captain Howson."

Chilly turns away, putting the coffee pot back. "Maybe less open, but hey, if I can answer without betraying Cap's confidence, I will."

Good man. I stay back even further, blatantly eavesdropping now. I may regret this, but I can't walk away now.

"Does he have a nickname?"

The guys all exchange glances—shit, that's not good. That means I do, but not one they use to my face.

"I mean, sure, we've all got the dumb names guys use for each other right?" Chilly taps his chest. "I'm Chilly." He points at Donelly. "He's Donuts Donelly, or just Donuts. Because when he was a probie, we convinced him it was station policy that probies had to bring donuts every shift for a month. And he fuckin' bought it, the gullible dork."

Jovie nods, pops a bit of muffin into her mouth. "Right, and I want to know what Jake's is."

Chilly waves her off. "Ahhh, it's stupid."

The guys in the break room are getting increasingly uncomfortable.

Jovie sits forward. "He does! You have to tell me. I think his buddies from Four almost spilled it, once, but I couldn't get it out of them. He was with me at the time, so that may be why."

I duck out of sight, then, hidden by the wall but able to hear, still—the silence which extends makes me imagine Chilly checking the doorway, and then lowering his voice.

"You can't tell him. It's...he'd probably get all pissy about it. You know how serious he is."

Jovie's voice is eager. "I won't. I swear. I just have to know."

"I'd never call him this to his face, but around the station, we call him...um. Well."

Jovie groans. "Come on, Chilly. It's me. My dad was your best friend."

He sighs, but the sigh turns into a helpless chuckle, as if it's just too funny to not laugh about. "We call him Big Hose."

There's a chorus of sputtering, snickering, and outright laughter.

I'm apoplectic. Stunned into paralysis. Big Hose? Fucking *really*?

Jovie is cackling. "Ohmygod, that's amazing."

"It just kinda happened," Chilly explained, over laughter. "When you see his name written down, it looks like it could be pronounced HOSE-son. But he's real careful about how it's pronounced, right? He'll correct you. Well, the first time he showered here, a couple of the probies saw him and his um...you know. I don't know what kind of relationship you have with the captain, but he's got a pretty big...uh...well, anyway. One of the probies said on break one day that Captain Big Hose had dressed him down for being slow into his turnouts for a call, and it kind of stuck. And now, around here, he's Big Hose."

I step into the break room, then. Part of me is pissed off, embarrassed, and seething, and another part of me recognizes the objective humor in the whole situation and is holding back laughter.

The room silences when the men realize it's me—Jovie is the last to catch on, turning in place, partly eaten muffin in hand.

Jovie carefully sets the muffin down. "Hi."

I pin Chilly with a glare. "You're an asshole."

He grimaces. "Cap, I was just—"

I scan the room, cutting him off. "If I hear that nickname from anyone, shit is going to hit the fucking fan, are we clear?"

There's a chorus of "yes sir" from the break room, and I spin on my heel, heading for my office. I slam the door closed and collapse into my chair, unsure if I want to dissolve into laughter or hit someone.

I hear my door open; I don't look, just lean back as far as the chair will go, face covered. "I'm not in the fuckin' mood, Chilly."

"It's me." Jovie.

I don't look at her. "I'm not talking about it."

"Come on, Big Hose. It's funny."

I pull my hands off my face and glare at her. "Yeah, and if people started calling you...I dunno, Yabbo, McGee? Or...or something?"

She snickers. "I'd shut it down and laugh behind their backs."

"Well, I'm not laughing."

"Okay, but Yabbo? Really?"

"I don't know, like the old-school weird term for boobs, yabbos? I couldn't think of anything better."

"McGee I got, like Tits McGee." She sighs. "And I

actually was teased pretty hard for my boobs. They came in early, and they came in *big*. I was like, fourteen, fifteen, and I had bigger boobs than most of my teachers. The stupid names people called me? I've heard it all. And most of it was from the girls. The guys were honestly too busy staring to come up with mean names. The girls were cruel, though."

"They were just jealous."

She laughs. "I know. I knew that then. Doesn't mean I didn't try to tape them down and wear two and three super compressive bras and stuff. Shit, I still do."

"You do?"

"Sure." She shrugs. "They're a liability. Running up or down stairs, jumping out of the bus. Shit, just in terms of dealing with people at work. Girls will assume they're fake and ask who bought them, shit like that. Guys will hit on me without provocation, just because they somehow assume a big chest means I'm easy or something. I don't know. So yeah, I wear compressive bras, for a lot of reasons. If I could get away with a shirt that was less form-fitting than this—" she gestures at her uniform shirt, "I would wear it in a heartbeat."

"How anyone could mistake you for anything but all-natural, I don't know."

She snorts softly. "They haven't seen them the way you have, Jake. It's much harder to tell natural versus implants when they're fully covered." Her voice is soft, quiet. "And it shouldn't matter anyway."

"No, it shouldn't." I look at her, then. Hold her gaze. See the turmoil behind her eyes. "I called you. Twice. I got the feeling you were screening my calls."

"Because I was."

I nod, frown, look away. Back to her. "Did I…did I upset you, somehow?"

She shakes her head, swallowing hard. "No."

"Then what? Because that night at my place…when I fell asleep, things between us were…"

She closes her eyes. "Jake, I…"

"Your oath."

She nods. "This is turning into something I'm not ready for, Jake."

I lean back in my chair. "I guess I should've seen this coming." I laugh, trying to not sound bitter. "I *did* see it coming. Shit, you *told* me it was going to happen."

"I'm sorry, Jake."

I sit forward again. "Your oath was made out of hurt and fear, and I get that, Jovie. I do. I lost my dad, and it fucked me up, and I won't lie and say this whole thing with you hasn't thrown me for a fucking loop, because it has. I don't know which way is up." I shake my head, sigh. "I don't know, Jovie. I don't know what to say. I get it, in one sense. You lost your dad. Your best friend lost hers, the same day. Your mom lost her husband. I get the vow, truly. But if there's something between us, something real. Something that could really *be* something? Wouldn't it be worth exploring?"

She rubs her face. "Answer me this, Jake: you get a call. Big fire. Your guys are inside. Something goes wrong, something collapses and your guys are stuck. You're going in, even if means you die. Right?"

I close my eyes, drop my head. "Yeah. I'm going in. It's the job. It's what I signed up for. I can't not."

She reaches across the desk but stops short of touching my hands. "And I get that. I respect it, Jake. I respect the hell out of it. I'd never ask you to be different. I'd never ask you to change. I've seen you do it, seen you act selfless and heroic."

"Don't use that word. It's just the job."

"Fine." She holds her hands up palms facing me. "My point is, I couldn't ask you to do anything less. But I also can't go through what my mom went through."

I groan, and sit back again. "She remarried, didn't she?"

Jovie nods. "She's not over Dad, though. She'll never be over Dad. She married Derek I think partly in an attempt to make herself get over Dad. Don't get me wrong, Derek is a great, great guy. I like him a lot. They're good together, and she does love him. But she's not okay. She hears a siren, and she flinches. Someone pulled a fire alarm by accident at her work, once, and firefighters showed up. She had a panic attack, like full shutdown, can't breathe hysterics. And that was ten years later."

"Jovie…"

"You didn't see her, Jake. Obviously. But Mom… after Dad died…I legitimately think if I'd been any older, if I'd been able to support myself, I don't think she'd have lived. She would have just willed herself to die. She nearly *did* die as it is."

I stare up at the ceiling. "But Jovie…even if I was…I dunno, a banker, or an accountant, or a plumber or something safe, I could die in a car accident. Or anything."

"I know that, Jake." She drops her eyes, picks at a loose thread on her pants. "I *know* there's a certain irrationality to it. But it's this…fear. Inside me. I had a panic attack after I left your place. As I was leaving, all the way home, and for forty-some minutes later in the shower. Just panic. Because being emotionally tied to you, and then knowing every single day you go to work, you could die? I can't. I just can't. And I'm sorry to do this here, like this. But it's safe here, for me. You can't kiss me to change my mind, here. You can't…" she shrugs. "It's safe here. And I'm sorry, but this is just…it's what I have to do. For my own self-preservation."

I nod. "I get it."

"You do?"

I shrug, hands out palms up, and slap them against my thighs. "I'm not gonna say I like it. I don't. I think you're chickening out without giving it a real shot. But you said at the outset you wouldn't get involved with a firefighter. I knew the score, Jovie. I took a chance."

"It'd be easier if you were a dick about it."

I laugh, a sarcastic huff. "I'm not doing that again, Jovie. I'm not going to be an asshole to make this easier for you. I like you. I see something in you that makes me feel alive, makes me feel…I dunno. Better than I've ever felt. I feel a connection to you, Jovie. Emotionally. And trust me, I've never allowed myself even close to an emotional connection. My dad died too, suddenly, tragically, and it fucked me up. Fucked my mom up—she's still single. She'll never remarry. But I also know that I'm willing to risk getting hurt. Because what I see being possible with you? It could be…" I trail off. "I don't have the words for it. I saw my mom's heartbreak, after Dad died. But I also remember how happy she was with him. How much she loved him. And I don't think she'd change anything."

"Goddammit, Jake. Dammit." She sits back, wiping underneath her eyes with her middle finger, trying gamely not to cry—she's losing the battle, and looking annoyed about it. "I fucking hate you for going there."

"Not gonna pull my punches, Jovie. I want a chance with you."

"You just say that because I gave you the best BJ you've ever had."

"Or will ever have."

"And because you fell asleep on my boobs."

"That was incredible. Both things were. And yes, I want more of all that. I want more of everything. I want to fall asleep with you and wake up with you still in my bed. I want to know what you're like when you're sleepy. I want you, Jovie. I just want you."

She shakes her head, choking. "I know. Part of me wants that too. But I...I can't. I'm too afraid."

"You don't see how it might be worth it?"

She scoots her chair back and stands up, visibly holding back tears. "Yes, I do."

"But you're still walking away?"

"I *have* to. I can't do it, Jake. I just can't."

I close my eyes. "Feels like a cheap cop-out, if you ask me."

"Fuck you."

"It does, okay?" I can't help the hint of anger in my voice. "I'm sorry. I'm hurt. It hurts—you're rejecting me."

A stifled sob. "Not fair. I don't want to reject you. I don't want to hurt you."

"But you won't even try."

"Because I don't have to *try* with you, Jake. It'd be the easiest thing in the world! I can see how it'd be. It would be the best thing. I would be *so* fucking happy with you," she says, sniffling. "And then you'd go into a burning building to save your guys, and I'd be a widow."

"You don't know that."

"Neither do you."

My eyes burn. "Jovie. Please."

She shakes her head, turns to face the door. Her shoulders lift…and then fall with a heavy, intentional, mind-clearing breath. "Goodbye, Jake."

"I'm not Hugh Grant," I say, as her hand hits the knob, stopping her. I stand up at my desk, fist clenched, because despite my words, I desperately want to chase her, to do anything to convince her. "I'm not going to chase you to the airport. I'm telling you right here, right now, I'm fucking telling you—I'm falling in love with you, Jovie. So…you know how I feel, and you have to know I have what it takes to see this through."

"I know you do," she whispers. "I don't."

She opens my office door, hesitating as if she has something else to say.

Or waiting for me to say something? What else is there to say?

There is one last thing.

"Jovie?"

She turns, visibly battling tears. I sit down again and grab a paper bag from the floor by my desk—the kind you get from the grocery store when they ask if you want paper or plastic—the opening is rolled halfway down.

I set the bag on my desk. "I, um. I found these. I was up in the attic looking for something and I came across this bag, just like this. I guess after your dad and Rossi passed, they left a few things…somewhere, and someone found them, meant to return them to you but forgot? I don't know. I don't know how they got missed, they should've been returned to you and the Rossis years ago, but they didn't, and I apologize on behalf of the department for the long delay."

With shaking hands, she opens the bag and reaches in. Withdraws the items within, one by one: a faded, battered, floppy ball cap with the department logo on the front—Jovie wouldn't know this, but the cap has MARTIN written in Sharpie along the inside rim; a crewneck fire department sweatshirt, stained with grease and sweat, ROSSI written in messy block letters on the tag; a Leatherman multitool in the black belt-carry sheath, without a name label; a Gerber folding pocketknife; a pair of ripped, stained mechanic-style work gloves, so old and well used that they retain the shape of the wearer's hands, again unlabeled.

The items cause Jovie to lose the battle against tears. "In the attic?"

I nod. "In that bag, just like that, rolled up like that, unmarked. Just sitting in a corner, forgotten. I was looking for a banner for a fundraiser I'm supposed to put together next month, and came across it. I'm really sorry, Jovie. It was before my time, obviously, but that's no excuse."

"You couldn't have known." She shakes her head, holding the ball cap in her hands—she checks the inside rim, as if she knows exactly where the name is written.

When she sees the name, she gives a little audible sob. "Daddy."

She's wearing a ball cap with the medical symbol, the blue six-pointed star with the serpent-and-staff in the middle; she removes that hat and puts her father's hat on; removes it, adjusts the setting, fits her hair through the back. She picks up the folding knife, next. It has a pocket clip and features a spring-open mechanism.

"This was his, too." The gloves, then. "So are these. Whenever he had a day off, he'd spend it in the garage, tinkering with that old Buick. I'm not sure it ever ran, or if he even wanted it to. He just like being out there, listening to Zeppelin and the Stones and the Allman brothers, wearing these gloves, messing with the Buick."

"What happened to the car?"

She shrugs. "Mom sold it after he died." She fits her hands into one of the gloves; it's too large by several sizes. The knife she fits into the pocket at her thigh, next to a penlight. "The Leatherman is Lia's dad's. I remember him carrying it everywhere. In fact, I remember him bitching up a storm one afternoon because he'd lost it. He was *pissed*. I guess Mama Rossi gave it to him for their anniversary one year and he thought he'd lost it. He was inconsolable for weeks."

"I only found that yesterday evening. I wasn't holding on to it or waiting to give it you or anything. Just so you know."

She nods. "Thank you, Jake."

"Jovie…"

"I have to go."

I stand up, round my desk, grab her by the arms, hold

her. "Give us a chance, Jove. Give *me* a chance. Please? You know we'd be good together. You know I'd take care of you. Who else could ever understand you like I do?"

Her face crumples, tears trickling down. "I can't, Jake," she says, her voice thick with tears; she drops her head, shakes it, shoulders heaving with silent sobs, and then she shrugs out of my hold. "I can't. I *can't!*" She piles the items back in the bag, snatches it off my desk, and bolts.

I watch her approach her bus—her partner scrambles out of the passenger seat and sprints to the driver's side, and Jovie climbs up into the passenger seat. I watch her shake her head at her partner's question, turning to stare out the window.

The ambulance makes a tight circle in the driveway, pauses, turns into traffic and rumbles away.

I'm alone, standing in my office, staring after her, the door wide open.

Chilly steps in. "Cap?"

"I need a minute, Chilly."

He closes the door, and I'm alone.

JOVIE

Mom, Mama Rossi, Lia, and I all sit around a small bonfire in Mom's backyard. No one speaks. Empty bottles of wine litter the grass around the fire pit, but there is no laughter. Mom holds Dad's gloves. Mama Rossi has her husband's sweatshirt, and Lia hasn't let go of the Leatherman since I handed it to her two and a half hours ago.

I stand unsteadily to my feet. "I need to sleep."

Lia reaches for me. "I'll come."

Mom glances at me. "Thank you, Jovie."

I shake my head. "Thank Jake Howson. He found it."

Lia knows the deal with Jake, but The Moms don't. I didn't see the point in explaining it all. It's over and there's no going back.

Except, as I turn to head back up to Mom's house, she calls my name, stopping me. "Jovie."

I glance back. "Hmm?"

"I wouldn't go back, you know." She closes her eyes,

holding the gloves to her nose and inhaling. "I wouldn't change a thing."

"I know."

"You can't block everyone out forever. Someday, sweetheart, some man is going to come along and he's going to knock down your walls. You're going to hate it. It's going to hurt." She finally looks at me. "I fought Derek for six months, you know. He proposed to me four times, and I turned him down four times."

I blink. "I...I didn't know that."

"I didn't want you to. But I think maybe hiding my struggle to let myself be with Derek was a disservice to you."

I shake my head. "It doesn't matter, Mom."

She snorts. "Of course it does. You think I don't know you're heartbroken? Of course I know, I'm your mom. I see it. You don't have to tell me a damn thing about him, if you don't want to. But I would guess he reminds you of your father in some way, and that scares the shit out of you. So you rejected him. Because it hurts too much to consider losing him too, right?"

I look at Lia, and she just shrugs. "Don't look at me—I didn't say shit to anyone about Jake."

Mom laughs. "Wait. The man who found these and gave them to you—*he's* the one you're in love with?"

Lia cackles. "He gave them to her *after* she rejected him."

I drop my head, hissing. "I didn't reject him. And I'm not in love with him."

"He wants to be with you, and you told him you

couldn't." Lia wraps an arm around me. "That's rejection, honey."

Mom sighs. Looks at me. "What does he smell like?"

I frown. "I dunno. Like a man."

"Be specific. Close your eyes and think about. Answer the question."

I close my eyes and inhale, as if he was standing in front of me. "He always smells a little like smoke, even if he's clean and hasn't been to a fire. He smells like...*clean*, I don't know. Shampoo, deodorant. He doesn't wear cologne often. Something kind of spicy, or musky. Sweat, but the clean kind of sweat, maybe that's stupid but...clean sweat." I choke. "He smells like...*Jake*. Like...*home*." My voice crumples on the last word.

Mom has me in a hug. "You wouldn't know what he smells like in that kind of detail if you weren't in love. If he smells like home to you, honey? It's because he *is* your home."

"I *can't*, Mom."

"He's a firefighter." It's a statement.

"Yeah."

She just holds me, refuses to let go. She gathers Lia close, and Mama Rossi is here, too, all four of us hugging. "You have to let go of that oath you guys took."

Lia and I pull back, looking at each other in shock.

"You know about that?" Lia asks.

Mama Rossi laughs, a wet, sniffling sound. "Of course we know. We're your mothers."

Mom kisses the side of my head. "I understand, Jovie. I do. But you can't go through life like this. A good man loving you only comes along so often in this life, Jovie. You'd be a fool to let him go."

"I'm too scared," I whisper.

She sighs. "Well, that's not who I raised you to be, is it?"

I have no answer for that.

A few days later, I'm still a disaster. But I've managed to pull my shit together for work, keeping the turmoil in my head and heart mostly at bay. I don't have to pretend with DeShaun when we're in the bus, posted up and waiting for calls. But I also don't have to talk about it. He just lets me stew in silence and plays pop songs way too loud, singing along off-key in a terrible falsetto. Making me laugh, or trying to, at least.

It's been a slow day, so far, only a few minor calls. But I'm restless. Antsy. Uncomfortable. There's a heavy feeling in my gut.

DeShaun feels it too, I can tell. He fiddles with the radio. Glances at me. "Tell me you're feeling what I'm feeling."

"Like we're waiting for something?"

He nods, uncharacteristically subdued. "Like the universe is pregnant with something terrible."

I sigh. "Yeah, I feel it too."

Right then, our radio crackles, dispatch coming through. "All units, respond to a plane crash and warehouse fire in progress..." she rattles off the address, a warehouse in a busy, industrial sector of the city. "Be advised, this is an MCI in progress—multiple casualties confirmed and more expected. Work with the incident commander for instructions."

Lights and sirens, hit the throttle. DeShaun slaps his seatbelt into place, answering for us as I bring us around and head for the location in question—he also inputs the address into the nav on his phone; it's the tail end of rush hour, and we're likely going to have to detour around stopped traffic. Indeed, we do, my knowledge of alternative routes bringing us around clogged main arteries.

We're still a few miles away when we first spot the fire. It's a BIG one. The flames are visible from here, and my heart sinks. This is bad. Very, very bad.

It's chaos when we reach the site itself. The response is still being organized, planned. Crews have water streaming at the fire, but so far it's little more than a squirt gun aimed at a bonfire. Sirens howl from every direction as more fire crews arrive, along with police cars to cordon off the area, as well EMS crews like DeShaun and me.

The IC is the Battalion Chief himself, Bruce Wells, a man my father knew and respected.

The wreckage of an airplane—a small personal jet, it appears—pokes up from the center of the blaze. The warehouse is one of several in the area, and the crews' immediate concern is to stop it from spreading. This being an active industrial area, these warehouses are staffed at all times, and I have to assume most of them have already been evacuated.

The fire has already spread to an adjacent

manufacturing facility—DeShaun and I are directed to join the triage area, assessing victims as the crews bring them out.

Time is a blur, then, as we treat burns and breaks and a whole assortment of injuries, one after the other. The blaze is terrible, the heat unbearable even from a distance—jet fuel. The spread is inevitable, especially when a strong wind kicks up, making the flames jump higher and spread faster.

DeShaun has been receiving the injured from the fire crews as they carry and assist them out of the burning buildings—and then, abruptly, DeShaun isn't there.

I grab a nearby firefighter, soot-stained, shell-shocked. "My partner. Tall, Black. Where is he?"

The firefighter points at the building. "He went in."

"*What*?"

"His buddy. From Station Two—Todd Walker, he went in and hasn't come out. Your friend went in after him. I couldn't stop him."

I know better. Of course I do. But DeShaun has been my partner for five years. There's no way I'm losing him.

A familiar voice calls my name as I sprint for the building entrance—this warehouse is kitty-corner to the main blaze, and I can see smoke and flames eating at the far back corner where it touches the edge of the wreckage. I ignore the voice. Within, it's dark, lit only by the rotating white flash of emergency lights. Smoky. I turn on my penlight and duck down, covering my face with the crook of my arm.

This is stupid. But it's DeShaun.

I'm in a foyer area, an office next to me—empty.

On the left, a break room, the punch clock, whiteboard, water fountain. Ahead, the main warehouse area, rows of manufacturing machines of some kind, bulky and huge, now silent. It's a maze of steel frames and short ladders and piping and wiring, crates of material stacked three and four high, empty Mountain Dew bottles lost beneath the machinery.

I see the flames in the distance. Hear shouts. "DeShaun!"

I run.

"DeShaun!"

Smoke obscures the ceiling overhead, growing thicker and blacker every moment, lowering closer and closer to the floor. It's so hot my lungs ache and my face feels red, puckering, tightening.

Ahead, shouts. Closer, now.

I can't see shit—the smoke is thicker here, lower. I see flames along the ceiling, spreading—toward me.

"DeShaun!" My voice cracks into a hacking cough.

"Jovie!"

I follow his voice, find him facing a fallen girder near the far back wall, close to the flames—too close. The girder is pinning a young Black firefighter, and DeShaun is straining at the girder, assisted by another firefighter, an older Hispanic man. They can't get it up on their own.

I move beside DeShaun. Add my strength to the lift—scream as I strain. Beside me, DeShaun is roaring through gritted teeth; the Hispanic firefighter is silent.

The girder moves—an inch. Two. Enough that the man trapped beneath is able to shimmy out from beneath it, and we drop it.

DeShaun throws himself over the girder and onto the man who'd been trapped beneath it. "Todd?"

"I'm okay," comes the faint response. "Leg just hurts…"

"Todd, baby, you're not okay." DeShaun's voice is wrecked. "We need to get you out. This fire is spreading."

I join DeShaun—his assessment is correct: the firefighter's leg has a terrible break—worrisomely high, very near his femoral; if the break has severed his femoral artery, he could bleed out before we even get him out of here.

The three of us work to lift Todd. He weighs a ton, groaning as we heave him over the fallen girder.

The flames are moving fast, licking along the walls to either side of us and creeping across the ceiling.

Something creaks overhead.

"We have to move," the Hispanic fireman says, his voice low, strained. "Fast. Very fast."

There's nothing for it but to run, despite the shouts of agony coming from Todd as we jostle him.

Something crashes behind us—I feel a wave of heat wash over my back. I smell burning hair.

Heat picks at my skull, sudden and painful.

DeShaun turns to look at me, to say something—his eyes widen. I see it happen in slow motion. I have no choice—I drop Todd's leg, patting at my head.

I whip the hat off my head and smack at myself with it, feeling the heat dissolve away. Another loud creak.

A crack.

A groan of something enormous dying.

The world moves in slow motion—something

huge angles toward me from the ceiling. In front of me, DeShaun and the other firefighter pull at Todd, hauling at his arms. DeShaun's eyes are on mine, his mouth open— screaming at me to come on, move, move.

I'm struck by the hand of God.

Or so it feels.

I must black out for a moment or two.

When I come to, I'm on the ground, pinned in place by something massive and hot—I'm being crushed and burned at once.

"Jovie!" DeShaun's voice.

"GO!" I scream, as loudly as I can. "I'm fine!"

"Don't you lie to me goddammit!" His voice cracks.

"You can't—" a wave of pain steals my words. "You can't help. Go!"

Nothing. Silence, except the roar of flames.

I assess: a girder fell, knocked me flying, and in the process knocked over and crushed a piece of machin- ery—I'm trapped beneath the machine, which is on an angle, leaning against the framework of another machine. I'm not beneath the full weight, or I'd be dead. But my left ankle is pinned, just enough to keep me here.

Just enough to kill me.

I push at it, but it's too heavy, too hot.

Flames crackle toward me.

I flop to my back, groaning. I don't want to die here, but there's burning wreckage between me and the exit, between me and rescue. The ceiling groans as the fire spreads. Any moment now, something else is going to fall, and that's it for me.

I close my eyes and try to just breathe.

Jake fills my mind.

And I realize, now that I'm face to face with death…

I'm an idiot.

He loves me.

I love him.

And I'm an idiot.

To think I could stay away from him… to think I could walk away.

It's so obvious that I burst out laughing, because it takes *this*, me about to die, to realize that my oath means nothing in the face of love. He loves me, and if I had it to do over again, I would just…go for it.

Maybe he'd die like Daddy did.

Or maybe he wouldn't. Maybe he'd retire in his sixties or seventies and we'd have had a lifetime together.

Maybe I'd be crushed.

But maybe I'd get a lifetime of love with an amazing man who understands me like no one else ever has—and I've barely given him the time of day. He just…*gets me*.

I breathe and wait for the end.

God, what I wouldn't give to see him right now.

If he's ever going to make an obnoxiously timely appearance, now is the moment.

I wait, hoping. Any second now. Right?

Please?

I want a second chance. A do-over.

JAKE

I'M SCRAMBLING INTO THE TURNOUT GEAR I KEEP IN the back seat of my truck. Watching the doorway through which stupid, stupid, stupid Jovie went.

Come out, please come out.

Figures emerge from the skirling pall of smoke and flicker of flames—her partner, hacking, sobbing, hauling a firefighter by an arm. Hauling on the other side, Luis Castalleno from Two. Paramedics appear with a stretcher as if by magic, transferring the wounded firefighter—Todd Walker from Two, as well. Another meets Jovie's partner with an oxygen mask, but he shakes it off, seeing me and beelining toward me at a dead sprint.

"She's in there!" he says, his voice hoarse and ragged, pleading. "She's in there."

I'm already in motion. "You *left* her?"

"She made me!" he shouts, sobbing, falling to his knees, hacking. Still waving off the oxygen—the paramedic insists, all but wrestling it onto him. "She's trapped and Todd, my Todd…" The way he looks at Walker tells the story.

I feel a presence beside me—there's no reason to look. I know who's with me. They're not even in my station, but we're still a crew, no matter what. I don't know how they know, how they're here when Four is supposed to be working on containing the main blaze. But they're here, and that's all that matters.

There's nothing to say; just do the job.

As we enter the building, José, Maks, and I each fit our oxygen masks in place—we do so almost in unison.

The heat inside is a killing pressure. Fallen girders create a three-dimensional maze.

"Jovie!" I shout, as loudly as I can—I doff my mask momentarily to send my voice further. "JOVIE!"

"Here…" a weak rasp—nearby. On the other side of a complicated X of fallen beams and toppled machinery.

"I'm coming, Jovie!" I call. "We're gonna get you out."

I have all of my emotions on rigid lockdown. Nothing in, nothing out. Just do the work. She's a victim, and it's my job—no more, no less—to get her to safety. Don't risk my men. Get in, get the victim, get out. Don't enter a situation I can't get out of.

Too late for the last one—this place is about to go, and we shouldn't be in here.

It's harder than it should be, getting to her. When we do, it's obvious time is very, very short. She's pinned by her ankle, scorched, singed, suffering from smoke inhalation which is growing more severe with each passing moment. The building is gone—crews are working to keep it from spreading any further, but this building is gone. It's going to collapse, and soon: I can hear it. I can feel it. It's in the groans of the walls, the creak in the ceiling. Something in the way the fire crackles and roars just so, where it's licking and eating, how the girders have fallen and where.

I just know.

Seconds matter. Instants.

"José—get ready to pull her. Maks, you and me lift. On three, ready? One….two…" Maks and I grip the beam, crouch, brace. Suck in a deep breath on two. It's just deadlifting. Except I can feel the heat of the metal through my gloves. Have to be quick. "THREE!"

We heave, straining every muscle, teeth gritted as we shout wordlessly through the effort. Just like deadlifting—you're not pulling the weight *up*, you're pushing the ground *down*. Metal protests, Jovie screams. José scrambles, hauling her backward with a rough jerk. Maks and I drop the weight, gasping.

Immediately, I scoop Jovie up and put my mask over her face. Maks leads the way back through the maze. It should be hard, ducking and weaving while carrying her, but adrenaline races through me—desperation to see her safe. It bubbles at me, that desperation. Eats at my insides like acid.

Behind, a deafening crash, followed by an ominous creaking rumble.

"RUN!" Maks yells, following it up with a repetition in Ukrainian.

Smoke burns my throat. Jovie coughs.

My legs churn—I'm not even thinking about the

route, I'm just blindly following and trusting in Maks to get us out.

The conflagration ignites to volcanic new levels as a portion of the ceiling in the far back corner goes in, sending a concussive wave over us followed by a billowing typhoon of heat and flames.

Sparks dot her hair, black flecks against stark black—I see them land in slow motion, wink, fade, die.

Something flaming catches on my arm—some kind of jagged debris lancing through the stiff, coarse, protective material of the turnout jacket. I feel it stabbing my arm. It hurts but it's not worth worrying about.

Ignore it.

How long have I been running through this burning building with Jovie in my arms? An eternity, it feels like.

Then, abruptly, I'm stumbling into a cool empty space. I stumble a few more steps, and then medics are taking her from me, replacing my oxygen with theirs. The mask dangles, hissing ever so faintly.

I take a hit from it.

Watch the medics check her over—one of them gives me a thumbs-up. Jovie will live.

That's all I need to know, right now.

I can't stop to be with her—I have a job to do.

But I can't help going to her, if only briefly. I hover over the stretcher, pull my hand from my glove so I can brush her cheek with my thumb. This causes her eyes to blink and flutter open.

"You're on fire." Her words are muffled by the oxygen mask.

I frown, following her gaze: the debris is still stuck

in my jacket—I use my gloved hand to pull it free, toss it to the ground. "You're an idiot, Martin."

"I know." She twists her head sideways, where her partner is fighting off medical advances in an attempt to get at Jovie. "But I'm *your* idiot."

"You are?"

She smiles faintly. "Looking Death straight in the face has a way of changing one's mind." She gestures weakly at her partner. "Will you tell DeShaun I'm fine and to quit acting a fool?"

Instead, I gesture—the medic follows DeShaun over with the oxygen, still trying to salve and bandage a burn to the back of his head at the same time.

He grabs Jovie's hand. "You weren't supposed to follow me in there, you dumb bitch," he sniffles, his smile turning the insult into a loving endearment.

"You weren't supposed to be in there at all."

He shrugs, glancing over a shoulder where Todd is being loaded into a bus for transport. "It's Todd," he says, with a shrug, as if that explains everything.

"I didn't know you had a Todd," Jovie says, pulling the mask away to cough, then replacing it.

"He wasn't ready to come out to the guys on his crew," DeShaun says. "So I kept it to myself."

Luis, the engineer on Todd's crew, joins us, having overheard—he's refused to leave Todd's general vicinity since emerging from the building. "We knew," he says. "He did not tell us, but we knew." A shrug. "Crew is crew."

DeShaun grabs Luis's hand—Luis looks a little uncomfortable with this display of affection, but allows it.

"You wouldn't have left him." It's somewhere between a question and a statement.

"No. You don't leave your crew behind." Luis squeezes DeShaun's hand.

DeShaun now looks at Jovie. "No, I guess you don't." He blinks hard. "I shouldn't have left you."

She fixes him with a glare. "That would have made the whole thing a waste, if you hadn't gotten Todd out. That's why you went in. And anyway, the beam fell between me and you guys. There wasn't anything you could have done, not with Todd."

"CAP!" Chilly's voice. "Chief Wells needs you, sir."

I squeeze Jovie's hand. "I have to go."

She pushes at me. "Why are you still standing here, you big dumb lunk? Don't you have a job to do?"

There are many, many hours of work, containing and then suppressing the blaze. It's well past dawn before it's fully extinguished.

Four people who'd been on shift when the plane crashed died, as well as four in the jet itself—it was a private charter flight, fortunately, only the pilot, copilot, and two passengers were aboard. Several more employees were injured, a couple of them quite badly. Six firefighters were injured, and of them, Todd Walker is the most severe, with a pulverized leg and second-degree burns.

I lose track of Jovie—she was transported to the hospital.

Finally, it's over.

After a long battle like that, it's always a little disorienting, simply…going home. The wreckage is still smoldering, and the forensics and investigators have to go over things, still. But my job there is done.

I get my crews settled, the ones who've been on duty fighting the blaze all night exhaustedly unwinding and getting ready to go as the new shift takes over. I have a mountain of paperwork to do, but it can wait.

I have someone to visit.

She's asleep when I get there.

All things considered, she's in pretty good shape, I think. Broken ankle, but it'll heal. Smoke inhalation, minor burns. Singed hair—fortunately it's a pretty minor and won't mean a drastic haircut.

I sit, intending to wait for her to wake up. Or, simply be with her. It's not visiting hours, but the old battle-ax who'd kept me out during visiting hours with Larry is on duty, and for some reason, she takes one look at me sitting at Jovie's bedside and says nothing. Recognizing something, I guess.

I must have dozed off.

I wake to something cold sprinkling my face. I blink awake, frowning, wiping at my face—Jovie, grinning mischievously, is dipping her fingers in a cup of ice water and flicking it at me.

"You're boring when you sleep," she says, her voice hoarse.

I laugh, sitting upright. "Yeah, sorry, I haven't mastered the whole *be entertaining while sleeping* trick yet."

She laughs, the laugh turning to a cough. "Ow." She sips at the water, her eyes on mine. "I was waiting for you."

I shrug. "Sorry I fell asleep. It was kind of a long day—"

"Not here, dummy. In there." She waves a hand vaguely outward. "When I was trapped. I knew either I was going to die, or you were going to rescue me. So, I was waiting for you. And you came."

"Of course I did." I scoot my chair closer to the bed so I can hold her hand. "Back there, you said you were my idiot."

"I blame shock. I would never have admitted to being an idiot otherwise." She grins, tangling her fingers into mine.

"The idiot part we can discuss another time. What I'm concerned with is the part where you said you're *my* idiot…"

"That part I meant."

"What changed?"

"Nothing. And…" She swallows, blinking hard. "And everything."

"You're not an idiot," I say. "He's your partner."

She sniffles. "He's my partner." That says it all. She studies the back of my hand. "Do you want to hear what changed?"

"Obviously."

"When I realized I couldn't get the thing off my ankle and that the building was coming down, something inside me just…broke. I dunno. I realized I was being so, *so* stupid. Like, obviously I…I love you." She sniffs a laugh. "I can't believe I just said that. But…it's true. And, I didn't want that. Not with anyone, but certainly not with a firefighter. Nothing has changed, like I said. I'm still terrified that I'm going to lose you. Today or yesterday or whatever—that could have gone differently."

I'm stunned that she said the words, but somehow not as stunned as she seems to be to have said it.

"You could have died. You almost *did*." I gesture at the hospital bed as evidence. "DeShaun could have—Todd, Luis, me. Any of us could have died, and you, Luis, DeShaun, and Todd all almost *did* die."

"Right. And I guess I…laying there, feeling the building shifting, feeling myself…I don't know. Facing death? Realizing I was helpless? Looking at the end of my own life and knowing I had a chance to be well and truly loved by a good man? And I refused it? I let it go? I denied it because I was *afraid*?" She shakes her head, laughing softly, bitterly, a raspy, hoarse bark. "I actually laughed out loud at how much of a dumbass I am. *That's* why I said I'm an idiot. I'm not an idiot for going in after DeShaun—I am my father's daughter, after all. I meant I was an idiot for… for…" she sniffles, trails off.

I lift her fingers. "Good thing I knew you'd see reason."

"You did, huh? You just knew I'd come around?"

I shrug, trying for casual and unconcerned. "I mean, yeah." I laugh, shaking my head. "I just…I couldn't see any alternative. You *had* to come around, because I couldn't figure out how I was going to keep living my life without you in it."

She tilts her head back on the pillow, blinking furiously. "God…*dammit*, Jake. Why do you have to make me cry? I'm not in the mood to cry."

"Sorry." I laugh. "What *are* you in the mood for?"

She picks her head up and winks broadly at me, licks

her lips. "Take off your pants and come over here, and I'll show you."

I cackle. "You're deflecting, number one. Number two, Ol' Nurse Battle-Ax is letting me stay in here past visiting hours, but if I do anything dumb, she'll for sure kick me out. And number three, the things I want to do to you would be kinda tricky with you all hooked up to monitors and IVs and shit. And you'll need your strength for them, anyway."

"Is that a promise...Big Hose?"

I roll my eyes at her, refusing to rise to the bait of my idiotic nickname. "It's a threat, Jovie Martin." I wink at her, because I know the wink drives her nuts. "The moment you get the all clear, I'm dragging you by the hair back to my cave and I'm fucking you six ways to Sunday."

At that exact moment, Nurse Battle-Ax waltzes in, eyes narrowing at me. "And if you don't let the poor girl get her rest, that'll be never. Can't you men ever think with your brains instead'a your balls?"

Jovie pats the nurse's hand as she fiddles with Jovie's blankets. "I started it, Ethel. And thank you for letting him stay."

Ethel huffs, checking the chart and monitor readouts and sundry other things. "As long as he behaves himself, meaning, keeps his big grimy paws off you till you're past the risk of infection. And if you want to regain your vocal health, you need to rest your throat, instead'a yakking up a storm like this. You suffered severe smoke inhalation, young lady." She pins me with a glare. "You think a fire-fighter would know better."

"I do, ma'am. But if you think I can tell Jovie to keep quiet, you don't know her very well."

"Only way to keep me quiet is to put something in my mouth," Jovie says, grinning at me even as she watches Ethel huff and bluster and blush.

"Oh, you young people. You only think about one thing." She seems satisfied that everything is fine, and heads for the door, pausing to point at Jovie and then me. "No monkey business. Just save it. Okay?"

"I'll be as proper as a nun, Sister Ethel," I say, Catholic school instincts kicking in rather randomly.

"Sister Ethel, he says." She snorts derisively. "I'm leaving the door open, and I'm *watching* you." She points at Jovie. "*Both* of you."

"Me?" Jovie mimics offended innocence. "I'm the invalid, here. I'm totally innocent."

Ethel just snorts again. "Right. And I'm Queen Elizabeth."

I restrain a cackle, barely. "There *is* a certain resemblance, actually."

A wave and another snort, and we're alone.

Jovie rubs the knuckle of my forefinger. "Do something for me?"

"Anything."

She grins. "Remember you said that, now." She lifts my hand and kisses my knuckles. "Go home. Jake. Sleep."

I shake my head. "I'm staying with you."

She arches an eyebrow. "You said anything."

"Except leave you."

"Nope. Too late."

"Jovie. I'm not leaving."

She kisses another knuckle, the middle finger knuckle, and then the ring finger. "Listen to me and listen good, Big Hose: I'm *fine*. I'm in no real medical danger. I'm a medic, remember? Broken ankle, sore throat from the smoke, some minor—and I do mean *minor*—burns. *You* need sleep. And I won't rest if you're here. I'll be too preoccupied thinking about all the things I want to do to you when I get out of here."

I sigh. "You're *not* calling me Big Hose."

"Why not?" She grins playfully. "I happen to think it a wonderfully accurate nickname for you."

"Fine, McGee."

She laughs, and the laugh turns to another hoarse cough. "Don't—gah. Don't make me laugh." She catches her breath. "See, I'm not embarrassed by my abnormally oversized yabbos anymore. I had that teased out of me years ago." She walks her fingers across the back of my hand, fore-knuckle to pinky. "And plus, I happen to know you are particularly attracted to that feature of mine."

"You called them yabbos." I sigh a laugh. "I'm not going to win this, am I?"

"Nope. The cat's out of the bag…Big Hose."

I groan. "God, it's so terrible! That's not even how you pronounce my name!"

"Which is why it's funny on so many levels." She sighs, closing her eyes. "I'll give you a little-known fact about me to make up for it, though."

I snort. "Ah, I see. Well, if I'm letting you call me *that*, it better be a hell of a good fact."

"It's about my name."

"Hmmm."

"When Mom was pregnant with me, they were fighting about whether to find out the gender or not. Mom wanted to know, Dad didn't. Complicating this scenario was the fact that Joe is a family name on both sides. My paternal grampa is named Joe, my maternal grampa is named Joe. I have no less than three uncles with some form of Joseph as their name. Joe, Joey, Joseph, Joey B, Joey P, Dad was Joey M. At a family reunion, you could shout Joe and twenty guys would answer, and that's just on Dad's side."

"Which means you were getting named Joe one way or another."

She laughs. "Because we're a very stereotypical Italian family, yes. Dad wanted me to be Joey Junior—I shit you not. Girl or boy, I was gonna be Joey Junior."

I laugh. "Cooler heads prevailed, clearly."

She arches an eyebrow at me. "But did they?"

"Your name is not Joe, or Joey…is it?"

She is significantly silent.

"You're kidding."

"I wish I was."

She sighs. "My parents *had* to have been drunk when they named me. It's the only possible explanation for the name on my birth certificate." She fixes me with a stare. "Not even Erin knows this. Only Mom and Lia."

"I won't tell a soul," I say, grinning. "As long as you don't call me Big Hose in front of anyone, not even the guys at my station who gave me the nickname—*especially* not them."

"You have a deal. It'll be my secret pet name for you."

I hold out my hand, and we shake on it.

"So," I say. "What awful name did your parents burden you with?"

"Josephina Victoria."

I stare at her. "They didn't."

"They did. Josephina because of the aforementioned prevalence of the name Joseph in my family, and Victoria because my mother and father had a mutual friend named Victor who passed away suddenly when they were dating."

I shake my head. "Your name is Josephina?"

"My name, legally, is Josephina."

"So then Jovie is a nickname?"

"Well, it's complicated. Jovie is the name I chose for myself." She takes my hand in both of hers. "It took me years of calculated silent treatment and refusing to respond to make the nickname I grew up with go away—all through my childhood I was Joey V. I shit you not. And listen...me telling you my real name *and* my childhood nickname? That's a real sign of love, Jake. I hope you understand how serious this is for me. Not even my mother calls me anything but Jovie, not even when she's spitting-nails mad at me."

"So how'd you come by Jovie?"

"Because growing up, I was just another Joey."

I nod. "Ahhh." I wince. "That's...rough. Because I'm assuming you probably weren't a tomboy."

"Yeah, no. I was...seven or eight? Around there. We were having a family barbecue—a Martin-Romano-Solinas-Ferrero reunion of epic proportions. So many freaking Italians. Turn around, someone was yelling for Joey or Joe, and it was just...chaos. And there was even another Joey V, my cousin. My mom and my cousin Joey

V's mom were standing together talking, and Mom kept yelling at me to quit whacking my cousin—another Joey, actually." She does a remarkable and hysterical impression of an irate Italian mother, albeit with a smoke-roughed and squeaky voice. "'Joey! Joey! Stop that! QUIT THAT JOEY! Don't hit your cousin! Joe V! Joe V! Stop that, Joe V!' And I kept turning around, thinking she was talking to me and I was going nuts, getting irritated, like, what? I'm not doing nothin'." She laughs, remembering. "And that was when it hit me. She kept saying Joe V, but all in one syllable. And I decided, right then and there, I had a new name: Jovie."

"It all comes together."

"So I marched up to my mom and Aunt Tonia and I was like, 'my name is Jovie from now on. Don't call me Joe or Joey or Joey V or nothin' else ever again.'"

I laugh. "You said it like that?"

She just shrugs. "Yeah. You think I'm sarcastic now? I've calmed down as an adult. I was real ball-buster as a kid."

"I can imagine."

"No, you really can't." She lifts her hands palms up. "From then, I wouldn't answer to anything but Jovie. I wrote it on tests, essays, everything. I even got sent to the office for ignoring my geography teacher, the ornery old goat refused to call me Jovie, and I refused to answer to Josephina. Eventually it stuck. By the time I was in high school, no one even remembered that I was ever anything but Jovie."

"Did you ever think about changing it legally?" I ask.

She shrugs, nods. "Sure. But after Dad died, I just

couldn't. It's a connection to him. I don't know. I just couldn't."

I nod, clasp her hands in mine. "Well, I love your name. And I promise I'll never call you Josephina." I can't help a teasing grin. "Unless you make me *really* mad."

"Call me Josephina," she says, glaring at me, "and it'll be the last thing you do, Jake Howson."

I laugh. "I'm teasing."

She presses the button to lower the upper half of the bed. "I'm sleepy, now. Go away."

I stand and bend over her, lightly kissing her lips. "Okay."

She pinches my chin in her fingers. "Get some rest, Jake." A saucy yet sleepy smirk. "You're gonna need it."

JOVIE

I'M IN THE HOSPITAL UNTIL THE NEXT DAY—ON strict orders to take it easy. I'm bandaged in a few places with the burns, my ankle is in a cast, and I sound like I've been a two-packs-a-day smoker for twenty years, but all things considered, I'm remarkably lucky.

I've got one thing on my mind, and one thing only: Jake.

Naked.

Having a broken ankle really puts a damper on things, as does the variety of burn placement. But I'm determined to not let any of that stop me from seducing the ever-loving hell out of the man I love.

Yeah, I'm trying that on for size—the man I love.

I'm escorted home by the whole crew: Mom, Mom Rossi, Lia, and Erin. They treat me like I'm made of glass and it's annoying the hell out of me, but I allow it because it makes them feel better. Mom goes to elaborate lengths—propping and fluffing my pillows, turning back my blankets, setting out the salves and antibiotics for my burns. I have to stop her from setting out my outfit for the next day like I'm five again. Mom Rossi comes equipped with cooking supplies: jars of her quasi-famous home-made sauce and homemade rotini, sausage and chicken… and proceeds to cook enough food to feed half the fire department. Which, honestly, is where most of it will probably go. Which I also think she knows.

Lia contacts our employer to verify my paid sick leave, and Erin sort of flits around cleaning.

I tolerate the tutting and hovering and babying for as long as I can, and then I loudly and ostentatiously yawn.

"Wow, I *sure am tired*," I say to the condo at large, in an overly obvious voice. "I should really get some rest. Alone."

Lia snickers, but The Moms pretend to miss the broad hint.

Mom, at long last, huffs. "You owe us the story, Jovie. I for one am not leaving until I get the full story."

I frown. "What story, Mom? There was a fire. My partner went in, and I went in after him. I got trapped. I was saved. The end."

Mom gives me a droll stare as only a fed-up mother can. "Jovie."

"Mom?"

"Don't make me bust out the full name, child. I will. I haven't used it in, what, almost thirty years? But I will, if you don't spill the tea right *now*."

I cackle. "Spill the tea? Did you find that phrase on a Buzzfeed listicle of hip phrases every senior adult must know?"

"Senior adult, my ass." Mom glares. "My coworker's granddaughter came by last week and was talking to Gloria. I guess there'd been some kind of major family drama and Gloria's granddaughter told her to spill the tea, as in share the gossip. I thought it was a cute phrase."

I sigh. "There's no tea, Mom."

"*Bullshit*," Lia says, attempting to disguise the word as a cough into her fist.

I turn a death stare at her. "You have something to share with the class, Lia?"

She arches an eyebrow at me. "Yes, Teacher, I do. What I said was bull…*shit.* As in bullshit there's no tea. Something happened in that warehouse, Josephina Victoria Martin, and we all know it."

Erin stares around the group, from face to face, landing last on me. "Your name is short for Josephina?"

Balancing on one crutch, I brandish the other in Lia's direction. "I oughta beat you senseless with this."

Lia grabs a throw pillow from the couch. "Try me, bitch. I'll club you like a baby seal. You have one working leg, so you *will* go down."

"Girls, girls," Mom says, in her most soothing mom-voice. "That's enough."

I gesture at Lia. "She used my stupid real name!"

"I said what I said." Lia sticks her tongue out, then hides behind the pillow.

I crutch over to the couch, lower myself laboriously down to it. Lean my head back, close my eyes with a sigh. "There was…a moment." I rub my face with both hands. I haven't allowed myself to think about it until now. "I… shit." I pinch the bridge of my nose, inhaling sharply, let it out with a shudder. "I was trapped. DeShaun had vanished, and a fireman told me he'd gone in. Which is not like DeShaun at *all*. He's careful. If we're faced with a risky option or a safe option for treating a patient, he'll go with the safe route. So I knew he had to have gone in for a very, very good reason. He's my partner. He's the best partner I've ever had, and I refuse to break in another one." My gaze connects with Lia—she gets it; we've both had good partners and bad, and we've goth lost good partners to trauma, transfers, and resignations. "So I went in. I had no choice. I mean, of course I *had* a choice, but…there was no choice. I found DeShaun and a firefighter trying to get someone out from under a beam."

I hesitate.

"The fireman trapped under the beam was DeShaun's boyfriend. He'd seen him go in, seen the back of the roof fall in, and knew that's where Todd was working. So, me, DeShaun, and Luis got Todd free and were heading for the exit. Another beam came down and hit me, knocked me flying, and trapped me. There was a big machine and the beam and it was all very precariously balanced. The fact that it only just barely pinned my ankle was a literal miracle of Saint Mary, I swear. If it had hit any more directly my ankle would have been just…pulverized. The beam trapped me, and was between me and the exit, and the other guys. They had no chance of coming back for me, and Todd was way worse off than me—in real medical danger, the immediate fire hazards aside. And it was just…even without Todd to worry about, DeShaun didn't have any protective gear, and Luis couldn't have helped me alone."

Mom winces, looking fearful for me. "Oh, honey."

I swallow, ignore her. "So, yeah. I made them go, made them leave me. And I...I knew there was no way out for me. I couldn't move the beam, couldn't even budge it. And I could hear the building creaking. It was coming down soon, and I knew it."

Mom and Mom Rossi exchange glances—the irony is not lost on me: this is how their husbands died.

"And I just..." I shake my head, struggling to find the right words. "I...I've never been face to face with death like that. I mean, I deal with death every day—for other people. Never for me personally, directly." I pause again. "I knew there was no way out unless someone came to rescue me. And somehow, I knew—I *knew* Jake would come for me. Sounds cliché as fuck, I know. Like a freaking rom-com or something, like *oh, I have peace because my hero will save me*." I snort. "It sounds so stupid to say out loud, but I was just...afraid, but somehow also...I wasn't. I just...I *knew*."

Lia's face tightens. She and I are going to have to talk.

"And then, all of a sudden, Jake appears, with José and Maks." I sigh again. "It was a near-death experience and I guess it really just made me think about a lot of things. And I'm still thinking."

"About Jake?" Mom asks—there's a tinge of hope-fulness in her voice.

"About a lot of things, Mom." I sigh, exhausted. "I really do need to sleep."

"We'll talk more later," Mom says.

"That would be good." I close my eyes and remain

JASINDA WILDER

on the couch as I hear them collecting their things and heading for the door.

I catch Lia's eye as she hesitates by the door, the last one through.

"I'll follow along later," Lia says to her mom. "I, um, forgot something." She closes the door and sets her purse back down, sits beside me on the couch. "What aren't you telling us, Jovie?"

"I'm not intentionally not saying anything."

"But there is something."

I lever myself upright and swing toward my bedroom, sit on the edge of my bed and lean my crutches against the foot end, and roll into bed.

Lia lays beside me, facing me. "Talk to me, Jove."

I can't look at her. I stare at the ceiling instead, and whisper. "I love him, Lia."

"I know you do."

"That was the realization I had when I knew I was either going to die or Jake was going to save me: I love him, and I'd be the worst kind of fool if I walked away from a damn good man who loves me just because I'm afraid." I finally have to look at her. "I don't know how to do it, though, Lia. How to love him. How to let him love me." I blink back tears. "How to tell you that I have to break our blood oath."

Her face crumples—a very rare show of emotion from Lia, who is normally even more stoic and unemotional than I am. "I knew you were going to from the first time you met him, Jove."

"You did?"

"The visceral, emotional way you reacted to him,

negatively at first, was all I needed to know. At no point in our entire lives has any man caused that kind of reaction in you. You've never talked about a man the way you talk about him. Never looked at a man the way you look at him." She holds my eyes. "With one exception."

"Dad."

She nods. Reaches out and takes my hand. Squeezes hard. "We were kids, Jovie. When we took that oath, we were crushed, brokenhearted, lost little girls. Our dads were our heroes, our first and only loves. Of *course* we were afraid. Of *course* we did something dramatic and kind of crazy like that stupid blood oath."

"It wasn't stupid."

"Yes it was." She laughs. "If we were so afraid of falling in love with firefighters, why did we both choose to be career paramedics, knowing we'd have to interact with them on a daily basis? Because we're intrinsically drawn to them. Our dads were our heroes, Jovie. We knew even back then we'd probably fall for someone like our fathers, and we were afraid of that. Rationally so. But now we're adults, and as rational and logical as that fear is, we have to let it go. You're ready, Jovie. I'm not, but you are."

"I'm not, though."

"You probably never will be." She touches my cheek. "You just have to jump, honey."

"In a way, I'm more scared of that than I was to die in the warehouse. And also, let's not forget that all the reasons we took that oath still apply. Nothing has changed in that regard."

"No, that's true. And if anything, the fire made it clear

it's entirely possible that the worst could occur, even if Jake isn't a frontline firefighter anymore."

I laugh. "Wow, Lia. Helpful."

She laughs, shrugs with faux daintiness. "I do what I can." She goes serious again. "All I can say is, you have my blessing." She hooks her pinkies with mine, pressing our thumbs together—if you look closely, you can still see very faint lines on our thumbs where we'd cut them to take the oath. "I, Lia Maria Antonia Provenzano Rossi, hereby formally and officially renounce our blood oath. In its place, I vow on our unbreakable bond as platonic heterosexual life partners that I will support you in any loving, healthy, meaningful relationship you pursue, whether it's a hunky fireman or a boring nine-to-five civilian with a spare tire and chronic gout."

I cackle. "You make that sound *so* appealing."

"You have to repeat the vow, dummy."

I sigh. "Fine." I take a breath. "I, Jovie Martin—"

"Ah-ah-ah. Full, real name."

"No."

"It doesn't count if you don't."

I groan. "Fine. I, Josephina Victoria Martin, better known as Jovie, hereby formally and officially renounce our blood oath. In its place, I vow on our unbreakable bond as platonic heterosexual life partners that I will support you in any loving, healthy, meaningful relationship you pursue, whether it's a hunky fireman or some boring nine-to-five civilian with a spare tire and chronic gout."

We kiss each other's thumbs, and then let go, sighing in unison.

"I actually feel a little better," Lia says. "Like a weight has been removed."

I roll my eyes at her. "You're just jonesing for a certain Latin firefighter whose name may or may not sound like schmo-zay."

She rolls her eyes, but her girlish giggle gives her away. "No. Not jonesing. Just…I find him attractive."

"Because he is attractive." I giggle with her. "And I happen to be fairly certain that he would jump your bones in a heartbeat if you were to so much as look at him crossways."

She frowns thoughtfully. "You think?"

"I know. He was staring at your ass every chance he got, when we were all hanging out at The Far Bar."

She shrugs at this. "That means nothing. Unless they're gay or into skinny-girl butts, all men are just helpless against the hypnotic allure of my ass." She gestures at me. "Like with you and your boobs."

I snicker. "In José's case, I think it's more than that."

She shrugs. "I'm not sure that's the direction I want to go. All I meant is that being free of the oath does feel better. I don't know why."

"Because you know that now that I'm falling for one, you're going to fall for a firefighter, too."

"You say that like it's a foregone conclusion."

"Because it is." I yawn. "I *am* tired."

"I may just sleep here," Lia says. "If you're okay with that."

"No, you have to leave," I tease.

Silence.

"Lia."

"Mmm?"

"How am I supposed to seduce him when I'm covered in bandages, sound like a seal, and am stuck on crutches for the next couple of months?"

"Good question." She pats my hip. "It would be kind of hard to be all sultry and seductive and sexy when you're stuck hobbling on one foot."

"Helpful."

"If he loves you, he won't care."

"That's not the point. We haven't had actual sex yet, and I really want to make it special."

"So make him wait until you're less…physically impaired."

"Lia, you're not helping."

"I'm being serious."

"*Wait*? For six to ten *weeks*?"

"Just till you get the cast off, at least."

"How do I sell that to him? How do *I* do that? He's all I can think about."

She's drowsing, half asleep already. "Date him. Tell him you want to establish a healthy emotional relationship with him before you go any further into your sexual relationship."

"That's way out of character for me."

"Which is why maybe it's a great idea."

"It's a terrible idea. I'll die of sexual frustration. Of whatever the female equivalent of blue balls is."

"I didn't say no sexy shenanigans at all. I said date him and focus on emotional connection. Just don't go all the way."

"It's all or nothing, I'm afraid. If I touch him, I'm gonna end up fucking him."

"That's a you-problem."

"It is. I admit it completely."

She sighs. "Maybe just talk to him honestly?"

"Psssh," I scoff. "Honesty is for losers."

"Right? What a dumb idea."

I doze off, and my dreams are a confusing montage of trapped-in-the-fire nightmares, wet dreams of Jake, and bizarre mashups of both, where I'm trapped in a fire while having hot monkey sex with Jake.

He's unable to get away from work the next day, and when he calls to tell me he's coming by, he sounds so exhausted that I make him go home with promises to come see me tomorrow.

It's almost three days after I got out of the hospital before he manages to find time to come see me, and it's nearly midnight when he does—after a multi-alarm fire woke him out of bed. Instead of going back home to bed when the call was wrapped up, he comes to see me, since I'm still awake.

It's too much work to change my clothes, so I'm still in the same pajamas I've been in for an embarrassingly long time—booty shorts and tank top sans bra. It's an outfit I know he appreciates, as frumpy and dirty as I may feel.

"Don't mind me," I say as I let him in the front door, hobbling out of the way on my crutches. "Showering and

273

changing requires a whole big process that I'm not quite ready to undertake just yet, so I'm riding dirty, since I'm stuck homebound for a while."

His gaze scans me head to toe. "I don't mind," he says, gaze pausing at my chest. "At all."

I roll my eyes, but it's with a grin. "Yeah, I figured."

He gestures at the couch. "Sit. I'll help us to something to drink."

"I'm not helpless, Jake. I can get us a beer." I plop down onto the couch, however, despite my protestation. "But I shouldn't drink anyway, since I'm on painkillers and antibiotics. You go for it, though."

He comes back with a pair of sodas. "Nah. I'm tired and hungry. One beer wouldn't do much to take the edge off anyway."

I turn slightly on the couch to face him, and he very gently lifts my feet up so they're resting on his thighs. I lean back and stretch out, enjoying the comforting thrill of his palms affectionately rubbing my legs from shin to thigh—affectionate, so far, rather than sexual.

"Hi." I sip, and smile at him.

"Hi."

"I have something to talk to you about," we both say in unison.

I laugh. "You first."

"Sure?" he asks.

"Yeah, I'm sure."

He sighs. "So, I'm kinda nervous about this."

"You?" I frown. "Nervous?"

"How to put it. What to say."

"Just be blunt, Jake. Whatever it is, just say it."

He nods, remains silent for a long moment, and then sighs again. "So, I've never actually…dated anyone."

I'm stunned—not by the admission, but by where I think he's going with this. I keep my thoughts to myself, though, and just nod. "Okay?"

"We've talked about this before."

"Yes, we have. For both of us, relationships have always been casual."

"To the point that I wouldn't really say I've ever had a real relationship with a woman."

I sip, nod again. "I'd say the same thing—I've never had what you would call a real relationship with a man."

He pauses again, tracing circles around my kneecap with a fingertip. "Meaning, more to the point, all of my…interactions…with women, have been primarily about sex."

I just hold his eyes. "Again, with you so far, and the same for me. What are you getting at, Jake?"

"I want you. You know I do."

"But?"

"What if…what if we didn't have sex yet?"

I can't help a grin, which I hide behind my soda can. "Why not?"

"You're laughing at me." His eyes narrow. "I knew this was stupid."

I take his hand. "Jake, Jake, no. No. I'm laughing, but not at you, and not for the reason you're thinking."

"So why are you laughing, then?" he asks.

"I'll tell you in a minute. First, explain your reasoning."

He arches an eyebrow at me. "Promise you won't

assume this has anything to do with my desire or abilities or attraction to you?"

I grin. "The way you ogled my boobs when you got here was all the assurance I needed that you're plenty hot for me, I promise."

He laughs. "This is about more than just your boobs, Jovie."

"Is that even a thing?" I tease.

He sighs. "Yes, it is. I mean, barely. Your tits are pretty much the second or third most impressive thing on the planet."

"The first being your dick and the second being what?"

He snickers. "This conversation is not going how I anticipated."

I pat the back of his hand. "No more jokes, I swear." I give him what I hope is a loving and supportive and understanding smile. "I do not in any capacity doubt you, your attraction to me, nor your desire or ability to pleasure me sexually, Jake. You have my unconditional promise on that."

He sighs as if this is a relief to hear. "I just…it's different with you. Totally different, and new, and unexpected, and…" a pause. "It's hard to navigate, and I want to do things right. I told you I love you. I feel like I know you, on a weirdly deep and personal level even though we haven't known each other all that long. But I…I don't want to do this the way I've done every other relationship or whatever you want to call it with women in the past— which is to just jump into bed and focus on that exclusively. And I'm not saying we got off on the wrong foot, but we have sort of approached this whole thing at an odd angle, you know?"

I laugh. "You mean, I resisted you tooth and nail? Or do you mean that it took literally almost dying for me to accept that I am in fact in love with you and that I would in fact be a total fool if I let you go?"

He chuckles. "There is that." He turns his palm face up, rests it on my thigh, my hand on top of his. "What I'm saying is, what if we just…dated, at first?"

"You mean, kept sex off the table for a while?"

He nods. "So we can keep the focus on…on building an actual relationship? I don't want to speak for you, but I know I personally have no fucking clue how to go about having a relationship."

"Me either." I sigh, closing my eyes and tangling my fingers in his hand. "The reason I was laughing is because that's what I was going to talk to you about."

He stares at me for a moment. "You're serious?"

I nod. "I am."

"So you agree?"

"I do."

He lets his head fall back. "I was worried you would think I was, like…I dunno. Less manly or some shit, if I said I wanted to put sex with you on hold."

I frown. "Jake. No. God, no." I reach for his face, touch his cheekbone. "It's *more* manly."

"Please don't mistake me, here, Jovie—I predict this will be extraordinarily difficult. But hopefully worth it."

"It will be worth it." I feel myself blushing. "I have to admit something to you, though."

He frowns. "Okay?"

"I have one minor ulterior motive for wanting to wait, in addition to everything you said."

The frown deeps with puzzlement. "Which is what?"

I lift the crutch, wiggle my injured foot. "This. If we were already in a relationship and had things all…I dunno…settled? It may be different. But I just…it's hard to put this without sounding stupid. I just…I guess as much as I fantasize about you every night, think about you all day, I want our first time together to be special, and it would be kind of hard to do that when I've got this stupid cast on."

He snorts. "Sorry, but that is kinda dumb. You think that would make a lick of difference to me?"

I sigh. "No, I'm sure it wouldn't matter to you. And it may be dumb, but it does matter to me."

He brushes my cheek. "Are you blushing?"

"I feel stupid."

"Don't, Jovie. It's not stupid. I get it."

"You do?"

He nods. "I do."

"So, what's the parameters of this?"

He shrugs. "We just…focus on us. On being together. Trusting each other. Learn how to be together without sex."

"So does that mean we go back to square one? Like, nothing?"

He sighs, closes his eyes. "Honestly, yeah. Mainly because I know myself, and I know that if I go there with you even a little bit, I won't be able to stop. I want you. I want all of you."

I squeeze his hand. "I feel the same way."

"You do?"

I snort. "Yes, Jake. You think you have a monopoly on desire for sex or a lack of self-control, sexually, just because you're a man?"

"I guess not."

"Who showed up at whose house for a sexy surprise?"

He sighed a laugh. "You did. But I guess I sort of assumed you'd done that mainly because you're...I dunno...like you'd done it for me. Like out of some kind of...selflessness or something like that." He actually blushes and laughs. "Sounds stupid when I say it out loud."

"It's not stupid," I say. "You can be forgiven for assuming that, because I think in a lot of situations it very well could be true. But in this case, it would be an erroneous assumption." I hold his eyes. "That was for me. Yes, for you, because I wanted to make you feel good, because you'd worked so hard for so long, but...it was as much for me. I wanted to do that for you because I *enjoy* it. I honestly don't do oral too frequently, not because I don't enjoy it, but because I do."

He frowns. "You're gonna have to break that down for me, babe."

I laugh. "I get pretty...enthusiastic, when I choose to give someone a blowjob. As you can witness. But I found out the hard way if I lead with that, if I go there with a guy, they have a tendency to expect it, and I like it to be special. I don't know if that makes any sense. I guess a better way to put it would be a guy has to be worth it for me... and as much of a judgy, superficial bitch as this may make me seem, not all guys are worth it for me. I may be okay sleeping with a guy—just to sort of scratch the itch, you know? But giving a guy head is…it's more personal, I suppose. Stupid? Maybe. And maybe that's backward from other women. I don't know and I honestly don't much care. To me, it's personal, and I'm only going to do that if I feel…safe. Comfortable. And, honestly, only if I feel a certain level of attraction."

He eyes me. "So I should feel pretty special and honored, then?"

I laugh, nodding. "Yeah, you really, *really* should. That was…" I shake my head, blowing out another huffing laugh. "That was special, Jake. The point of all this is that I did that out of my own personal sexual desire to do so. Not because I'm some selfless saint or anything, doing something I dislike simply out of service for you, or something."

He hums, musing. "Actually, I like that even better. I wouldn't want you to do anything with me, to me, or for me unless you personally want to do so."

"Don't worry, I won't."

His eyes fix on mine. Heat up, blue fire in his handsome face. "It *was*, very truthfully, the single hottest thing that's ever happened to me."

I notice the way his zipper tightens. This conversation is going sideways in a hurry. "Funny—it was super fucking hot for me, too. But, I have to say, that day you ate me out?" I point at my bedroom door with a jerk of my thumb over my shoulder. "*That* was the hottest thing that's ever happened to me." I smirk at him. "Sucking you off so good you forgot your own name was a close second."

He groans, plucking at his zipper, his fingers almost errantly, randomly, traipsing up my bare thigh—did I mention I'm not wearing panties under the booty shorts? "This conversation is not making it easy to hold to what we just agreed we'd do."

I set my empty soda can on the floor beside the couch and lay back with my head on the arm of the couch. "I mean. Just saying. But…we *could* start that tomorrow."

His fingers graze up my thigh, to the hem of my shorts, pushing them up, up, sliding inward to the gusset. Pushes it aside, revealing my bare pussy—he groans. "*Fuuuuuuck*, Jovie. I'm trying to be good, here."

"Good can start tomorrow. We can be bad right now." I say this breathily, as his fingers trail over my seam. "Also, we don't have to think of it in terms of good or bad. This isn't bad. It's not wrong. We just agreed we'd focus on our emotional connection, on our relationship. That we'd wait to have sex for a while and get to know each other."

"You're making excuses."

I nod, laughing, biting my lip as his fingertip slides down my sex and back up. "Yeah, I am. I just really, really, *really* fucking want you, Jake. Anything I can get." I arch my back, hating the cast and the ache, needing his touch. "I need you to touch me, Jake."

He slides his finger into me. Slow, delicate. "Like that?"

I nod, gasp. "Yeah, like that. I need it, Jake. And if you need excuses, how about this one: touching you and being touched by you helps me feel emotionally connected to you. So really, this is helping."

He laughs. "I like helping."

I forget words, then, as he lazily fingers me, moving his finger up and down my seam, sometimes delving in deep only to slide out and smear my clit with my juices, then up and down, up and down…in, plunging a few slow strokes into me, then back out, circle, circle, circle…until I'm gasping and writhing.

I groan in needy frustration, eyes opening and fixing on his—he has a smirk on his lips, a knowing one. "Jake," I moan. "Please."

He gently, carefully settles my injured foot aside and leans into me, nuzzling my cheek with his nose, lips sliding across the corner of my mouth, a laugh huffing from him. "Yes, Jovie?"

I turn my face into his, claiming a kiss, a slow, scorching one, tonguing his lips and teeth and sucking his tongue into my mouth, assaulting his mouth with mine, communicating my desire as clearly as I can via the kiss.

And then I break free, holding the back of his neck. Fix him with a hungry grin—I pull his head down toward my sex. "Down, boy."

He rumbles a laugh. "Woof," he says, slithering sinuously to his belly on the couch, pulling at my shorts.

Working together, we get them off my good leg, and then down my injured one, where they catch on the cast. Bare to his gaze, now, I quiver, clench. He kisses my thigh, my hip.

I rip my shirt off, needing to be naked, grab one of his hands and press it to my breast, and then I tangle my fingers in his hair and none too gently guide his mouth to my sex. "Eat me out, Jake. Now."

He answers with actions rather than words—he

fuses his mouth to my sex, tongue sliding up my seam and pushing in, darting, slithering, devouring. Fuck, I need this. I need it. I need his mouth. I need his hand on my breast, squeezing, kneading, pinching, flicking. I need his tongue on my clit. I need him. What am I thinking? Agreeing to *not* have sex with him? For *weeks*?

In this moment, it's inconceivable. Need for Jake is everything.

And he gives me everything.

His fingers slide into me, three of them all at once, palm up, fingers in a triangle inside me and then spreading, curling, scraping and massaging my G-spot, tongue flicking my clit until I'm gasping and writhing, and then he only renews his assault, fucking me with his fingers and devouring me with his mouth. Eager, wild, tireless.

I come with a scream, and he keeps me there, rocking his fingers into me, and letting me tumble gently back down to earth…

Only to lavish oral attention on my breasts, licking and suckling my nipples, teasing my clit with his fingertips. Masterfully, unhurriedly, he brings me back up the mountain, taking his time, now. Kissing my sex as if making love to my mouth. Fingers driving in, curling, slowly withdrawing. Tongue languorously smearing around my clit.

How long?

Five minutes?

An hour?

I lose track. All I know is his mouth, his fingers. My breasts ache, feel full and heavy, nipples tight buds, hardening to diamonds under his touch. Hypersensitive already, each flick and pinch and caress of my breasts sends me higher, makes me writhe, makes me growl and mewl. Having come once already, it would have been quick and easy for him to take me there again immediately. Instead, he holds me at the edge, not teasing, necessarily, just...not letting me reach the height of climax.

The longer he keeps me just this side of orgasm, the more I need it—the more my whole being aches with the tension, the more I crave release. It's a burgeoning weight inside me, a fullness, a nascent explosion. And each kiss to my clit, each sweep of his touch inside me, each pluck of my peaked nipple adds fuel to the fire.

He pulls me to the edge of the couch, my ass now on the opposite arm of the couch from where my head had been, my entire lower half suspended in the air. My casted leg hangs down his back, my other spread wide, hooked over the back of the couch. His mouth is wild, now, suddenly furious and aggressive, tongue whipping side to side, lashing me up the peak toward climax.

"Oh fuck, Jake!" I cry, my voice a ragged raw whimper.

He just growls, and begins sliding his fingers in and out of me, slowly at first. But as his mouth on my clit drives me to the edge of climax, his fingers send me over. Plunging faster, I feel the ache grow into a burn, and he pinches my nipple hard, until it hurts. The beautiful twinge of that pain is delicious, and turns the burn in my core into a nova, a chaotic swirl of heat and pressure and wild tension. A hot line tugs at me, from nipple to clit— and he's plying me with every ounce of skill, wilding me to screaming orgasm.

But when I'm crying out, hips flexing with the speeding thrust of his fingers and tweaking twist of my nipples, crying his name as I find my release...he proves he's only begun, then.

He moves so he's hovering over me, mouth fused to my pussy, two middle fingers inside me, his other hand at my breasts. His fingers begin to fuck me, hard and fast. His mouth thrashes side to side, and he pinches my nipples in turn, one and then the other, hard, hard, *hard*—it's all too much. I can't take it—I'm already coming, but even as I fly into climax, something he's doing makes me feel like I'm going to explode even more; a bigger, wilder, deeper climax.

I'm there.

Coming, and coming—but teetering on the edge of something *more*.

And then...it's just all too much.

He pinches, sucks, fucks—it all converges inside me, intersects and reacts.

I'm already gasping through gritted teeth, whimpering, thrusting at his mouth...

I dissolve.

Break apart.

SCREAM.

I'm on fire. I'm being ripped apart from the inside out by a galaxy of orgasms, a countless billion of them all at once, shredding me and flinging me to the farthest edges of human experience.

Something breaks inside me.

I'm sobbing, literally sobbing.

Heat floods through me. Out of me.

He doesn't let me go, wrenches me through a swirling, distorting, crushing vortex of orgasmic chaos, so flooded and wild with abandoned sexual fury that I have words, no control, no self.

There is no me.

There is only Ecstasy.

He brings me down slowly, gently.

And *that's* when I pass out.

When I come to, I'm in bed, and Jake is hovering over me, kissing me everywhere—shins, thighs, hips, belly, sternum, diaphragm, breasts, arms, face, temples. I catch his face, bring his mouth to mine.

Kiss him until we're breathless.

The kiss turns wild, however, and I find myself clutching at his shirt…which is wet.

I break the kiss, frowning—realizing. "I squirted?"

His lips move against mine, smiling. "You did."

"You seem pretty proud of that, mister."

"I am. You squirted *and* you passed out."

"That's embarrassing."

He shakes his head. "No. It's hot as fuck." He licks the corner of my lips. "I have a new standard for making you come."

I shake my head, laughing, blushing. "I think it just means I peed on you. It's not grossing you out?"

He lifts his shirt and sniffs. "Nah. Not pee. Don't know what it is and don't care. It was hot as fuck."

"Hot as fuck, huh?" I caress his head. Tangle my fingers in his hair. "If you think so, then that's all that matters, I suppose."

He kisses me, and pulls away, standing at the side of my bed. "You should rest. It's late."

I laugh, snagging his shirt. "Oh, I'll rest. But I'm not sure where you think you're going."

He frowns. "To let you rest?"

I grab his buckle, grinning up at him. "You're not going anywhere."

He frowns. "Jovie…"

I sit on the edge of the bed and undo his buckle, grinning up at him as I let his uniform slacks drop heavily to the floor. He's wearing a fire department polo with his name and rank embroidered on it—I push at it, and he peels it off.

"Jovie…you should—"

"I should do exactly as I please?" I interrupt. "I'm so glad we agree." I grip him.

He huffs, eyes closing. "Oh fuck, Jovie."

"Talk to me, Jake."

He widens his stance. "I want it."

I stroke him, slow twists of one hand around him, root to tip. "Tell me what you want, Jake."

He watches me. "I want your mouth, Jovie. I want to watch you take my cock as far into your pretty little mouth as you can."

I grin, and then the grin transitions—I press a closed mouth kiss to the tip of him, smiling up at him, and then slowly open my lips, tongue swirling around him as I take him into my mouth. Back away. "Like that?" I ask.

He wraps my braid around his fist. "Just like that, baby." He guides me back to his cock. "Except this time, don't stop to talk."

I laugh. "Your wish is my command…Big Hose."

His laugh trails off into a long groan as I move on him, then. Mouth around him, sliding from glans downward, inch by inch, until he's at my throat and I don't want to take anymore. I keep him there, bobbing on him, cupping his big heavy taut balls in my hand and caressing them as I work him with my mouth.

He's more forceful, this time, showing me the pace he wants—not too fast. Nice, long strokes, lots of tongue. All the way down. He groans, huffs, thrusts. I take his thrusts, move with them. Faster, then.

"Oh fuck, Jovie. Fuck, fuck, fuck." He holds my head and face in both hands, guiding me. Pulling me down, letting me rise up to catch my breath, and then back down.

I pull away, use both hands to caress his length in the twisting plunging strokes he likes so much, and I put my mouth to his sac, licking, suckling. When I feel him huff, hear him groan, feel his body tense, feel him throb in my hands, feel his balls tense, I take him into my mouth, all the way, all at once.

Slow, now.

He wants it fast, but I do the opposite. Slow, loving, sloppy, wild. It's noisy, and I fist him at the root, twist and pump, other hand cupping his sack. Finger along his taint, pressing.

He arches, hips pushing forward as his shoulders pull back, lifting up on his toes.

"Jovie!" His grip on my hair tightens, goes rough, tugging twice in warning.

I moan as he comes, then. I moan, for him. For the beauty of him as he unleashes. For the power in his voice, the erotic way he takes over, holding my face and hair and thrusting into my mouth. He tastes like my forever. A hot flood of his cum surges into my mouth, more than I can contain, more than I can swallow. I can't help but pull him free to gasp for breath; he's still exploding, grunting a wordless roar of climax, and a spurt of cum splashes onto my throat, another onto my clavicle, and again onto my breasts, trickling down between them.

He's breathing as if he sprinted a hundred yards up a hill. "Fucking hell, Jovie."

I wipe at my lips. "You didn't think you were getting away that easily, did you?"

He crouches and claims a kiss. "What the hell did I do to deserve you, woman?"

I kiss him back. "Nothing. You don't deserve me." I kiss him again. "Any more than I deserve you."

He laughs. "You had me there for a second."

"I hope I have you for more than a second, Jake."

"You have me for a hell of a lot longer than a second. Longer than a minute, or a year, or fifty years."

"Promise?" I rub my thumb over his lower lip.

He just laughs again. "Remind me how we're sup-posed to go from *that* to no sex for who knows how long? Why did we think that was a good idea?" He drops to his knees, and I know what's on his mind. "Because right now, it seems flat out impossible. It feels like if I'm not inside you in the next couple minutes, I may just die."

I plant a hand on his chest. "I feel the same way." I kiss him, and then grab both of his hands. "But right now, what I need you to do is clean up this mess you made on my tits."

He nods. "I have an idea."

"Does it involve sex?"

"Mmmm…" he bobs his head side to side. "It could. Doesn't have to."

I laugh. "Mysterious."

"I'll be right back. I promise. Don't go anywhere."

I snort. "I'm naked, covered in semen, and you knocked my crutches across the room with your wild caveman flailing."

He shoves his legs into his trousers, commando. "That wasn't me, that was you."

"It was not. And where are you going?"

"Getting supplies from my truck."

I frown. "Supplies?"

He's already halfway to my front door. "Supplies. Just hang tight. Thirty seconds."

"Better be quick, Jake!" I call. "May I remind you, I'm covered in your sperm."

I hear a choked laugh from Jake as the door closes. "Um, hi. She's kidding. It's just a little joke she likes to make."

Shit. My neighbor was out there when I yelled that. Great. Mrs. Callahan is old, conservative, and cranky.

I wait—it feels way longer than thirty seconds before Jake comes back; he must have grabbed my keys, as he lets himself in. He has a roll of duct tape and a roll of industrial-grade garbage bags.

"Was that Mrs. Callahan?" I ask.

He yanks a bag free from the roll and rubs it between his palms to separate the opening, fitting my foot inside. "Short, white hair, big glasses, looks like she bit into a lemon even *before* you yelled for the whole building to hear that you were covered in my semen?"

"That's her."

I laugh. "Good thing my lease is up in a couple months. She's liable to report me. She reported someone down the hall for burning incense."

He chuckles as he wraps the bag around my calf. "Oh, she's reporting you, all right. She looked like you'd set a flag on fire, peed on a cross, and then called her the C-word."

I cackle. "Yeah, no, that's how she always looks."

He peels a long strip of duct tape with that distinctive *zzzzzhhhhwww-WHOOOP* sound. "Unpleasant lady, then."

"I was getting my mail once, and she was getting hers. Another building resident came in with her little son, and her son was laughing, like that belly laugh cackle that little babies do? And I swear, Mrs. Callahan told the kid to stop laughing so loud."

"Damn. Little babies laughing is the happiest sound on the planet." He runs another strip of tape around my leg, sealing the cast off. "There. Up you go."

I stand up—with more than a little assistance from Jake. Meaning, he pulls me to my feet…foot…with no effort on my part at all. As soon as I'm upright, he hands me my crutches and precedes me into the bathroom. Turns on the shower.

I eye him. "A washcloth would have sufficed."

He just smirks. "And miss an opportunity to be naked in the shower with you? Hell no." He winks. "Plus,

I figure you may need some help. You know. With those hard-to-reach places."

"It's my ankle, not my arm." I lean against the sink for balance and pretend to reach for my pussy, act as if I'm stopped by an immovable force—or at least, that's the goal, I've never been good at charades. "Nope, can't do it." I flop my arms out as if giving up. "You definitely better get in the shower with me."

He nods seriously. "I mean, what would you do without me? Babe, vagina scrubbing just got a whole lot easier, now that you've got me around."

I cackle, accepting his hand and hopping toward the shower. He picks me up by my waist and sets me in the shower, pulls the glass door closed behind us, setting me under the hot spray.

"The question now," he asks, "is how hot do you like your water? Hot? Very hot? Turn you into a lobster? Or All the Fires of Mordor?"

I grin. "I'll take All the Fires of Mordor, please."

He twists me to face the water stream. "What a co-incidence—I too like to scald my skin off in the shower."

"If I'm not beet red by the end of the shower, it's not hot enough."

"If I'm not blistered and peeling at the end of the shower, it's not hot enough."

I laugh. "So we both like the water *really* hot?"

He rubs water over my chest, rinsing away his cum. "Means we can take more showers together." He ducks his head under the stream. "I've got multiple sprayer heads in my shower."

"We're definitely going over there next time, then."

I move so he's under the stream, take my turn splashing water on him. "This is nice, though."

He plucks my hair out of the hair tie and flips it free of the braid it's been in since the hospital. "There's only one thing that would make this nicer."

"I just did that," I say with a saucy smirk.

He laughs, pouring body wash onto his hands and glopping it on my chest, taking quite the liberties with my breasts in the process, scrubbing and rubbing and fondling until a thick lather coats me…in just that one particular area.

"I think they're clean, Jake," I say, droll.

He snickers. "Oh. Um, yeah. I may have gotten carried away."

I pour body wash into my hands, scrub it onto his chest, over his abs, to his cock. "Well, better make sure this is clean, too."

"Better be careful, Jovie." He lathers the rest of me, shoulders and back, waist, belly, thighs. "Once you start to get my motor runnin', it ain't shuttin' off."

"At what point did I give you the impression that I wanted anything else?" I feel him responding, thickening. "Haven't you gotten it by now? I'm hornier than you are, Jake."

He growls, carving his hands over my ass, soap making his grip slippery. "Is that a challenge, Jovie?"

"I'm competitive as hell, Jake. Something you'd better learn now. Not only do I not back down from challenges, I'm often the one throwing them down."

I caress him to full life, his cock a ramrod in my fist, sliding my soap-slick grip over his many, throbbing inches.

He rinses me, caressing away the suds, and then his fingers find me. "You're really trying to compete with me over who's hornier?"

"Yes I am."

"What happened to waiting till your cast is off?" he asks. "What happened to establishing an emotional relationship first?"

I whimper as he shows yet again what his talented fingers can do—make me wet and turn me to a puddle of orgasmic goo in seconds flat. "That…that starts…tomorrow—oh *god*, Jake."

He shows no mercy. "So anything goes, just for tonight?"

"All I care about right now is you, doing that, and not stopping." I clutch him, stroke him in time with his circling fingers.

He brings me to the edge, my belly trembling, leaning back against the shower wall with the water splashing over his back and my front. I curl forward, head dropping, wet hair slapping aside. He grips my bad leg, pulling up at the back of the knee so my thigh is along his hipbone, providing leverage and balance. I stroke him, his thick cock plunging through my fist, and I feel him heave, tensing.

He knocks my grip away, then, tangling our fingers together and pressing the back of my hand against the wall overhead, guiding my other hand to grip the back of his neck. His face buries in my throat, his voice a rough snarl. "I fucking need you, Jovie."

I whisper against his stubble. "I need you too, Jake."

He nudges his hips against mine, pressing the head

of him against my opening. "I know you wanted to wait. I know you wanted special."

"Fuck waiting." I grind, fitting him to me, splitting myself on him. "This is special."

He touches his forehead to mine. "I want what you want, Jovie. But I just…I fucking *need you*. Is this what you want?"

Rather than answer with words, I cling to his neck and sink down, letting my weight drive his cock into me. I whimper, tasting his skin and the water and his heat as I bite his neck, nipping the tendon at the side of his neck, the one that tenses just so. He groans, and lifts my bad leg higher, pushes me back against the wall. I'm utterly supported by him, balanced. His other hand cups under my ass, lifting me, and then he thrusts upward, and now I'm impaled on him, only my toes touching the floor of the shower. He lowers my weight and surges upward, driving until he's so deep into me that he's all I feel, all I know.

"Oh fuck, Jake. God, I love you." I lift up onto my toes, sink down, gasping—the gasp turns into a breathless whine as he drops down and then rocks back up, thrusting hard, dragging a whimper from me. "You better not stop, you beautiful man."

He growls. "Not a chance. You feel too fucking good, Jovie."

My breath comes back with a rough growl, and I knock my forehead down against his shoulder, writhing on him, now, aching with him. Crammed full of him, bursting with him. He yanks me hard against him, breasts squashing against the hard wall of his chest. His nose buries in my wet hair, and he snarls wordlessly as he thrust into me again and again. As he thrusts, I surge downward, crying out, screaming.

It's the most beautiful thing I've ever felt, ever known, ever experienced, this moment with Jake. "Oh god, it's perfect," I gasp, clinging to him and clutching him and riding his thrusts. "So perfect. You're so perfect, Jake."

"I love the way you fuck me, Jovie," he growls.

I can't respond—my words are being ravished out of me. All I can do then is scream into my climax, clinging to his neck with both hands as he levers my thigh higher, lifting up onto his toes to fuck into me. He's so strong, so powerful, his muscles rippling in the water, holding me effortlessly—I couldn't bear to close my eyes, couldn't bear to miss a moment of the beauty of him, of me, of us together. I watch his cock disappear into me, watch my pussy swallow him, each thrust ripping a scream from my throat. He fits inside me as if made for me, just barely too much, so I ache and burn beautifully with every wild thrust, my sex pulsating around him, rippling around him, split apart by him.

"Jake, Jake, Jake…" I chant, gasping for air between helpless screams. "Oh fuck, Jake, I'm coming!"

"I want to fuck you forever, Jovie," he snarls, slamming into me. "I don't want to stop."

I claw my nails down his back, rolling my hips against his. "Fuck me harder, Jake. Please—fuck me harder!"

He does a partial squat, dropping at the knees and hips, scooping his hand under my other leg, now. Lifting me aloft. Still impaled by him. I'm weightless. Clutch his neck and shoulders, foreheads touching, gasping in unison. I quake around him, circle his neck with one arm to free my other. Find my clit and rub it delicately, lightly.

"Now?" he rumbles.

I nod against his forehead. "Now, please now."

He pins my shoulders and upper spine to the wall, allowing my weight to drop a little lower...and then he begins slowly pumping into me. I've already come once—and now, braced and balanced like this, injured leg hanging in space and painless, fingers drifting lazily around my aching, swollen clit, I feel another building inside me. Each thrust of his huge, hard cock into me drives me higher, my circling fingers only adding to the tumult of sexual stimulation whorling together into a hurricane of sensation.

Fuck, I feel him. All of him. Every inch. I gasp and whimper, lips stuttering against his cheek and stubble, eyes closed, memorizing the feel of him inside me. Focusing on the eroticism of the moment—my helpless dependence on him, held aloft by his powerful physique, fucked by him so beautifully, his strokes steady and slow, long plunging slides of his shaft through me, veins slicking against the stretched walls of my sex.

"Harder, Jake."

He gives me what I beg for—harder thrusts, faster strokes. He's unstoppable, endlessly virile, fucking me until I'm delirious with it, teetering on the edge of a second orgasm, this one more powerful than all the others I've ever had combined. I'm swollen with it, a balloon on the cusp of popping, every fiber and every synapse and every nerve ending attuned to Jake, to our joined bodies, to our enmeshed souls.

"I have to come, Jovie," he gasps, his wild thrusting going ragged, rhythm faltering into staccato surges, fucking in hard, pulling back slow. "I have to…I can't hold it back any longer."

I squeeze him with every muscle, fingers digging into his shoulder until I'm certain he'll have marks, later. My sex clamps around him, my orgasm stuck, unable to release until it's triggered by his.

"Come for me, Jake," I whisper. "Now, please."

"I'm not wearing a condom," he growls.

"I don't care." I bite his earlobe, whisper. "I've been on the shot for ages. I trust you. I love you. I need you. Just fuck me, Jake. Come for me. Give it to me."

"I'm clean, I swear I am."

"And I'm protected," I murmur, writhing my hips on him. "Please. Please, Jake. I need you. I need it. I need to feel you come inside me."

He hoists me higher, adjusting his grip, pressing me harder against the wall. His mouth finds mine, a kiss that's all lips and teeth and tongue as he slams up into me, all the way, hard, deep. So thick, so long. Filling me and over-filling me, stretching me to perfection, pumping into me, kissing me, kissing me, fucking me, loving me.

"Oh fuck…*Jovie!*"

"YES!" I scream, feeling him unleash, then, and it finally triggers mine, a rippling orgasm concussing through me, wrenching me into a dizzy delirious paroxysm of united ecstasy.

"Jovie…my Jovie…" he thrusts, whispering instead of roaring—and it's somehow all the more potent for the whisper, because his thrusts are primal in their ferocity in rife counterpoint to the delicacy of his whisper.

I cry out, then, words again dissolved by the sheer primacy of sensation—he's coming, I feel him pouring into me, feel his veins tense, his balls pulse, feel his cock throb thicker. I come around him, come with him, feeling myself clamp around him so hard it nearly hurts, helplessly spasming, my scream wrenching into breathless aching silent open-mouthed wonder, tears starting in my eyes.

Sobs rip from me, then, sobbing in the rhythm of his thrusts as he now growls and fucks. "Jake, oh god, Jake!"

"I love you—Jovie, I love you. I love you…"

His mouth finds mine but we're too wrought to kiss, can only touch lips and gasp together.

"I love you, oh god I love you," I answer. "I fucking *love* you!"

We come together for an eternity.

JAKE

W HEN I FINALLY HELP HER SLIDE DOWN TO HER ONE good foot, she nearly crumples, legs still jellied.

"I don't know if I can stand up," she says with a laugh. "You fucked me into temporary paralysis."

I scoop her up again, and she opens the shower door. I step through, and she snags the towel off the nearby rack. I bring her to her bedroom and set her on her foot—she clings to my neck for balance. I take the towel from her and dry her with it.

She plops down to the end of the bed, bends forward at the waist to flip her hair upside down, and twists her hair into the towel. "I need another towel," she says, reaching for the bathroom as if trying to summon one with Jedi powers.

I laugh, and fetch another one for her, still dripping wet myself. I toss it at her, expecting her to wrap it around her body; instead, she grabs my ass cheek and pulls me closer, reaching to dry me everywhere she can manage while seated. She doesn't let me go, when I'm as dry as I'm getting. Instead, she lets the towel drop to the floor, wraps her arms around my waist, and rests her face against my belly. I hold her.

"Braid my hair for me?" she murmurs, and I feel the huff of her words on my skin as much as I hear them.

"Sure," I answer. "Where's your hair stuff?"

"Drawer to the right of the sink."

I fetch a hair tie, a comb, and a brush—as I'm gathering the things to braid her hair, I hear her removing the wrapping from her cast. I slide behind her on the bed, framing her with my thighs, and pull the brush through her thick wet hair until it's smooth and pin-straight. My hands work automatically—I did this for Mom at least once a week for months, and even though that was years ago, my fingers know the work still.

I make quick work of plaiting her hair into a decent braid. "There you go," I say, touching a kiss to her shoulder.

She turns her head to the side, looking at me from the corner of one eye. "Thanks. Now put me in bed."

I set the comb and brush on the nightstand, and then help her to the left side of her bed, her side, I can tell from the phone charger, dog-eared paperback romance, tube of lip gloss/chapstick, and squeeze bottle of lotion. Once she's settled into her pillows, I pull the blanket up around her shoulders, bending to kiss her.

She cups the back of my head, whispering in my ear. "You didn't think you were leaving, did you?"

I huff a laugh. "I wasn't sure."

"Get your big ass in the bed with me, Jake Howson. I require post-orgasm cuddles, stat."

I laugh as I crawl across the foot end and slip under the covers, slide up behind her, pull her ass against my front, clutch her breasts in my hand, nose against her nape. "How's this?"

She sighs, a deep, peaceful exhale. "Perfect."

"It is pretty perfect."

She mewls wordlessly, snuggling further backward into me, clutching my hands. "Two firsts at once," she says. "Go you."

"Which two firsts?"

"First time shower sex has ever been good, and first time I've ever asked a man to stay for post-orgasm cuddles."

"Wouldn't you know? Same two firsts for me."

She turns her head slightly, not quite looking at me. "Really? You're not just saying that?"

I shake my head. "I've had shower sex before, obviously, but you just make everything so much better. I don't know how or why, just that everything you do, and everything I do with you is infinitely and inherently better than the same thing in the past with someone else." I inhale her scent. "And I've never wanted to stay for post-orgasm cuddles before either."

"What's your usual exit strategy?" she asks.

I laugh. "I don't have an exit strategy. I just say thanks, I enjoyed it, gotta go."

"You say thank you?" She sounds puzzled.

"Yeah. Is that weird?"

She shrugs. "I dunno. No guy has ever thanked me, nor have I ever thanked a guy."

"It just felt…polite, I guess. Thank you for your time,

for your attention, for sharing your body with me? I don't know."

"You haven't thanked me."

I laugh. "Because I'm not going anywhere—I'm nowhere near done with you."

"Oh." A light huff. "I like that reason."

A long, sleepy silence. "Jake?"

I'm drowsy. Not normally the type to fall asleep after sex, I resist it. It's hard, though, because she's so soft, so comforting. She fits in my arms like a puzzle piece I never knew I was missing.

"Mmm?"

"Can we just agree that the conversation about holding off on sex was laughable at best? Well-intentioned but laughable?"

I kiss between her shoulder blades. "It was, wasn't it?"

"Because I feel no shame in admitting that I'm going to need you to fuck me like you just did at least once a day. Cast or no cast."

"The cast doesn't bother me. I can work around it."

We drowse together.

Once more, she whispers my name. "Jake?"

"Mmm?"

"I love you. I just thought you should hear me say it again."

I squeeze her. "Love you, Jovie."

She mewls again. "Okay. Bye-bye."

I huff a laugh, settling into sleep.

I'm disoriented at first, when I wake up.

I'm not at home, and I'm not alone.

Jovie is on her back beside me, sprawled out, blankets around her waist, breasts bare, face turned to the side.

I just watch her for a while.

Sleepily, she rolls to her side, and I slide up behind her, wrap her in my arms again. Holding her like this, sleepy and warm, I have never been so happy in my life. Scratch that—I never knew such pure joy could exist.

Feeling me even asleep, she sighs, wiggles backward into me.

God, what beauty.

Her, us. This. It's just...perfect beauty. I'm safe. I'm loved, and I love.

I have no control over my body, over my instinctive, helpless reaction to her naked body, her warmth, the soft squish of her ass against my front, the hot weight of her breasts in my hand. I harden, ache.

This wakes her. "Jake." Her head turns to the side, eyes fluttering, finding me.

"Hey, you." I nip her earlobe. "Morning."

She wiggles her bottom against me. "Mmmm. A *very* good morning."

She reaches behind her with one hand, burying her fingers in my hair; with her other hand she reaches between her thighs to grip me. Guides me to her opening. There's no hesitation, no waiting to savor the moment.

She fits me to her seam and rolls her hips to take me into her.

"And it just got a whole lot better," she murmurs, gasping.

I curl around her, push in deep, inhaling her scent and groaning as her tight hot sex clamps and ripples around me. Rolling to my back, I bring her to lay on me, her back to my front, head on my shoulder. I grip behind her knees and thrust into her. She twists her head to the side, lips finding mine, and now there's nothing but her mouth and our union, tongues tangling as our bodies meet in perfect rhythm, gasps stolen and whimpers kissed, thrusts met and heights reached in unison.

I hold her knees high and wide and I kiss her, and she touches herself and writhes on me, crying out against my lips.

I had wondered if last night was a fluke, if it was as powerful and intense as it was simply because it was the first time together after so much buildup. This proves it wasn't—if anything, this connection with Jovie is more than last night. Better. Deeper—spiritually, emotionally. More intense.

She comes, sobbing, and her orgasm triggers mine—I couldn't hold out if I tried, and I don't. I simply give in, even though I've only been inside her for a matter of moments, but it doesn't matter—I need her. This is overwhelming, an agony of ecstasy tearing through me, an orgasm so intense it steals my breath, leaving in its place only the capacity to whisper her name as a prayer, as a benediction.

I come so hard I see stars behind my closed eyes.

Hold her thighs pinned together and pulled back so her knees touch her belly, my other hand clutches at her breasts, each of them too much for one hand, my attempt to grasp them both at the same time meaning they spill out of my hand.

She screams my name, and I whisper hers, and we match breaths, groans synched, whimpers joined with growls.

We come together, moving and breathing in perfect harmony.

When it's over, I roll to my side once more, cradling her against me.

"Now I need another shower," she says, laughing. "You spooged me again."

I groan a laugh. "Way to ruin the spirituality of the moment with your relentless levity."

She rolls in place—a somewhat laborious process with her cast. Cups my cheeks and jaw with her hands. "Jake, I can say with no exaggeration whatsoever that making love with you is the most mentally, emotionally, spiritually, and physically intense and meaningful event of my entire life. I may make jokes because it's just my nature, but that doesn't mean it's not the most important thing I've ever experienced."

"Would I be off base in suggesting that this *is* the emotional connection we were talking about?" I ask, putting her head into the nook of my shoulder. "Because I don't know about you, but I feel pretty fucking connected to you."

She laughs, nuzzling closer, throwing her good leg over mine. "What if we just make a conscious effort to date each other *and* engage in what we could call emotional orgasmic connectivity training."

"Emotional orgasmic connectivity training," I echo. "I like that. So we go on dates and gaze lovingly into each other's eyes and tell each other every last detail of our lives, and then we go home and fuck each other senseless." I huff. "And by fuck, I mean—"

She interrupts. "Love each other…aggressively?"

I snort. "Precisely."

After a few moments of silence, she looks up at me. "Would it be too soon to talk about one place versus two?"

"Way too soon." I laugh. "Mine, yours, or we find one together?"

"Find one together? Between your station and mine?"

"Sounds good." She nuzzles her face under my chin, peppering little kisses to my throat. "My moms will want to meet you."

"Moms, plural?"

"Lia and I have referred to her mom and mine as a single collective unit, The Moms, since we were like, eight. After our dads died, they actually lived together, for like, ten years, up until Mom finally agreed to marry Derek, Erin's dad."

"And they want to meet me?"

"The man who finally not only caught and tamed me, but a firefighter no less? Yeah, they're gonna want to meet you."

"I'm thinking I'll spring you on Mom this weekend. She and I do Sunday brunch together twice a month. We have a standing reservation at a hotel restaurant a few blocks from Station Four—we've been going there since I joined the department." I sigh happily. "I've never once brought a girl to Sunday brunch, and she's given up asking."

"I've never introduced a guy to The Moms, either. We do a girls' day at this little place off the highway near Mom and Derek's, usually the last Sunday of the month. Usually we go for dinner and end up closing it out."

"So we do brunch with my mom and dinner with yours?" I say.

"And fuck like bunnies in between?" She sounds so eager, so hopeful, like we didn't just finish an epic mutual orgasm.

I'm starting to wonder if maybe I've actually met my match—someone who can out-horny me.

She's my match in every way, honestly.

EPILOGUE
JOVIE

YOU WANT TO KNOW EVERYTHING, DON'T YOU?

What's his mom like? How was brunch? What's our first condo together like? Does he get along with The Moms? Do we have epic sex four times a day or just three? Does he propose? Do I say yes? Where's the wedding? Who's my maid of honor? How many kids do we have?

It's happily ever after. That's what it is.

It's a lifetime of love woven from a dozen threads. It's family, his, mine, ours. It's learning to accept that he simply won't ever get his dirty socks into the hamper even if it's a foot away, but he makes up for it by always having coffee ready and making me breakfast—and many mornings, he makes me breakfast and makes *me* breakfast, wink wink nudge nudge.

It's third shifts and barely seeing each other for a week. It's my heart stopping when I find out a building he was in collapsed with him in it, according to reports—only to find out the reports were wrong and he got out before it collapsed.

It's missing my period and feeling a mixture of fear and excitement…until the test comes back negative, and then feeling equal parts relief and regret, because we hadn't exactly planned for that just yet.

It's him luring me to the station late at night while both engines are out on calls, and proposing to me in his office, on one knee, while haltingly reciting a love poem by Shakespeare.

It's a first responder wedding, half the firefighters and paramedics and cops in the city congregating in our park to watch us say I do.

It's that test coming back positive the first time we actually "tried" for a baby.

It's a house in the 'burbs with an actual white picket fence, and barbecues with friends every weekend.

Oh, you want to know about my friends and his?

Those are their stories. It's up to them to share them with you.

Maybe they will, maybe they won't.

All I know is, I got my happily ever after. I never asked for it, and it was with the last person I expected it to be.

And it's perfect.

ALSO BY

JASINDA WILDER

Visit me at my website: **www.jasindawilder.com**
Email me: **jasindawilder@gmail.com**

If you enjoyed this book, you can help others enjoy it as well by recommending it to friends and family, or by mentioning it in reading and discussion groups and online forums. You can also review it on the site from which you purchased it. But, whether you recommend it to anyone else or not, thank you *so much* for taking the time to read my book! Your support means the world to me!

My other titles:

Preacher's Son:
Unbound
Unleashed
Unbroken

Delilah's Diary:
A Sexy Journey
La Vita Sexy
A Sexy Surrender

Big Girls Do It:
Boxed Set
Married
On Christmas
Pregnant

Rock Stars Do It:
Harder
Dirty
Forever

From the world of *Big Girls* and *Rock Stars*:
Big Love Abroad

Biker Billionaire:
Wild Ride

The Falling Series:
Falling Into You
Falling Into Us
Falling Under
Falling Away
Falling For Colton

The Ever Trilogy:
Forever & Always
After Forever
Saving Forever

The world of *Wounded:*
Wounded
Captured

The world of *Stripped:*
Stripped
Trashed

The world of *Alpha:*
Alpha
Beta
Omega
Sigma
Gamma
Harris: Alpha One Security Book 1
Thresh: Alpha One Security Book 2
Duke Alpha One Security Book 3
Puck: Alpha One Security Book 4
Lear: Alpha One Security Book 5
Anselm: Alpha One Security Book 6

The Houri Legends:
Jack and Djinn
Djinn and Tonic

The Madame X Series:
Madame X
Exposed
Exiled

The Black Room
(With Jade London):
Door One
Door Two
Door Three
Door Four
Door Five
Door Six
Door Seven
Door Eight

The One Series
The Long Way Home
Where the Heart Is
There's No Place Like Home

Badd Brothers:
*Badd Motherf*cker*
Badd Ass
Badd to the Bone
Good Girl Gone Badd
Badd Luck
Badd Mojo
Big Badd Wolf
Badd Boy

Badd Kitty
Badd Business
Badd Medicine
Badd Daddy

Dad Bod Contracting:
Hammered
Drilled
Nailed
Screwed

Fifty States of Love:
Pregnant in Pennsylvania
Cowboy in Colorado
Married in Michigan
Christmas in Connecticut

Goode Girls
For a Goode Time Call…
Not So Goode
Goode to Be Bad
A Real Good Time
Goode Vibrations

Billionaire Baby Club
Lizzie Goes Brains Over Braun
Autumn Rolls a Seven
Laurel's Bright Idea
Standalone titles:
Yours
The Cabin
The Parent Trap

Wish Upon a Star

Non-Fiction titles:
You Can Do It
You Can Do It: Strength
You Can Do It: Fasting

Jack Wilder Titles:
The Missionary

JJ Wilder Titles:
Ark

To be informed of new releases, special offers, and other Jasinda news, sign up for Jasinda's email newsletter.